Praise for Alice J. Wisler's debut novel, *Rain Song*

"Ms. Wisler balances small-town North Carolina, eccentric southern relatives, and barbecued chicken with the serene culture of Japan and Harrison Michaels' Japanese cuisine and koi garden. Her graceful writing had me sighing and reading certain passages over again with pure delight."
—Cheryl Klarich, *Writing Remnants*

"You will come to love Nicole's eclectic family and you will cheer her as she makes her very cautious discoveries. I look forward to more beautiful stories from this very talented writer!"
—Kim Ford, *Novel Reviews*

"Wisler paints her characters with sure, vivid brush stokes. We instantly recognize them even as we recognize their uniqueness. Wisler lets us believe that finding romance can be magical, if we only take the time to look and have the heart to experience that great adventure."
—*My Romance Story*

"Alice's slow, Southern style, filled with Grandma Ducee's Southern Truths, will carefully unwind the burial clothes that enshroud us and set us free. . . . Alice is an author to watch, and to fall in love with."
—Deena Peterson, *A Peek at My Bookshelf*

"The style of writing just pulls the reader in and connects you with the characters. This was a wonderful debut by Alice Wisler . . . I am looking forward to reading any future books by her."
—Deborah Khuanghlawn, *Books, Movies, and Chinese Food*

"*Rain Song* is a truly wondrous book, funny and wistful and wise and brave at the same time. It's full of tiny exquisite moments, marvelous descriptions and astute insights. . . . It's a book about ties that bind and traditions that truly make a family. It's a book about true beauty that sometimes lies deep within. . . . More than anything, it's a book about love in its many incarnations."
  —*Reader Views*

"In Wisler's likable debut, a young woman is offered a chance to find romance and make peace with her past. . . . Faith fiction fans will appreciate the strong faith of Nicole's influential grandmother, Ducee Dubois, who helps Nicole face her fears."
  —*Publishers Weekly*

"A worthy first novel with a Southern flair, this title addresses dealing with a painful childhood in a realistic way."
  —*Library Journal*

"Alice is both a talented and gifted writer."
  —Eugene H. Peterson, author of *The Message*

". . . a fresh narrative that will be appreciated most by those who enjoy a story with characters real enough to be a neighbor next door, or your own family members. *Rain Song* breathes hope into our troubled world."
  —Nancy Leigh Harless, author of *Womankind*

"Reading *Rain Song* is like eating a delicious Southern meal— well-balanced in tastes of family, love, and life."
  —Stella Sieber

How Sweet
❧ It Is ❧

Books by Alice J. Wisler

Rain Song

How Sweet It Is

How Sweet It Is

ALICE J. WISLER

BETHANY HOUSE PUBLISHERS

Minneapolis, Minnesota

Published by Bethany House Publishers
11400 Hampshire Avenue South
Bloomington, Minnesota 55438

Bethany House Publishers is a division of
Baker Publishing Group, Grand Rapids, Michigan.

Printed in the United States of America

Library of Congress Cataloging-in-Publication Data

Wisler, Alice J.
    How sweet it is / Alice J. Wisler.
        p.   cm.
    ISBN 978-0-7642-0478-4 (pbk.)
    1. North Carolina—Fiction. I. Title.

    PS3623.I846   H69   2009
    813'.6—dc22

                                                2009004739

For all who wish to expand their horizons,
this is for you.

When one door of happiness closes, another opens;
but often we look so long at the closed door that
we do not see the one which has been opened for us.

—Helen Keller

one

When single people pack up to relocate, they often have a dog. With deliberate caution, they load cardboard boxes into the car, along with a few framed wall pictures, a blender, one or two trusty saucepans, and a tightly rolled sleeping bag. The dog jumps onto the passenger seat, the driver lowers the window a few inches, and as the car slowly backs out of the driveway, the canine shoves his twitching nose over the glass. When the car picks up speed, the wind ruffles the dog's fur and he opens his mouth as if to lap up the fresh air with his tongue. This animal is as carefree as the day he was born. All he has to do is tilt his head, breathe deeply, and enjoy the ride. No tedious job of consulting the creased road map. No watching road signs. No making conversation. He didn't earn the title "man's best friend" due to any special skills in flattery.

I, however, do not have a dog. I'm allergic to dog fur and

men who break hearts. I do own a blender—all chefs should, according to Chef Santiago Bordeaux. Chef B claims that a blender is the most versatile cooking apparatus. "Cooking apparatus" is what he calls any kitchen device, including a saucepan. My KitchenAid blender is packed in a box along with my cake-decorating supplies—all carefully wrapped in T-shirts to protect them during the trip.

Today I'm leaving Atlanta and all the cooking apparatuses I have grown to love in the kitchen at Palacio del Rey. I'm headed to the green area on the map, right there in the fold—the mountains of North Carolina. But I'm still a Georgia girl, born and bred.

As I carry a box of faded dish towels topped with oven mitts to my Jeep, my Peruvian neighbor, Yolanda, dabs at her glistening brown eyes and reminds me, "You are Georgia girl, Deena. What will you do in Carolina?" To herself she mutters, "No, no sabe. Ay, ay."

I've been over this with her before. I've already told her the same thing I told my parents who live in Tifton, my pastor at First Decatur Presbyterian, and my boss, Chef Bordeaux: "I'm going to live."

"What do you mean?" they have all asked in some form or another. When he questioned me, Chef B had a ladle in his fist that he waved wildly, as though he wanted to use it to knock some sense into my head.

I've replied, "I'm going to live. I'm going to North Carolina to live!" I wanted to tell them that just because it's called North Carolina doesn't mean it's a Yankee state. Some consider it as southern as Georgia. I've even seen North Carolinians drink sweet tea.

I'm going to live. That's all.

Chef B placed his ladle on the counter next to the restaurant's stove as the large pot of French onion soup simmered on the front burner. A puzzled expression came over his face. Not since his asparagus soufflé fell the previous October had I seen him so bewildered. He said, "And you tell to me, why can't you live here?"

I almost died here, I thought. But that's not something I would say out loud to anyone. People don't like to talk about death. If you want to see how quickly a person can change the subject, just bring up the topic of death.

I've no idea what life will be like for me in North Carolina. All I know is I'm ready to say good-bye to Atlanta. *Say good-bye to Atlanta*—that sounds like a line from a country song. I consider singing as I wave one last time to Yolanda, who is now biting her lower lip and shaking her head in a way that makes her long ponytail swing like a beagle's tail. However, everyone knows I can't carry a tune in a double-boiler. And I think in order to be a true country singer, there is one important criterion: You have to own a dog.

two

Somewhere outside of Gainesville on Route 23, it starts to rain, and when the drops begin to splatter wildly across the windshield, I pull the Jeep over to the side of the road. My hands tremble; the engine idles. The next thing I know, I'm rocking back and forth, my kneecaps jarred by the steering wheel. As my eyes close, my memory flashes with a vision of crunched metal—ugly and jagged. I hear glass shattering and the shriek of tires. My eyes open; I'm not in a wrecked vehicle. I grasp the seatbelt strap across my chest and swallow three times. My friend Sally taught me to do this. "When you swallow, your body relaxes," she repeats whenever she finds those deep lines of panic displayed across my face.

An officer pulls up behind me, and I hear the crunch of the gravel under his heavy shoes as he comes to my window.

He uses a gloved hand to knock on the glass and then asks if I need any help.

I stop rocking, find the button to lower the window a few inches, and clear my throat. "No." Chilling rain dribbles into the car, streaking the sleeve of my windbreaker.

"Are you sure?" His breath smells of coffee, which reminds me that I have had no caffeine today.

I speak to his shiny badge, which I'm sure includes his printed name, but my eyes are too blurry to read it. "I'm fine."

Just three and a half months ago, another officer had asked me how I was as I lay in the passenger's seat of Lucas's 1987 Mustang. I'd passed out after that. I don't want to look into this man's face right now.

"Well, miss, you will need to move along." His tone is compassionate, in an authoritative sort of way.

Nodding, I tell him, "I will." My voice sounds tinny, like I'm talking through a pipe.

When he leaves in his red-domed patrol car, I resume my rocking. This time terror rumbles through my head like the wheels of a tractor plowing a dirt field, flattening every stem, every weed. If I look to my right, I'll see a woman slumped over in the passenger's seat, blood smeared on her forehead, shards of glass protruding from her arms. Gritting my teeth— a habit I have only recently formed—I look to my right. The passenger seat holds my worn brown suede purse. Jerking my head toward the back seat, I see only the gray upholstery. I'm really all alone.

Post-traumatic stress syndrome is what the doctor called this. PTSS for short. To me, that sounds like a brand of hairspray. Or the sound of air slowly escaping from a lidded pot cooking collards on the stove.

I hear a scream identical to the one I recall hearing during the accident and realize it belongs to me. Clutching my elbows, I try to steady my breathing. But my breath is a series of gasps, and then a loud sob rushes out of my mouth. Tears much larger, I'm sure, than these falling raindrops slide down my cheeks.

I should have taken Sally up on her offer. She said she'd drive me and my belongings to Bryson City. She's a doctor—her patients are the kind I'm allergic to. "You don't do well driving," she gently told me one evening when we were at Burgalos for dinner. "It's natural after what happened for you to have fear. Just let me drive you. I'm off next Saturday."

I let her comment slide off me like a loaf of bread out of a well-greased baking pan. She must have seen my knuckles turn harder than concrete last Tuesday when I dropped her off at her clinic because her car was in the shop. I was doing well until a trucker in front of me slammed on his brakes. "What is he doing?" I cried.

"The light's red," she told me. "Cars tend to stop at those." She smiled, but I couldn't return her smile. It was too hard just to breathe.

"Swallow, Deena," she urged me.

This morning's rainstorm was not predicted. I wouldn't have chosen to leave Atlanta on a day with rain. Had I known the weather would be like this, I'd have waited. I would have sat cross-legged in my almost empty, one-bedroom apartment, dressed in a pair of gray sweat pants and billowy T-shirt, and listened to Antonio Vivaldi's *The Four Seasons*. At lunchtime, I would have eaten takeout from the Chinese place down the street and talked to Sally on the phone in between her canine and feline appointments at her clinic. She would have told me how nasty the rain makes pet fur, and I would have remembered again why I chose not to be a vet.

When the windshield begins to fog, I switch on the defroster.

"Are you going to just sit here paralyzed forever?"

Oh no, now I'm talking to myself.

I reply, "Well, no."

"Then get moving, miss." I make my voice firm, without any hint of compassion.

"Now?" The sky still looks dark.

"Now or never."

These conversations between my reluctant-fearful self and my trying-to-motivate self have become more and more common since the accident. I'm not sure which self I like—or loathe. Often it depends on the weather.

As my hands clutch the steering wheel, I consider calling Sally on my cell phone. I've flipped open the phone and my index finger is poised to jab at the first number. Instead, I toss the phone across the seat and say, "Think of something pleasant."

So I think of a stream with rocks and clear, cool water. Daisies, petals touched by dew, bobbing in the gentle wind. Peach pie with a mound of vanilla-bean ice cream. Rich velvet cake with buttercream icing that melts on your tongue. An autumn morning walk with Dad across the harvested fields, pointing out geese that soar overhead, picture-perfect against a blue sky, and later, just before breakfast, going to the barn to feed the plump piglets that were born in late spring.

Soon, I'm driving again, visions of piglets prompting a tiny smile. But when the rain gushes over the Jeep like a waterfall, I feel panic set in once more. Cars pass me; some even have the nerve to honk. As their tires spray water against the sides of my vehicle, I mutter, "I'm going thirty miles per hour." Which, despite the 55 MPH speed limit signs, seems to be the only safe speed for this soggy day.

Through the torrents of rain, I spot a lopsided billboard with the words *Good Eatin'* on it. I am more than ready to stop. I drive another slow mile and then see a small burgundy diner on the right. A few of the letters are burned out in the neon sign that flickers, so it reads *God in.*

A place where God is present—what more could anyone ask for?

———

Inside the fluorescently-bright restaurant, I'm greeted by the smell of bacon, hamburgers, and something strong, like bleach. A waitress in a rust smock and matching lipstick seats me at a sticky table in the back. She hands me a menu stained with grease spots. I try to smile as she comments, "Looks like a day for ducks and my petunias."

As I study the menu, I wipe my neck, which is moist from my wet hair. Since I couldn't remember which box I'd packed my umbrella in, I just ran from the parking lot into the restaurant. The rain felt clean and strangely comforting, as though its pellets were trying to bathe away my worries. I even considered standing in the rain for several minutes and getting completely drenched, just to see if nature's bath could rid me of all my discomfort.

The waitress waves toward a car parked outside. "Ah, look at that, would you? Someone forgot to roll up the windows.

Well, he'll be in for a surprise." She clucks her tongue and then chuckles as she walks toward the front of the restaurant.

I take a few gulps of air, shiver. I know I rolled up my windows. That's not something I have to worry about. My right arm jerks, and I massage it with my left hand. A nurse gave me a massage in the hospital; I wish she could come over every day and repeat that wonderful, soothing act. If I ever win the lottery, I'll hire a personal masseur. And a chauffeur, so that I won't ever have to get behind a steering wheel again.

When the waitress comes by with a white memo pad and number two yellow pencil, I order sweet tea and French fries. Large for both. I haven't eaten anything all day, even though Yolanda fried eggs and tomatoes for me this morning. "You eat for to be strong," she encouraged me. When she was looking for a pair of clean socks for her son, I opened her garbage can and let the eggs and bits of tomato run into the black Hefty bag right next to last night's potato peelings.

From my purse I dig out a bottle of Extra Strength Tylenol. Right after the accident I had prescription stuff—the good stuff—which they freely gave me as I lay in the hospital bed. Upon discharge, I was given a prescription for what must be the world's most wonderfully strong pain-zapper. When the prescription ran out, although I begged, Dr. Bland told me he didn't want me addicted to codeine. "You should be feeling better," he said as he took a moment to study me over the black rims of his glasses. "It's been three months."

"Yes, but I still have pain all over," I told him, hoping to sound refined, with only a mild strand of desperation. What I really wanted to say was, "Which pain were the drugs supposed to cure? The pain in my legs or the pain in my heart?" Somewhere around March, two months after the accident and a month after my grandpa Ernest's death, I'd realized my life was in shambles. I didn't know how I would ever be normal again. And somewhere around that time, the physical pain went away and the heart pain set in.

Just like death, people don't like to talk about pain—well, unless it belongs to them. They want you to move on, get over it, resume your life, whip up an omelet, frost a cake, be happy, play the saxophone. But I still carry pain—and Extra Strength Tylenol is not getting rid of it.

When the fries arrive on a chipped blue plate, I squeeze Hunt's ketchup into a mound and dip one crispy slice into the red circle. I chew loudly, making a smacking noise, just to hear the sound. I figure table manners don't count when you dine solo, although my mother would surely disagree. "Deena, Deena, you must eat like royalty," she once said. I don't know where that idea of hers came from. I'm the daughter of pig farmers and have yet to feel regal.

The next time I sink a fry into the red condiment, all I can think is that the ketchup looks like a pool of fresh blood.

three

Covering my plate with three white paper napkins from the dispenser, I recall the first time Chef Bordeaux taught our class how to make crispy fried potatoes. He called them by a fancier name, yet they were just one step above French fries. He coated them in a seasoning of salt, pepper, garlic salt, cayenne pepper, and olive oil. Then he baked them at 400 degrees for thirty minutes, taking them out of the oven once to stir them. "So as not to burn," he said. We ate them when they were done, and we were all impressed with the soft insides and flavorful taste.

"You like potatoes?" he asked us.

"Yes," we said, in between bites. We were all in training. I'd only been working at his restaurant for a month. Anthony, just off the boat from a small village outside of Lyon, France, said never had he had potatoes so "delicate." He then switched from English to French, and none of us understood him. Chef

B grew up in San Sebastian, Spain, but he tried to follow the young Frenchman's enthusiasm. After all, Anthony had been recommended to him and the Palacio del Rey from a two-star restaurant in Lyon.

Anthony makes the best braised duck in orange sauce I've ever tasted. He knows how much I like it, so he made the dish for my going-away party. Chef Bordeaux made wild rice seasoned with garlic and fresh rosemary from his own garden. The rest of the meal included shiitake mushrooms filled with cheese and baby shrimp, mint sorbet, and basil and parmesan Tuscan loaf bread. The party couldn't have been more flavorful or beautiful, unless perhaps it had taken place on the *Queen Mary 2.* It was too bad the occasion was that I was leaving the restaurant.

The event even included a gift. Everyone chipped in and brought a set of cake pans for me. There were three—an 8-inch, 9-inch and 13-inch—and each one was wrapped in silver-and-purple paper topped with a large bow. I almost cried when I opened them, and I don't cry easily. My mother taught my sister and me the art of sucking in not only your stomach but also your emotions. "A woman cannot be easily read," she told us. "A woman must cover her body and her heart."

I pull another napkin from the metal dispenser and lay it like a veil over my plate of half-consumed food. Hunger grips my stomach, so I decide to eat a few more greasy potatoes, in spite of what the ketchup brings to mind. I lift one edge of a napkin and take two fries from the plate. They will never compare to Chef B's potatoes, but sometimes you just make the best of what you have.

Suddenly, I want to make a list of all the food we had at my going-away party, and I'm sure it's because I don't want to forget any part of the event that was held in my honor. After all, how many good-bye parties does one get in a lifetime?

Before I grab a napkin to jot down the names of the various dishes from my party, I see another gift—one that begs my attention—and I pull it from my purse. It's a hardcover journal Chef B gave me. "Writing down your heart is healing," he told me when I opened the blank journal. "One lady, father die, then her sister, then her cat. Next, she does not want to keep on. She write her heart onto the pages of her journal. She find some peace."

The shiny cover of the journal features a slice of peach pie next to a goblet of a clear liquid and a white mug of a dark beverage—my guess, Costa Rican coffee with a rainforest blend.

"Write each day. Date on the page," were Chef B's instructions to me.

Writing and I have never gotten along. Writing makes me remember a creative writing class I was forced to take in high school.

"How many writing courses did you have in high school?" Sally asked me once when I complained about my lack of desire to write.

I was icing a coconut chocolate cake in my apartment for my friend Jeannie's thirtieth birthday. I thought a moment as Sally swiped a dollop of buttercream frosting from the bowl. "One."

"One class?"

"Yeah, one creative writing class."

"And it was awful?" She licked her fingers, then wiped her mouth with the back of her hand.

"It was terrible."

"Why?"

I needed no other prompting; I told her. "The teacher went on and on about the muse and words and the value of them. Her husband had Alzheimer's, and she had to tell him good-bye long before he actually physically died."

"One class?" said Sally. I don't know why she felt she had to repeat that again.

I took a spatula from a drawer and used it to scoop the thick, creamy frosting from the mixing bowl into my decorator's bag. "Her husband loved roses, and she'd pick one from their garden each morning. She always placed the rose in a slender crystal vase—one he had given to her the first time he'd ever bought her roses. Then she'd push his wheelchair to the kitchen table and ask him, 'What color is it?' He would stare at the rose and answer whatever color it was. Until one morning when she brought in a red rose and her husband called it yellow."

"Sad," said Sally. She thought a moment longer and repeated, "Sad."

"The teacher read a poem she wrote about it, and then a short essay, and then another poem. All about her husband and this rose."

"Alzheimer's is a nasty disease." Sally had a faraway look in her eyes, and under other circumstances I would have thought to ask if she'd had experience with a loved one with Alzheimer's, but no, I was on a roll.

"She even wrote a letter to the editor of the paper about her husband and the rose." My voice had somehow reached that annoying high-pitched timbre. I took a breath and added, "All these tips on how to deal with losing your loved one before he's really gone."

Sally sighed as she watched me pipe fleur-de-lis—three shells—along the sides of the cake. "So you really hated that class, then," she concluded. "You make it sound like you've suffered through dozens of creative writing classes."

True, I've only had one creative writing class, but it felt like a dozen.

Does Chef B really expect me to write down my feelings? When pigs fly, I think as I snap the journal shut. If the slice of peach pie on the cover were real, it would have fallen onto the floor from the force of my closing the cover.

I need a slice of peach pie.

The door swings open, and I look up to see a couple walk into the diner. They are both young and beautiful, laughing as they wipe themselves off from the rain. Her hair is thick and brown. As she shakes her head, I'm reminded of the fleece of the Shetland sheep our neighbors in Tifton raised. He—tall and muscular—smiles, places a protective arm around her, kisses her cheek. They stand together, waiting to be seated. Inseparable. Able to face anything because love is the strongest force against a world of uncertainty. I wonder if they're engaged or married. I wonder if he runs his finger along her jaw from her earlobe to her chin and then cups her face in his hands, all the while telling her that there is no one but her in his universe. Has he called her to say that a day without hearing her voice is not worth living?

I have to turn away. Sometimes other people's happiness brings an ache in my gut so large and deep that I wonder if I'm sinking. Sinking into my own gut—now that's a medically unsound concept. Sally would dismiss it with a wave of her surgically adept hands. "Deena," she'd say. "You can't drown from your own sorrow. I know it might feel like you could, but . . ." Then she'd smile because she doesn't like to be serious for too long.

When the waitress refills my iced tea, she stares out the drenched window and asks if I'd like anything else. Oh yes, there are a few more things I would like. Happiness. A fiancé who stays faithful. The ability to forget the car accident. "Peach pie," I answer. "With ice cream on—"

"We're out," she says flatly.

My mouth must be hanging open. "No peach pie?"

She shakes her curls and sticks her pencil into a few loose ones on the right side of her head. This is Georgia, I think. Every car parked in the lot outside this rainy window has a peach on its license plate. How can Good Eatin' be out of peach pie? How can they call this place *good* if they don't have enough peach pie to go around?

"We have chocolate," the waitress volunteers with a smile.

"Chocolate?"

"Let me make sure." With her face turned toward the kitchen, she yells, "Hey, Harry! We got chocolate pie back there?" Waiting for his reply, she taps her fingers against the pencil in her hair with one hand and pats her generous waist with the other. She reminds me of one of those wind-up toys where the monkey frantically claps the two cymbals together until he winds down.

"What?" comes a tenor voice from the back, somewhere over the long, empty counter.

"Chocolate?" A louder tone. "Listen to me, Harry! Do you hear me?" Through her frown she shouts, "Chocolate pie!"

A few rows in front of me, the happy couple cover their ears with obvious hands.

"It's okay," I quietly tell her. "I'm fine."

She stops tapping and patting, shrugs. "Our chocolate pie

is good. Creamy. Rich." She keeps going. "We make it with whole milk. None of that skimmed, low-percent, by-product stuff."

"That's all right." I don't tell her that I don't like chocolate pie. Waitresses don't really want to hear about your menu likes and dislikes, anyway. I muster a smile, or something that resembles one. "Thanks, though." Mom would be proud of me.

When the waitress ambles toward the cash register, I take another look at the journal. This time when I open it, surprisingly I have the desire to write something. This is a moment I can't let get away. Focusing on the first page, I uncap my pen. I run my finger over the smooth, lined paper. Concentrate on writing as neatly as you can, I tell myself. Such a hard thing for me to do.

April 15th, diner outside Gainesville. I ordered iced tea and fries. I wanted a slice of peach pie, but they were out. They have chocolate, but I am almost allergic to that. The rain acts like it doesn't want to stop. I'm on my way to Bryson City. I am leaving Atlanta.

Putting down the pen, I think, "That wasn't too bad." I have Tylenol to mask my physical pain and this journal to tackle my emotional pain. What can go wrong?

Before leaving, I place two dollars on the table for a tip. Then I add another dollar, and from the bottom of my purse, a quarter, two dimes, and a shiny nickel. I feel sorry for the waitress having to work in a place that isn't well stocked with peach pie. After I gather my purse and my small amount of courage, I plunge out into the rain again for the rest of my journey.

four

W ell, well. It's been a while, Shug. Look at you—all growed up."

Aunt Regena Lorraine is wearing a bright orange dress, a color that might appear on those decoratively-painted Ukrainian eggs featured in travel books and posters. Light swirls of white and yellow are mixed in with the orange, giving the dress an intricate look. Her gray hair is tied in a ponytail, though a few tendrils float free, one curling along a large gold hoop earring. She poises a pudgy bejeweled hand—I count three silver rings—against the side of her lined face and studies me through leopard-spotted glasses.

I'm twenty-seven years old; I hope I'm grown. And on the other hand, she just saw me less than five months ago at Christmas. I haven't *growed up* since then.

Aunt Regena Lorraine shifts her attention from me to a shaggy creature she fondly calls Giovanni. The dog is golden with a patch of olive on its left front paw. "He got in that paint I was using in the downstairs bathroom," she explains as Giovanni sniffs my knees.

"Nice color," I tell her while I watch the animal circle two times and make himself comfortable on a striped rug by the sliding glass door that leads to the deck of the A-frame cabin.

My aunt waddles into the kitchen, gives a sigh as large as she is, and starts opening cabinets. As she moves, I smell her perfume, which is light and sweet. I recall her wearing the same scent at Christmas when I sat next to her on my parents' couch and she showed me photos of her father's recent trip to Venice. Grandpa Ernest traveled from North Carolina to Italy to Greece to spend Christmas at his favorite island, Kos.

My aunt mutters as she fingers various items she pulls out from the cabinet shelves. "I can't believe he didn't get rid of this," she says as she touches a fondue pot. She notes a bowl with a crooked rim. "Oh, he kept this all these years. Well, well."

The "he" she is talking about is Grandpa Ernest, who, until his recent death, occupied this cabin. Perhaps she never had the opportunity to look through his kitchen cabinets while he was alive and today she's enjoying the chance.

When she takes out a tin can with Santa's jolly face painted on the side, she muses, "I gave him this years ago." Opening the tin, she cries, "It's still full of licorice!" Then she laughs, takes out a piece of the black sweet, and pops it into her mouth. After a moment of chewing, she says, "Mmmmm. It's still good. Well, I can't believe it!" To me she says with confidence, "Licorice stored tightly in a tin keeps." She finishes the piece and scans the container. "This must be . . . let's see . . .

Christmas of '99. No, must have been 2001." She laughs again. "I know I gave it to him."

I am not allergic to licorice, but it also is not one of my favorite things.

Suddenly my aunt calls for tea and fills a stainless-steel teakettle with water from the tap. "The sink water here is good," she tells me. "At the coast, my stars. You could kill a few dozen seagulls with that nasty tap water. Always buy bottled when you go to the Outer Banks."

As though on cue, and in doggy agreement, Giovanni produces two barks.

I'm not sure what to do with this tidbit of advice. So I do nothing but stand watching my aunt take out two mugs from a cabinet. One says *Cherokee* on it and has a painted bear. The other says *Blowing Rock* and has the face of an Indian maiden with large, dark eyes. From a tote bag that has *You must do the thing you think you cannot do* boldly scripted across it, she produces a Ziploc bag. "Shug," she says as she spoons the contents of the bag into each mug, "you are going to like it here."

The Ziploc's contents look to me like a dime bag of marijuana you would buy from a dealer in an Atlanta alley. What is Aunt Regena Lorraine doing with it?

"I just love sassafras tea, don't you?" she exclaims as she lifts the whistling teakettle and pours water into each mug.

I don't know; I've never tried it. Except for sweetened iced tea, I'm not a tea drinker. Hot coffee suits me, and I know where almost all of the Starbucks are located in Atlanta. I move to the sink to wash my hands and remove the slobber Giovanni placed there. As I dry my hands on a cotton towel, I see a can opener hanging on a small nail. I stoop to read the inscription on the stainless-steel handle. In a bold lime green font it states

Always open with love. This strikes me as funny because I don't think I've ever opened a can of condensed milk or cherry pie filling with love. Determination and frustration, for sure, but not love. My eyes scan the small kitchen to see other utensils hanging in odd places around the room.

I am about to study more of them when Regena Lorraine summons me into the dining room. "Don't want the tea to get cold, Shug," she says. "Sassafras tastes best with steam rising from it."

As we sit across from each other at the wooden dining table, I think to myself that my aunt is my only connection to this small town called Bryson City. I don't know another soul within a one-hundred-mile radius. And as eccentric as my sister Andrea and I have always thought our aunt to be, knowing her is better than knowing no one. I'm sure she'll guide me on where to hand out my brochures and maybe even show me other venues for advertising my cake-decorating business to this mountain community.

With satisfaction, Regena Lorraine breathes in the aroma of her mug of tea. Steam is rising from the liquid, causing her glasses to fog. "When is your first day to be at The Center?" she asks.

I wonder where my grandpa keeps the sugar. "What?"

"Have you called them yet?" Taking off her glasses, she wipes them with the fabric around the neck of her dress.

"Called who?"

She laughs, but I can't see what is so funny. "They are going to love you!"

"Who?" I ask. I want to say, "What in the world are you talking about?" but I don't. My mother would consider that pure rudeness. I think of how to rephrase the question so that it will come across as polite and make my mother proud of me. "Can you explain this to me?"

"Explain? Oh my, Shug." My aunt places her glasses on the bridge of her nose and then takes a long drink. "Delicious!" she says, and laughs again.

Uncertainty lines my face; I can feel it in every pore.

Fingers gripping the mug's handle, Regena Lorraine peers at me. "You don't know?"

five

Suddenly I am back in the hospital with my body covered in sterile bandages. Sally and Jeannie are giving each other glances—knowing glances. *You don't know, Deena? Lucas has been two-timing you.*

"Lay it on me, Auntie," I want to say. I don't think I am capable of being shocked by anything anymore. But the boldness doesn't surface in my tone; my voice merely utters a weak, "What?"

My aunt prolongs her answer by first taking a doggy biscuit from the pocket of her dress. "Here, Handsome," she calls. Giovanni raises his large head, jumps up, and races to her side, drool rolling off his mouth.

I wouldn't call him handsome.

She hands him the treat, and her adoration for her pet is evident. As he chews, she gently runs her fingers over his coat. I start to ask what kind of dog he is, but then I think:

Does it really matter that I know the individual breeds of the very animals I am allergic to?

When he has devoured every crumb, he searches for some under the table and, finding none, resumes his position on the rug. Only then does my aunt give me her full attention. But she still doesn't answer my question. "How are the pigs, Shug?" Her voice penetrates the darkness that has formed over the mountains outside the sliding glass door.

"They're fine." I think of my parents' farm as a strange longing curls through my stomach. I wonder if Dad is filling the troughs with dinner for the animals now. I can almost hear Clementine, the spotted sow with an attitude, quacking at him in a tone that makes us think she is part duck. I say, "Clementine had a litter of nine last month."

"Nine? Did you say nine?" Regena Lorraine clasps her hands together as if she's ready to applaud. Laughing, she adds, "My stars! I bet your dad was happy. Lots of cash in those."

"He's always happy," I suppress the urge to say. If only some of that energy for living would rub off on Mom. And me. "So about what you said . . . ?" I hope to guide my aunt back to the original topic.

She nods while rubbing her fingers over her rings. Some have tiny jewels and others are plain silver. "Do you know where I got this one?" she asks, polishing a silver band with an index finger.

I shake my head. Swallowing, I want to say, "Rings make me sad." But as surely as Giovanni likes dog treats, such a statement would cause my aunt's interest to pique, and suddenly we'd be talking about Lucas.

She gives my hand a pat, a gesture that makes me feel that I'm five years old. "You're supposed to teach."

Detach before returning

Laboratory Corporation of America

Dear Patient,

Your comments are an important part of our efforts to continuously improve the service we provide to you. Please take a moment to complete the survey on the other side. Just drop the completed survey in any mailbox or leave it with our staff.

Thank you for making LabCorp the lab of your choice.

LabCorp Customer Service

Visit LabCorp's website at:
www.labcorp.com for additional locations.

LabCorp
Laboratory Corporation of America

DETACH HERE

Would you like to be contacted?

Please rate our patient service center based on today's visit.
Mark a bubble from 1 "Very Dissatisfied" to 5 "Very Satisfied".

Overall experience . . . .

Convenience of location . . . .

Waiting time . . . .

Professional and courteous treatment . . . .

Staff skill and knowledge . . . .

Cleanliness of the service center and staff . . . .

Use of safety precautions (gloves and labcoats) . . . .

Hours of operation . . . .

Have you used LabCorp before? . . . .

Would you use this Patient Service Center again? . . . .

Would you recommend us to others? . . . .

How long did you wait for service? . . . .

Did you come here from your: . . . .

How far did you travel? . . . .

How were you referred to LabCorp today? . . . .

A more convenient location for you would be near: . . . . . .

"Teach?" The word sounds hollow and foreign, like when I'm trying to repeat a word my missionary sister has taught me to say in Chinese.

"At The Center. Ernest's request."

"What's The Center?"

I wait for her reply while she takes a long drink from her mug. Wiping moisture from her mouth onto a tissue she pulled from somewhere out of her robust chest, she says, "The Center is a program for middle-school-aged children. It's held at the church along with the preschool."

I picture a group of preadolescent kids and swallow again. The thought of preschoolers makes my nose itch. When I was small, I was known for squirming in my chair. I would move my bottom left and right, driving my mother to the point of glaring at me. "Deena, Deena, young ladies do not twist in their chairs." The urge to twist is strong right now. I scratch my nose instead.

My aunt gently tells me, "Ernest started the program at the Presbyterian church in town. They get donations from local people and businesses."

But what does this place have to do with me?

She tucks her tissue into her chest and smoothes her dress. "Ernest wanted you to teach there. The older kids, I mean. That's why he left this cabin to you."

No. No, I don't have to teach. Teaching is not my gift. I cannot sing and I can't teach.

"He wanted you to live here and teach." She studies my face. "With pay, of course."

At last I find my voice. "Teach *what*?"

"Flower arranging and martial arts." She pauses to glimpse my expression.

I have no smile, just a solemn look.

Laughter overcomes her again. Even her glasses shake as she gives in to amusement. "Cooking, Shug! Cooking."

"Why?"

"Because you're a cook!" Her words expand to the wooden ceiling, bounce off, and vibrate against the cedar walls. "Ernest loved to cook. Knowing Ernest, he probably had hundreds of other reasons, too."

I wonder what plan he had in mind when he dangled kitchen utensils around the cabin. There is a whole assortment displayed in every room. There's even a stainless steel whisk hanging over the washing machine. Did he whisk his clothes?

"He was so proud of you going to cooking school," my aunt says warmly.

That much I know to be true. "He wrote and told me that," I say. The letter arrived shortly after I started my first year at Chef Bordeaux's. It was on paper decorated with drawings of figs and grapes, bananas and lemons. He wrote me many times after that, and I would reply with descriptions of my courses because that was what he wanted to hear. He seemed especially excited when I sent the recipe for mussels in tomato and garlic. Weeks later, he wrote, *I think it's wonderful to learn that my little Georgia granddaughter is creating Greek food—clearly, some of my favorite.*

My grandpa was always traveling, so I never got to see him much, but through letters and recipes, over the miles, and as he traveled around the globe, we somehow connected. Somewhere in my belongings is the picture he sent of himself standing at the miniature village called Madurodam in Amsterdam. Towering over the replica with the tiny shops behind him, he looks larger than life. I think that must be the way his daughter, Regena Lorraine, will always remember him.

"Well, my goodness." She produces another light laugh. "Now you can share your love of cooking with the sweethearts at The Center."

The sweethearts? I want to ask an obvious question: Why didn't anyone mention this before? All I heard was that a cabin awaited me in the beautiful and serene Smoky Mountains. My father told me Grandpa had left the cabin to me because I was surely Ernest's favorite grandchild—just like he was his father's best-liked son. Mom said it was because nobody else wanted a cabin stuck on a remote mountain peak. No one ever mentioned anything about teaching children.

"I'm executor of Ernest's estate. Have you seen a copy?"

First it's a cabin, then teaching children at a church, and now an estate? Hesitantly, I ask, "Of what?"

"The will."

I shake my head.

Massaging a dimpled elbow, she explains, "Well, it's all in there. Ernest states that you are to teach cooking at The Center for six months. Then this cabin will be yours."

"Six months?"

She lifts a hand to view her wristwatch. The face sports Minnie Mouse in her typical polka-dotted skirt. Using her elbows, Regena Lorraine pushes her body from the table. Her smile is captivating, as if she knows a secret and is clearly amused by it. "So glad you're here safe and sound, Shug." Standing, she adds, "Gotta go."

"You're leaving?"

"Time for Clue."

"Clue?"

"Yes, the game of Clue."

"I've played Clue."

"Ernest did, too. That's how he got most of these kitchen utensils." She points to a spatula dangling from the edge of a cabinet. "Some of these things he got, I have no idea where they came from. What do they say about one man's junk being another man's treasure?"

Confusion weaves itself around my mind. "What?"

"He sure enjoyed playing to win," she comments as she scans the decorated walls of the cabin. "We've played for kitchen utensils for dozens of years." Grinning at me, she adds, "I'd tell you how it works, but really, that's a story for another day."

Giovanni is already standing at her side, his tail wagging like the windshield wipers on my Jeep. My aunt opens the passenger door to her truck, and the one hundred pounds of fur hops in, tail still moving.

After Aunt Regena Lorraine backs out of the gravel driveway, managing with magnificent skill not to go over the cliff, I walk around the house and spend time viewing all the cooking utensils. There's a grater with a round rooster's face for a handle. A three-pronged fork has *Atlantic Beach* inscribed on one of its silver tines. A red corkscrew suspended from a hook in the kitchen over the stove has *Kiss the Cook* in gold letters. A red, white, and blue plastic spatula near the sink reads *Panama.* On the wall by the Kenmore refrigerator, a large wooden spoon declares *I Left My Heart in Athens* in green and red lettering. Above the fridge is a round egg-yolk-colored form that looks to be made of plaster. I, too, wonder where Grandpa Ernest got some of these items. The piece looks like a chunk of rock from another planet. On the bottom side of it sits a metal hook. If it is a utensil, what does it do?

As I walk through the dining room and see a variety of bottle openers, pizza cutters, and corkscrews mounted on the walls, I conclude that Grandpa must have been a good Clue player. He must have known every motive Miss Scarlet had in the library with the candlestick.

———

Halfway through Vivaldi's "Spring" concerto, I begin unpacking my Coleman cooler. To the rhythm of the instruments played by Neville Marriner's orchestra, I place the items that were in my apartment refrigerator and freezer earlier this day in the cabin's white Kenmore. I glide across the linoleum floor the way I used to when I was a tiny girl with the desire to become a ballerina. Vivaldi is one of my favorite composers, although my friends think I'm loony for enjoying classical music.

Grandpa's refrigerator holds one lemon, single, alone, lying on its side on the middle shelf. I can see the faint blue word stamped against the yellow peel—*Sunkist*. I wonder if this is his lemon, one he purchased. I see him driving down the winding roads to Ingle's to buy ingredients for a meal he planned to make—perhaps one he had invited others to. But, the question is, why it is the lone item in the refrigerator? He's been dead three months now. I'm assuming that, like most of us, his refrigerator contained half-used jars of mustard, ketchup, and mayonnaise, and a bottle or two of his favorite salad dressing. Maybe even a container of some cheese dip he bought a year ago that he wasn't sure he really liked but kept on the back of the bottom shelf, just the same. A healthy head of lettuce, a few yellow onions, some carrots in the produce bin, and since I know he was fond of vine-ripe tomatoes, a cluster of those. Maybe the freezer held some frozen peas, lima beans, and corn. Someone emptied this refrigerator—most likely Regena Lorraine. I can picture her tossing out all the bottles, perhaps hanging on to the produce and later making a tossed salad with the vegetables, tears in her eyes, thinking that it was the last salad she'd ever eat made with Daddy's lettuce, Daddy's carrots, Daddy's onions, and Daddy's tomatoes. If she cleaned out the fridge, why did she leave the lemon? I finger its cold surface and scratch it with a fingernail. It still smells like a lemon should.

I add the contents of my Coleman. A bunch of red seedless grapes, a jar of Hellmann's, five sticks of butter, a bag of Starbuck's Dark Roast, and two bags of frozen corn. From a large brown sack I lift out five baking potatoes, a plastic bag of purple onions, a box of cake flour, a loaf of wheat bread, and three cans of green beans. I find places for them on the pantry shelves. In the next couple days, I'll head to the local grocery store for milk, juice, and half-and-half for my coffee. Every cup of java needs half-and-half, an indulgence culinary school taught me.

I peer into every cupboard and into the pantry, trying to find the sugar. Finally I find the sugar bowl—a tomato-red dish with a green lid. Inside sits a tiny spoon with the word *Kos* printed on the handle.

From a lumpy box, I unpack my cake-decorating ingredients, tips, frosting bags, blender, and new pans. All were protected by items of my clothing—my worn T-shirts, my sweat pants. Finding space in a bottom cabinet for the pieces of my life—the tangible parts that help me define who I still am—I feel a small tinge of hope.

Vivaldi plays with vigor as I make the kitchen my own.

Over the instruments I can hear Chef Bordeaux's voice from when I first studied under his tutelage: "A real chef needs a kitchen to make her own." He must have seen this printed in a cooking magazine or heard it on some culinary video because this phrase is the only sentence the chef speaks using proper English grammar.

I sneeze, and I'm sure the cause is dog fur. Of course the only person I know in this town would have to be a dog owner.

six

I've decided I'll try teaching the kids. Grandpa Ernest requested it, after all, and it was kind of him to give me this cabin. It's peaceful here; I want to stay. And if teaching is what it takes, I'll try it. I can't go back to Atlanta.

Chef Bordeaux would beam with happiness if he found out I'm going to teach. His eyes would dance with excitement as visions of cherry strudels and minestrone sashayed through his culinary mind. His enthusiasm I cannot handle right now, and perhaps that's why I haven't called to tell him about my new surroundings or *situations*—the topic he said he wanted to hear about.

They are middle-schoolers, so I suppose I'll start at the beginning and teach basic cooking. From a cardboard box labeled *Books*, I dig out one of my basic cookbooks. The lettering in the title, *Easy Cooking*, is made to look like yellow icing piped onto a creamy white cake. The only trouble with the cover is that forming perfect letters like that with frosting is not *easy*. I flip the first few pages and see the headline *How to Boil an Egg*. I don't like boiled eggs, so I don't consider them a basic cooking need. Besides, what would you use a boiled egg for? Chef salad. Cobb salad. Deviled eggs—or for those who don't like the word *devil* in their culinary experience, stuffed eggs.

Thinking about teaching, coupled with last night's restless sleep due to some disturbing noises outside the loft bedroom's window, does not make me ooze with excitement. From the medicine cabinet in the bathroom upstairs, I reach for my bottle of Tylenol. As I take two tablets, I wonder why the doctor wouldn't just let me get addicted to codeine.

In the living room, I note a charcoal drawing of an Asian boy in a straw hat riding on the back of a water buffalo. The boy has one hand on the wide back of the beast and the other raised as if he's waving to someone. Maybe his mom is standing nearby and he's waving and telling her that he's okay this time, unlike last time when he slipped off and fell face-first into the rice paddy.

When my cell phone rings, I rush around the cabin, trying to find where I placed it before going to bed last night. I find it on the kitchen counter and answer just before it goes to voice mail.

The familiar voice of my dad is on the line.

"Hi, Dad. How are you and how are the pigs?" I picture him in his usual attire—denim bib overalls, red shirt, and a wide-brimmed straw hat he bought last year at the state fair.

"Grumpy today." Even after nearly forty years in Georgia,

his accent still sounds like that of western Pennsylvania, that Yankee state, where he grew up.

"And you?" My accent is Southern, and I don't care what people say. I'm a Georgia girl.

"Grumpier."

This is our typical greeting. My parents are pig farmers in Tifton, which is a small town near Jimmy Carter's Plains, Georgia. All my life I've been the daughter of pig farmers, and I must say, I'm surprisingly proud of this heritage. My sister finds the comments she gets when she tells people what her parents do for a living embarrassing. To avoid these comments and cackles, she has shortened the truth to, "My parents have a little farm." Quaint, cute. Most people don't want to know more than that.

My dad asks about my trip, and when I answer, I omit the fact that I was almost too paralyzed to continue the drive once it started to rain.

I try to sound cheery and optimistic about beginning my new life in Bryson City. I tell him that the scenery is gorgeous and that the mountain air is almost as fresh as the air in Tifton.

Dad asks if I've seen the train that runs through the town. "Smoky Mountain Railroad has its headquarters in Bryson City," he informs me like a travel guide would. "The train goes to Dillsboro, and they have gourmet meals aboard some of the trips." I know he is tossing in the gourmet meal part to try to entice me.

"Oh?" I think I recall a set of tracks near the Methodist church along the steep, windy road up to this cabin. Trains do not impress me the way they do my father. He will stop whatever he's doing whenever he hears a train whistle or sees a train coming down the tracks. He says trains remind him of his years as a hobo, but I know he's only teasing about that.

Then my mother is on the phone, asking how long the trip took, if I have food to eat, if I took my vitamins this morning, and would I like her to send me some pickled pig's feet? I have never liked pig's feet, and I don't know why she doesn't remember that. Perhaps she thinks that for some reason they will taste more agreeable to me at this elevation. I expect to hear her tell me to sit up straight, and as we talk, my shoulders do rise and I stick out my chest.

"Sit up straight," my mother once told me when I was growing up. "You don't want to become hunched over. My aunt Lavonna Dewanna was *such* a hunchback."

I never heard the rest of her reminiscing because I couldn't believe that anyone would be named Lavonna Dewanna. I asked if that really was her name, and my mother said, "Yes, but we called her La De."

"La De!" I laughed so hard that I rolled off the bed. I was only six, but after seeing my mother's expression, I knew that I would never joke about her aunt La De again. Apparently, Mom didn't think there was anything funny at all about her aunt's name.

When I was in the hospital, sitting for any length of time, especially with my shoulders squared, was difficult, but Mom's words rung out sharper than my pain. *Sit up straight, Deena.*

I view my reflection in the mosaic mirror that hangs in the upstairs loft bedroom. I have no recollection of having climbed the staircase to the second story; my mother's voice often takes away my own reminiscences.

"Is there a washer there? How about a dryer?"

Mom's questions make me feel like I'm a child. I relax my

jaw, trying not to grit my teeth, and then slowly answer her questions in the affirmative. I can tell that she is pleased to know her daughter will be able to wash and dry her clothing. When Mom and I hang up, I meander around the loft, and then make the bed, pulling the lavender quilt over the sheets. Someone made this quilt; I finger the fabric as I study the stitches. I wonder if my grandmother, Grandpa Ernest's wife, was a quilter. She died before I was born, and I know almost nothing about her.

Downstairs, in the sunny living room, a scarlet quilt drapes over the back of the overstuffed sofa, and I note the pattern of leaves. Jeannie quilts and has tried to interest me, but I can't say I really care to learn. There are things in life you hope to do some day—like ride in a hot air balloon or go to Paris—and then there are things that you know you will never do because, in a nutshell, the desire isn't there.

On the wall behind the sofa are two pictures. The one that catches my eye is a framed print of a woman in a gold and deep-red kimono. The cloth of the kimono looks shiny and smooth. A bright fan the color of cherry blossoms covers the right side of the woman's delicate face. I wonder why she has the fan in that position. Perhaps the right side of her face has a huge mole or wart. Or maybe she was in an accident and her face is scarred. Maybe she had to have 179 stitches. Perhaps she even had plastic surgery. Suddenly, I feel an attachment to this painting. I stand back and give it another look. Then my cell phone rings again.

"Where is the nearest store?" Dad asks anxiously.

"What?"

"Your mom wants to know what the closest grocery store to you is called. She forgot to ask you."

"Ingle's," I say.

"Ingle's," Dad repeats, and I can hear my mother say, "Oh, okay." I can't tell whether she approves of this grocery store chain or not. I know her favorite place to shop for fresh produce is Publix. She will drive an extra ten miles for the opportunity to buy carrots, lettuce, red peppers, and peaches at Publix.

My dad says that Mom thought this was Piggly Wiggly country. I wonder why she makes such a fuss over supermarket chains.

Dad tells me he loves me, and suddenly I wish I were in Tifton, walking with him in thigh-high black rubber boots, feeding slop to the newest batch of rosy piglets and listening to him talk about the latest gadget he might buy. His "I love you" is tender, just like it was when he first came to see me in the hospital after the accident. There I was a mass of white bandages, and he found my cheek and gave it his signature kiss.

I tell him I love him, too, and when he hangs up I still feel the warmth of his voice through the phone.

I forget the kimono woman and her hidden face and head up the stairs to the bathroom by the loft. Earlier, I had my first breakfast (wheat toast with butter) in the cabin and I'm about to take my first shower.

The bathroom is painted forest green with tan molding along the ceiling. From the window I see the gravel driveway where my Jeep is parked and the thin, winding road that took me up here yesterday afternoon. I shudder and back away from the view. Sometimes it's best not to see just how high up the mountain you are.

After my shower, I dry off using a towel I brought here,

even though the cabin's closets are stocked with fluffy, soft towels and rose-scented sheets and pillowcases. As usual, I'm trapped into looking at my ragged scars. I can cover the one on my abdomen with clothing and avoid short skirts or shorts so that the ones on my thighs are hidden. I wonder how I can make it through a summer without exposing my arms, though. I follow the deep indentations with my finger. Train tracks—I have my own set. Two long lines run from just above my wrist up to my bicep on my right arm. Sometimes I think of them as the Tigris and Euphrates rivers.

"Do people ever name their scars?" I asked Dr. Bland one afternoon as the clouds filled the sky and the weatherman predicted snow by midnight.

He smiled and told me my scars would fade.

Chef B joked that it was good that Dr. Bland was a doctor and not a restaurant owner because who would want to eat at Bland's Restaurant? "Not good for the business," the chef said in his Spanish accent. "People think food won't be spicy or very flavor."

I am still in my bathrobe with my wet hair dripping down my neck when Sally calls. At first I can't find my cell phone again. I rush down the stairs to answer before it goes to voice mail. I have no idea when I placed my phone on the kitchen counter.

"Glad you made it to North Carolina," Sally says. "You sound out of breath. Are you okay?"

"So far, so good."

"How's the cabin?"

I think of the first thing that came to my mind when I entered the cabin yesterday. "Sunny," I say. Sunlight had filled every inch of the downstairs area as it poured through the windows, even the windows in the sloping ceiling. Light streamed across the hardwood floors—floors partially covered by a collection of round and square throw rugs. Even the purple Mexican hat with yellow tassels hanging by a nail on the wall by the hallway glistened festively. I was so glad to see the sun after the downpour I'd experienced when leaving Georgia. "There're windows along all the living room and dining room walls," I tell Sally.

"Is there a fireplace?"

I know Sally thinks a fireplace makes or breaks a place. She told me that during her years at the veterinary school in Vermont, her apartment's ceiling leaked whenever the upstairs tenant ran his dishwasher, the pantry had a live-in mouse, the odor of fried fish permeated the walls, and yet there was one saving factor: the apartment had a fireplace. Sally lit a fire every night during the cold months—of which apparently there are many in Vermont—and studied by the glowing flames.

"Yeah," I tell her as I walk over to the white stone fireplace. "And even a hot tub out on the deck." I push a blue drape back from the window to view the hot tub. Actually I don't even know if it works. The thick tan cover spreads over it like a skin, and it looks too heavy for one person to remove. Maybe my aunt can help me with that, I think. Then, like a bolt of lightning, a memory hits me. The last time I sat in a hot tub, Lucas was with me. He asked what kind of engagement ring I wanted. He took my hand, caressed my fingers, and then kissed each fingertip. "When we get married," he said, "let's get a hot tub."

"So"—Sally bursts into my thoughts—"what's next? How are the brochures?"

The brochures are part of my plan to start my own cake-decorating business here in the mountains. Eventually, I want to expand to a full-fledged catering business, but I'm going to start with cakes and see how it goes. I did a mockup of the cover weeks ago, but I still need to work on the inside copy. Sally wants to hear something positive, so I say, "It's so beautiful here. I know I'll be inspired to work on the brochures."

She sounds relieved. And I'm grateful I can protect her from how I really feel. I don't want her to worry. Let me be the one who worries in this friendship. There's no point in both of us filling that role.

When the conversation ends, exhaustion fills me, as though I've just made a five-course dinner in record time. I slide onto the bar stool. Resting my chin in the palms of my hands, my elbows supported by the counter, I stare at nothing. Then I feel warm tears fall along my fingers. Growling like a captured animal, I start to form the words. "I hate him." The sound of my own voice scares me; the tears fall faster. "I hate that he left me," I cry to the walls, the kitchen utensils, and the pictures. I turn to see the woman with the fan hiding half of her face. Annoyed that the picture is there and that I have no idea why she has that fan covering her, I yell, "I hate you, too!"

I don't even know her.

My gaze rests on my right arm, and although my arm is fully covered by the sleeve of my terry-cloth bathrobe, I know what lies beneath. I shouldn't take a shower or bath. There is just too much damage to see. Who knew a Mustang was so sharp? The word *shattered* comes at me like a large grizzly, teeth bared and ready to pounce.

———

As I pull on a pair of khakis and a pink long-sleeved shirt, I remind myself that I won the Georgia Teen Cook Award at the state fair when I was a senior in high school. This reminder is supposed to make me feel better—alive, worthy, and capable. The mayor presented me with a gold-embossed certificate and a check for fifty dollars. He told me that my winning entry—a strawberry cream pastry—was surely a sign that my life would be filled with "everything sweet from here on out." Easy for him to say; he was the mayor of Atlanta.

When I push open the sliding glass door leading to the deck, I think of how I spread the mounds of thick whipped cream onto the buttery crust of that pastry over a decade ago.

Two squirrels scamper over a mossy tree stump, reminding me that I'm not in Atlanta anymore. I take in the serene vista from the wide deck. Here at the end of April, the landscape of distant sloping mountain peaks still holds a wintery feel. There is promise of gentle green, but for the most part, the hues are still stark and brown. Except for the evergreens. Their bushy limbs spread across the pine-needle-covered terrain around me and soak up the sun's rays.

As a sparrow darts toward one of the limbs, I stand as tall as I can, lifting my chin toward a pale sky with broken clouds. I breathe in the moist earthy air and then attempt a smile. My tear-stained cheeks feel raw; I smile as broadly as I can—hopeful.

"I'm here for a new start," I say aloud, and am surprised that my voice does not waver or crack as it glides toward the mountain peak. From behind the cabin, the familiar mew of a catbird replies. Catbirds greeted me every afternoon in Tifton when the bus brought me home from school. Whenever I hear them I can't help but think of my customary after-school snack of milk and peanut butter oatmeal cookies.

Through a cluster of tree trunks to the right of the driveway, I can see one distant house the color of oregano. A gravel road winds around it. No other houses are close by, and I have the feeling that, except for nature, I'm alone.

When a breeze picks up, I head inside to continue the task of unpacking. I find room for *Easy Cooking* in the narrow bookcase that rests against the wall by the fireplace.

The case sits under an ink drawing of an ornate elephant. The beast is draped in cloths that flash red and blue jewels. On his head is a crown with sparkling diamonds. His trunk is raised and mouth opened. He is either protesting all the adornments or proud to look so majestic.

I think to myself that I probably own more cookbooks than Julia Child. I unpack each of the colorful books containing glossy photos of prize-winning desserts; each tome is almost as heavy as a sack of cake flour. I have a complete set of *Southern Living* cookbooks and one by James Beard that has a burned patch on the cover.

Am I really going to teach children how to cook? Why would my grandfather make this request of me? Why would he think I could do it?

A cookbook that does not belong to me catches my eye. The spine reads *101 Ways to Create Fabulous Cakes.* I take the book from the shelf, and the layered lemon cake on the cover looks good enought to eat. When I open the first page, something falls from it onto the floor. I pick up a white business-sized envelope. When I turn it over I see my name printed in bold letters: *FOR DEENA.*

seven

Easing myself onto a throw rug the color of raspberries, I cross my legs. I've sat like this since I was a little girl in Girl Scouts. I feel like a kid now, getting ready to open something that holds an element of surprise. I finger the white envelope for a moment. Then I guess. From the feel of it, the contents must be thin, like a sheet of paper. It could be a photo wrapped in paper. A check? Cash?

Inserting my finger under the back flap of the envelope, I open it. Reaching inside, I take out a folded legal-sized sheet of yellow, lined paper. I unfold the page to view a handwritten letter addressed to me.

Dear Deena,

Life is never as we expect it.

The love of my life died early. Your grandmother was only

sixty-one. But she could have been seventy-one or ninety-one—any time to lose her would not have been a good time.

She encouraged me, Deena. She loved her children and grandchildren. She loved life, the rolling hills in the summer, green with life, the frozen pond in the winter. She taught me how to ice skate, how to listen for each bird and learn its call.

Sometimes I have wondered why we have to face so much sorrow in this world. Our sorrows often multiply, our disappointments increase, and our hearts are heavy. Perhaps this life is not the one we would have chosen. Ah yes, we would choose ease over growth, riches over courage.

How can one live amidst all the barbs of this life? I have struggled to find out how, and have always come up with the same answer: Trust God. Put your whole hand in His, not just one finger or two. Get to know the feel of your hand in His. This is the only way I have found to live, really live.

"The greater part of our happiness or misery depends on our dispositions and not on our circumstances." Martha Washington said that, and I can't help but find a great deal of truth in her statement.

So I must conclude that life is never as we expect it. Life is what we make it.

I want you to try my recipe for Southern Peanut Soup. See if you can taste all the flavors. Sometimes you have to concentrate on the good in order to experience it. The good stuff in life doesn't always come with a big sign around its neck. We have to look, to seek. You can't help but find when your hand is firmly encased in His.

> *Love,*
> *Your Grandpa Ernest*

P.S. Eat the soup from the bowl with the raccoon.

I read the letter aloud two times. In between I sniff the

paper, note the curve of his letter T, and then study the envelope. I wonder why he never mailed it. There is no date on the letter, no postage. How did he know I would come to live here? Did he write it long ago or just before his stroke? He died instantly, they said. One minute he was enjoying a ride on a sailboat on the coast of the Greek island of Kos, and the next, he toppled over into the ocean. But here is this letter to me, hidden in a cookbook, of all things.

I finger the cookbook, open it, and note the inscription: *To Grandpa Ernest, with love from Deena.*

When did I send this book to him? Did I mail it? I try to recall, but I'm blanking out on any memory of giving this cookbook to my grandfather.

I read the letter again, pausing after each paragraph, wondering what he hoped to convey to me. Why did he feel the need to write these words to me? I know that in his will, he left instructions to give me this cabin. I'm still not sure why I am the one he bequeathed it to; he has seven other grandchildren. One lives in Los Angeles and has been on TV commercials for toilet cleaners and stain removers. He looks honest as he tells viewers that there is no other product that can do the job like Insta-Clean and Foam-Away. Why did Grandpa choose me over him?

To add to my confusion, now there's this letter that talks about God and peanut soup. If Grandpa wrote it after my accident, perhaps he was trying to encourage me. But how did Grandpa know how I was feeling? *"Sometimes I have wondered why we have to face so much sorrow in this world."* As I read the words this time, I feel the backs of my eyes stinging. Giving in to tears again will surely leave me useless the rest of the day. And I have unpacking to do, and a heart to mend.

When the doorbell rings, I hope it's Grandpa Ernest so I can ask him the questions that have formed tangles in my mind.

I open the door to find a man standing on the stoop by the chopped firewood. His back is to me, and it looks like he is testing the railing of the stoop by kicking the wood with his leather boot.

eight

The man is wearing dark jeans, a checkered shirt the color of roasted duck, and a bright yellow bandana around his head. In his hand is a large wrench. He turns to greet me with a boyish smile. "Well, hello."

He is not my grandpa back from the dead. Tentatively, I say, "Hello." I'm in the mountains—home to boiled peanuts and apple cider. Surely everything is congenial and kind here. This man isn't on "America's Most Wanted." I've left Atlanta behind.

With arms crossed around his trim waist, he says, "You must be Deirdre."

"No. No, I'm not."

He raises an eyebrow and I say, "Maybe you have the wrong house."

In a methodical tone, as if from memory, he tells me, "Pass the red barn, Memorial Methodist Church, first right."

Is he giving the location of this cabin? I'm surprised he didn't mention "And turn down the gravel path that is too narrow to be called a road—the one with no guardrails and no room for any large vehicle." I thought I was heading over the cliff yesterday.

His eyes are brown and deep-set, and his hair is auburn streaked with wisps of gray. He has the widest mouth I've ever seen. When he smiles, I see what appear to be hundreds of teeth stretching for yards. "You're Ernest's granddaughter," he says. "His granddaughter."

That part he has right. "Yes."

"Yes siree. Regena Lorraine told me about you." He shuffles his shoes, looks at them, and then peers again at me.

"Oh?" I imagine my aunt sitting down with this man and spilling out my recent past, fretting over my romance-gone-bad as she encourages him to drink a cup of sassafras tea. If she's told him all about me, why did she forget to tell me about him?

With a grin, he says, "Told me you're from Atlanta. Yes, yes, siree." His tone has a halting quality about it, almost as though he is reading his words from a script he isn't fully comfortable with.

"I'm Deena."

His large, calloused, warm hand grips mine. "I'm Jonas. I'm here to fix the pipes."

"Is something wrong with the pipes?" I have visions of water leaking while I sleep and waking to find my bed being carried by torrents out of the cabin, over the cliffs, down to Fontana Lake.

He winks. Few people can pull off a wink without looking corny. He is one of the few. "You can never be too sure.

Never too sure." With that, he enters the cabin, his heavy work boots crushing the hardwood. He seems harmless and a little different.

He sees I've been unpacking. I watch his eyes rove among the boxes sitting on the sofa, the countertops, the dining room floor.

"Don't let me bother you, Deirdre. You go right on doing what you need to do." He swings his wrench a little too swiftly for my comfort. "Yes siree. I'll be checking."

This time when he smiles, I think part of his mouth has stretched clear to Tennessee.

nine

Miriam runs The Center at the Nantahala Presbyterian Church in Bryson City. I suppose her title would be Director. She's part Cherokee and part Swiss, she tells me. Her eyes are the kind of blue that makes me think of an autumn sky, and her skin is creamy brown. Her hair is shiny, like the coat of a seal. Immediately, I am surprised to see that although she is dressed in Ann Taylor's newest spring line—a scoop-neck aqua satin blouse and black skirt—on her feet are grass-green tennis shoes.

She tells me that my grandfather was a big supporter of The Center and of her desire to establish a 501(c)(3) organization to keep kids off the streets after school and during the summer months. I am learning new things about my grandpa every day. It's like Christmas, opening all of these surprising revelations. I used to think all he cared about was food and travel.

We stand in Miriam's office, a tiny compartment to the left

of the hallway in an annexed section of the church. I wonder why a director doesn't wear heels. She tells me how the younger kids in the preschool program at the church enjoyed having my grandfather read books to them. "Dr. Seuss was never the same for me after your grandfather read *Oh, the Places You'll Go.* We all miss him here." Her smile is warm; her eyes sparkle.

I am glad to know my grandpa was thought of so fondly, but I'm not sure I can recall *Oh, the Places You'll Go.* I make a mental note to brush up on my Dr. Seuss and then have a fleeting thought that maybe Grandpa gave my sister and me *Green Eggs and Ham* one Christmas. As children of pig farmers, we were used to getting books, cards, and comments about pigs, ham, bacon, tenderloin, and pork chops.

When I was small, my grandparents still lived in Pennsylvania, where Dad was born. Dad moved to Georgia in his twenties after attending business school. I recall him telling me that as a child, kinfolk would comment that Edna, his mother, must have forgotten which town she was in when she had her sixth child, which was my dad. Ernest and Edna hadn't lived in Lancaster since 1930, so why did they name my dad Lancaster? Dad was born in 1945 in the brick house where they lived in Altoona. He has always been grateful his mother didn't name him Altoona. "Lancaster is a fine name," he has told me over the years. "Lancaster has a solid ring to it." Such a nice ring, in fact, that my middle name is Lancaster. Growing up in the South, I longed for a more debutante-quality name like Deena Ann, Deena Joy, Deena Marie, or even Deena Sue. But no, my dad had to provide me with a *solid name.*

The Center's kitchen smells like a mixture of day-old popcorn and lemon-scented cleaner. The gas stove is clearly industrial, though not as large as the one at Palacio del Rey. A stab of pain jabs at my heart as I wonder what everyone at the restaurant is doing today. Do they miss me? Is the new baker as good as I was? Does she take the time to pipe perfect roses for the tops of the vanilla crème cakes? Does Anthony ask her to taste his sauces to see if they are seasoned just right?

Miriam's voice breaks into my thoughts. "Would you like to buy the ingredients you'll need and give us the receipts and we'll refund you? That might be easier than one of us here shopping. We might not buy the right items."

We stand by the kitchen's pantry. The pantry door is ajar, so I can see stacks of white china plates and coffee cups. I consider the options and decide I'll purchase the ingredients for the classes, because that way I can be assured I'll be cooking with the correct products. The Center can reimburse me—if I can manage to keep track of the receipts.

Miriam asks if I can start teaching tomorrow afternoon and teach a class every weekday afternoon right after the kids get off the school bus. I start to say that I don't really care because I'm obligated to do this as part of my grandfather's instructions, but then I decide that would make it seem as if I don't really want to teach. Actually, I would rather bungee jump off the Blue Ridge Parkway than teach, but I can't let Miriam discover that. She hands me a form to fill out and asks, "You want your paycheck directly deposited or mailed to you?"

My bank is in Altanta, but I think they have a Bank of America office here, too. I make a mental note to check on that. They do have many of the other modern conveniences like Burger King, McDonalds, grocery stores, and gas stations. I tell her that direct deposit will be fine and stuff the forms into my purse.

She demonstrates how to use the dishwasher, the sink,

and the disposal. I nod and thank her for showing me. I'm tempted to say that I have worked in kitchens for a long time now, that I am a graduate of a fine culinary school, but I really don't think boasting in church is acceptable.

"The sink does drip," she tells me as three droplets sail from the faucet. "Our plumber should be by to fix it one of these days."

I wonder if I should recommend Jonas to her. He knows how to tighten every pipe with his swinging wrench. When he left yesterday, he told me, "All your pipes are working good" and I had to smile.

We pause by the window over the sink to watch a group of kids play basketball on a paved court. A tall man with curly blond hair that bounces as he goes for the rebound is with them. I watch him quickly reach for a pass and stretch his arms to toss the orange ball through the hoop. A short boy wearing red sneakers tries to block the pass but doesn't succeed. Basketball and I haven't had much experience together. I played in high school only when the gym teacher required us to do so fall semester of my freshman year. Since then, I haven't picked up a basketball, and like creative writing, I don't miss it.

Miriam smiles. "He's a cutie," she says.

I assume she means the man, although the young boy with the red shoes is cute, too. He turns so that his face is visible, and I notice his large, brown eyes under straight, black hair.

The curly-haired guy's face breaks into a smile as the boy pulls the ball from behind him and dribbles it down the paved court. The man's smile doesn't go to Tennessee like Jonas's, but it looks confident, secure, self-assured—if all those things can be displayed in a smile, and seeing his, I'm certain that they can. He has all the characteristics I no longer possess.

He and I may be at the same church, but we are not on the same planet.

Suddenly, into the kitchen comes a woman with hair the color of a pumpkin, skin darker than Miriam's, and a glare that shouts of hatred. As her voice bellows across the counters, I cower behind Miriam. My fingers are knotted balls.

"Felicia, you are not to be here," Miriam says boldly. "I will call the cops."

"Zack told me I can see my boy."

"Only when you have an appointment."

"He's my son. I can see him whenever I please."

"That is not what the terms are." Miriam's eyes are cold; no sparkle from earlier remains.

"I'm not in jail anymore. I'm free. I can do whatever I want to now."

"You will land back in jail with that attitude."

"Where is Darren?"

"Felicia, you need to leave now."

"Make me!"

"I'm calling the cops." Miriam pulls a cell phone from her pocket and flips it open. She punches numbers.

But it is not a cop who steps into the kitchen right then. It is the tall basketball player, dripping with perspiration. "Felicia," he says with strength and calmness, "you know the rules."

"I want my boy. I just want to see my boy. Please, Zack." The woman's voice cracks with each word. I think she is on the verge of tears.

Zack glances at Miriam, who shrugs her shoulders. Turning to the distraught woman, he says, "Come with me," and gently ushers her out of the kitchen as Miriam follows with halting steps.

I stand alone next to the industrial stove. The sink drips twice, pauses, and then lets out four more droplets, all of which end up in a blurry mass.

ten

Back at my grandfather's cabin, I make a dinner of fried potatoes and onions—one of the quick-and-easy recipes I've grown to love and will probably still be making when I'm ninety. As I smell the comforting aroma of onions sizzling in butter, I think to myself that I should have told her. While Miriam and I stood there at the church kitchen window watching Zack play basketball with the children, before Felicia's unexpected arrival, I should have said, "Well, guys aren't important to me now. Cute or otherwise."

But what if she had asked why not? Would I have been able to tell her about Lucas? I still don't want to talk about him.

I use one of my grandfather's stainless-steel spatulas to flip over a slice of potato. I study it to see how brown it's become. "Never tell people too much about yourself at first," my mother always told my sister, Andrea, and me growing up. "Leave room for them to ask about you. Besides, no one really cares." Another mixed message from my mother; those little pieces of wisdom have become part of the woven fabric of my childhood. Do this, but don't. Mom's advice on dating was, "Be coy around men, but don't play games."

If you're not supposed to talk about yourself and you are supposed to wait for people to ask about you, and yet people don't really care to hear about you, then how will you ever get a chance to share about yourself?

When Andrea and I hear something that doesn't make sense, we'll say, "Sounds like one of Mom's expressions." Andrea and her way-too-handsome husband, Mark, are missionaries in Taiwan now, and she often feels she's getting mixed messages. *You should see some of the English translated by Chinese—totally confusing,"* she wrote in an e-mail message shortly after she and Mark arrived in Taipei. *"I think Mom's influence is strong even in Asia."*

As I set a place for one at the wooden dining table, I decide that it is just as well that I didn't mention anything about Lucas to Miriam.

———

I wake and look at the digital clock on the bedside table. Two minutes after three. What woke me? Did I have pain in my legs, or my arms? What is that noise? I turn on my stomach and cover the back of my head with a pillow. This is a crazy thing to do because who can sleep with a pillow smothered over your head? The pillow feels heavy and stifles my neck. I can't breathe. I toss the pillow aside. The noise is still there. Sitting up, I realize that it must be the hooting of an owl. Once, we had an owl living in our oak tree by the barn. My mother wanted to call the county extension service to come and rid us of its disturbing cries. But Daddy said the owls were in Tifton long before humans were and that we had to just let it be.

I'm wide awake now. I've slept through the sirens that blare throughout Atlanta, but sleeping through nature's cries will take some getting used to. I wonder how Yolanda is doing. I miss the Peruvian delicacies she would share with me. My thoughts of arroz con pollo and leche asada are replaced with thoughts of my little apartment. My bedside table not only held an alarm clock but also a framed picture of Lucas. The thought of Lucas causes my skin to itch.

One thing I don't do well is lie awake at night. Getting out of bed and doing something helps me when I can't go back to sleep. After the accident, I woke at all hours, so I invested in a number of jigsaw puzzles. I sat at my kitchen table many nights while sirens blared around my neighborhood, working on finding the pieces to quiet forest scenes.

I leave my bed, pull on my bathrobe, climb down the loft stairs, and head outside onto the deck via the sliding glass door.

The night is chilly, but the fresh air feels good against my face and in my lungs. I stand with my hands on the deck railing and watch the stars glitter above me. They look so near; if I just reached out, I could gather a few hundred in my hand.

The owl continues his own concerto. Unlike the stars, he wants to remain unseen. I once wondered aloud what it would be like to listen to an orchestra play Vivaldi's *La Stravaganza* in total darkness. No viewing of the musicians playing violins—just an audience sitting and listening to the notes in the blackness. Lucas asked me how the musicians would read their music if there was no light. I hadn't thought of that. I suppose it would be too much to ask them to memorize it all.

Lucas said it was an intriguing idea, however, and gave me that smile of his that seemed to encompass total appreciation for me.

"Ha!" I cry into the air. There is strength in the sound of my own voice. "Ha!" I repeat and hear the echo in the forest around my cabin.

I now wonder if Lucas's smiles meant anything at all. When did he stop loving me? I once told Sally that perhaps he was trying to kill me that rainy night. She shook her head so hard her curls flung into her eyes. "Oh, Deena, no. No."

"He was angry at me. We'd been arguing. Maybe he did want to kill me," I said as Sally continued shaking her curls.

I don't know why on this beautiful mountain night I have to spoil everything by thinking about Lucas, but my mind will not stray from these thoughts. Leaving Lucas and Atlanta was supposed to make me forget.

Finding out your boyfriend is secretly seeing someone else, and has been for a long time, makes your stomach feel like a bully wearing spikes just kicked it. When you're a couple going to the movies on Friday night, when you've pledged your hearts to each other, and he asks someone else to dinner on Saturday, well, that burns.

It happened to me. And she's pretty. Very. There I was picking out wedding invitations—contemplating over gold-embossed or silver-lined and imagining the elegantly wrapped gifts guests would send us—and Lucas was wrapping his lips around Ella Loloby.

The nurse had just given me one of my Toradol pills when Sally and Jeannie entered the room and told me this. They asked how I was, but I could tell that was not why they were glancing at each other, avoiding my eyes, and refusing to smile.

They waited to tell me until after the nurse took my temperature, checked the bandage around my forehead, and left the room.

Sally bit her lower lip. I've noted her habit; it's always the right side of her bottom lip she sinks her pearly whites into. "Lucas is seeing Ella Lolly."

"Loboly," corrected Jeannie with certainty.

"Lobolo," said Sally as she reached for my bandaged arm.

I moved my arm away from Sally's hand. "What do you mean *seeing*?" I asked. My throat felt like someone was stuffing toast down it.

Sally moistened her lips, then bit her lower one. "Dating her," she said. I could see the surge of pain in her eyes. I wanted to comfort her and tell her not to be so sad.

"They were out together Saturday at that new Italian restaurant."

"The Mona Lisa," I said. Lucas and I ate there often. I loved their portabella mushrooms served with creamy fettuccini. "She's a wedding planner," I told my friends. "Maybe he was asking her for tips about our wedding."

Jeannie moved closer to my bed. "Honey," she said, "the only tip he was getting was on how to make out with the wedding planner after dinner and before dessert."

Suddenly, just like that, a cloud appeared in my hospital room. It must have entered from the vent right over the bobbing purple *Get Well* balloon. Lucas and Ella? "But . . . but she isn't even a Braves fan!"

Sally looked at me like I had lost my mind, but Jeannie murmured, "I know, I know."

I wanted to jump out of the bed, pull off the bandages,

and run. Run to a place where things were still bright and perfect.

"You're going to be just fine, honey," Jeannie said, and this time I let Sally hold my hand as Jeannie stroked my other arm. "You'll be okay."

Jeannie should know about these things. She's been divorced twice. She's only thirty-two. She's also prematurely gray.

I waited until they left to let what they had told me sink in.

When the nurse came in at midnight to check my vitals, I was sitting up in the bed crying into the bouquet of white lilies, red carnations, and baby's breath my parents had brought the day before. The nurse sat on the edge of my bed and rubbed my back with slender fingers. At last she said, "It's gonna get better."

She didn't say a word about the long-stemmed red roses that swam in the toilet bowl. Later that night she sent an aide to fish them out. He wore latex gloves and a funny grin. As he left, I wondered when Lucas had brought the roses for me. Was it before or after he went out with Ella? Did he call the florist and order them at the same time he called the Mona Lisa to make dinner reservations for himself and Ella?

Red roses were delivered to the restaurant where I worked when Lucas and I first got engaged. I felt so excited when I saw them in the tall narrow vase. Chef B grinned like a silly schoolboy. The whole restaurant staff couldn't stop smiling. I was engaged to Lucas; we were going to be married within a year! Delight spilled out of me that night as I prepared and decorated a chiffon cream cake. Never was there a more joyfully decorated border on a cake. Anyone who looked closely could see that each dot had a smile; every pearl was as exquisite as a wedding bouquet.

I step back into the cabin, close the sliding door behind me, and lock it. I'm from the city, so I believe in locking things with as many deadbolts as possible. My apartment had three locks. Yolanda invested in four.

The moonlight shines on the sofa where my journal lies. I haven't added a line to it since the morning I traveled here, and that seems like weeks ago. Out of consideration for my former boss, I feel obligated to use this hardbound book. Obligation—how much of what we do is just because of a sense of obligation? I am obligated to teach cooking, thanks to my grandpa. I am obligated to listen to my mother share about her oddly named relatives and her messages of wisdom. As a child, I was obligated to attend state fairs and hand out flyers on ordering a ham from our family's pig farm.

As the owl continues his or her nighttime noise, I pick up the journal and open to the next blank page. The pages are so crisp, so white, so unoccupied. If I write my thoughts and feelings, the pages will become gray, ugly, damaged. I hear Chef B's instructions: "She write her heart onto the pages of her journal. She find some peace. Write each day. Date on the page."

Stretched out on the sofa, I cover myself with the quilt and write: *3 A.M. Grandpa Ernest's cabin.* I don't bother with the date because I'm not exactly sure if it's the 28th or 29th.

Okay, what next? How does one go about writing her heart? I place a hand over my heart as though that gesture will help me know the exact words to jot onto the journal page. After a moment, I am able to write: *Lucas heard about my scars and left.* Placing the cap back on the pen, I stare at the words I've just written. They won't let me leave them alone. Pulling the cap off the pen, I add the lines: *No, he left way before the accident. He was going out with Ella before Christmas of last year. My scars had nothing to do with him cheating on me.*

That is all I write. I am afraid that if I write more, I might not be able to go back to sleep. Lucas is a two-timer. Lucas is history. He will never come through the door and apologize. He didn't want to marry me. He just didn't know how to break up.

I am halfway to the loft when I come back down the stairs to pick up the journal and add more thoughts. Seated on the edge of the couch, I write one more line: *My only crime is that I loved the wrong person.*

I ease into bed and the calling owl disturbs me for a bit longer. Finally either I have tuned him out or he's moved to a tree farther away. Surprisingly, sleep comes over me, accompanied by a peaceful dream. In the dream, I'm in a parade, complete with billowing banners and helium balloons. The float I'm riding on is not for the homecoming queen, but rather for the girl who found out her fiancé was cheating on her before she married him. The mayor is even there, handing out free cake samples. He congratulates me on learning the truth before it was much too late.

eleven

The idea for my cake decorating business came from Jeannie. When I told Jeannie and Sally one night over a dinner of garlic scallops, tomato risotto, cranberry spinach salad, and herb rolls that I had inherited Grandpa's cabin and was considering a move to Bryson City, they wondered aloud how I could quit my job at Palacio del Rey.

"How will you pay the bills?" Practical Sally wanted to know.

"My aunt said that the utility bills will continue to be paid from some bank account," I told her.

Sally raised her eyebrows. "Sounds a little mysterious." Nodding, she said, "I like it."

"Maybe the neighbor pays them with money he and my grandpa stole together on some venture in the Caribbean."

Sally's eyes lit up like they always do when she thinks a topic is fascinating. "Yeah, and the cops are after your neighbor and they come to your grandpa's cabin to ask you to open a safe that is locked up in the basement."

We laughed and ate slices of peach pie for dessert. I had tried a new pie recipe, one that used brown sugar and rolled oats in the crust. "Every cook should willing to try the new," Chef B told us in his basic cooking class. With a crooked smile, he added, "And willing to accept the old might still be best." Although I like oatmeal and brown sugar, I prefer standard white flour crust for my peach pies.

"All right," said Sally as she finished her slice. "So the utilities are paid for and there's no mortgage or rent. What are you going to do for food and clothes and Band-Aids and gas money?" Again, the very practical vet.

"Maybe you could get a job as a pastry chef in the mountains," suggested Jeannie. "Or," she added as a smile crossed her lips, "build your own catering business."

"I don't know," I said.

Jeannie persevered. "How about a cake decorating business?"

That's when we all smiled.

I have the brochure's design on a file on my computer. Jeannie took a picture of my chocolate swirl ice cream cake and I placed that on the cover. The cake is no tiramisu, but it does look regal in the photo.

I wanted to put a picture of the seven-tiered wedding cake I created for Chef B's sister's wedding last fall on the cover. While Jeannie said the cake was "definitely classy," she wondered if it was too fancy. "People in the mountains," Jeannie explained, "want a delicious cake that is simple."

Sally said to make sure I put something in my brochure about working at Palacio del Rey as a pastry chef. She felt that would give me clout. "And the fact that you studied in Atlanta," she added. "People think of Atlanta as the New York City of the South."

I thought, *They do?* but didn't question Sally. When Sally has that I-know-what-I'm-saying look in her eyes and tone in her voice, I know not to question my friend. Her clients' owners don't ask, "What do you mean my cat has a hairball?" or "Why are you suggesting that my dog needs eye drops for his red eyes?"

Of course, Jeannie and Sally didn't really think I'd leave Atlanta to move to the home of a grandfather I rarely saw. They were just trying to go along with my cake business plan to keep my mind off Lucas. When I told them I was moving in April, they acted as though I'd told them I was marrying Elvis.

Sally and I rented a U-Haul, and with the help of three friends from church, we were able to load up my apartment's furnishings and drive them to my parents' for storage. Sally and I spent a night on the farm, ate blueberry pancakes with maple syrup and a side of thick bacon strips for breakfast, and then she drove me back to my apartment in Atlanta. As we entered my kitchen crammed with partially packed cardboard boxes, she said in a soft tone, "You don't have to carry through with this, you know."

I had taken all my furniture to my parents and was planning to spend my last two nights in Atlanta in my sleeping bag. On the hard floor. I wasn't going to quit my plan to relocate.

———

Standing in the checkout line at Ingle's, I suddenly have a hard time believing that the people in this town would care that I've studied and worked in Atlanta. I envision most of the locals shrugging their shoulders and saying, "Who cares?"

Thank goodness I've decided to start out just with cakes and not a full-fledged catering service.

As small as this store is, they still have a rack by the checkout line crammed with glossy women's magazines, just like any grocery store in the big city. I used to subscribe to *People,* but now I avoid its cover. I look away from the issues of *Glamour, Elle, Good Housekeeping,* and *Allure.* I don't need to see perfect smiles and skin today, or any day.

I keep my eyes on my shopping cart or, as the real Southerners call it, buggy. I stare at what I've placed there—the tiny carton of half-and-half, whipping cream, gallon of milk, clear jug of orange juice, blue plastic bag of confectioner's sugar, head of lettuce, can of jumbo olives, balsamic salad dressing, and two gray cartons of large eggs. A rack of donuts placed by the checkout catches my eye, and my stomach agrees that donuts always make a home cozier. I pick out a bag of Krispy Kreme mini crullers.

When the woman in front of me—dressed in an emerald wool cap that reveals pink puffy curlers secured in her gray hair—starts to complain about not getting to use a coupon, I can't help but look up from the donut box to see what is going on. However, once I look up, it's as if the newest issue of *Glamour* is taunting me to take a peek. Lowering my eyes, I place the donuts in the buggy.

"Those bodies are all air brushed," Sally told me shortly after my accident. "You don't believe that those celebrities have no moles or laugh lines, do you?"

"Well . . ."

"Come on, Deena. Everyone has a scar or two. Be realistic. These Hollywood starlets never fell off their bikes or got stitches?" She looked at me and smiled. "Every other day one of them steps up to admit she had plastic surgery. I bet most of what they show off on the covers isn't real."

Still, as it is with so much of life, it depends on what others think is real. Other people think celebrities really are just that flawlessly beautiful. And compared to them, I am a train wreck. The scars on my right arm glare at me through my long-sleeved shirt. They remind me every day that I am no longer beautiful. I was the homecoming queen in high school and now look at me! People used to say my brown hair and eyes were prettier than Julia Roberts's. Now I just have a pair of rivers, the Tigris and Euphrates. If you look closely, you can even see the fertile Nile River Valley where the scars meet just an inch from my wrist.

"The scars will fade in time." Dr. Bland's voice usually enters my thoughts when I get on this well-worn path called Feeling Sorry for Myself.

The cashier, a young girl with several moles dotting her arms, is trying to help the woman in curlers. "That coupon expired last month," she says sympathetically.

The woman raises both hands. "Then that means I can't buy the dog food?"

"Well, you can buy it," the cashier tells her. "You just can't use the coupon."

The woman lowers her hands, shakes her head. "I have been shopping at this store all my life!" she blurts out and then takes a breath. "I can't believe you won't let me use the coupon!"

"Ma'am, it's expired."

"What will Sinatra do?" She lovingly strokes the twenty-two-pound bag of Kibbles 'n Bits. "What will he do? I can't bear it. I can't."

I am assuming Sinatra is her canine.

"He had surgery last week. This may be the last dog food I get to buy him," she says, turning to me.

I don't know what to say. I keep my mouth shut, afraid that instead of showing empathy I'll shout out "I'm allergic to dogs!"

The cashier notes the line forming behind me. A man in a Hurricanes cap clears his throat; another customer rattles change in his pocket. The cashier asks, "Ma'am, what are you going to do?"

The woman eyes her and states firmly, "That's my question. I think you should let me use the coupon. Where is the manager?" Her eyes are beady, like little tan pellets, perhaps similar to the dog food she wants.

The cashier sighs, and the next thing I know, she shakes her head and punches some buttons on her keypad. The woman with the curlers is now wearing a smile as bright as the curlers on her head. She pays for the dog food and teeters out of the store like she's just won the blue ribbon at the state fair, her bag of Kibbles 'n Bits towering in her shopping buggy.

"I know that woman," the man behind me says to no one, to all of us. "Marble Gray," he spits out. "She'll cheat you out of your underwear, if she can."

Marble Gray with a dog named Sinatra? Aunt Regena Lorraine with a furry creature named Giovanni? What happened to the traditional pet names like Fido and Daisy? Sally and Jeannie will never believe these names when I tell them. Especially not Jeannie, believer that folks want *simple* in these parts.

———

I put on a long-sleeved blue cotton shirt and a denim skirt

to wear to teach my first cooking lesson. The long sleeves are a must for me; they cover even my wrists. I don't need middle-schoolers asking me questions about my injuries.

When school lets out at 2:50, the kids will ride the bus from Swain County Middle School to The Center, arriving at 3:05. Miriam told me that my class will start shortly after that. She also said that about halfway through my lesson, I should allow one break so that the children can play basketball outside. "We like them to get their exercise," she said.

I stare at myself in the round mirror with the mosiac frame. I smile, hoping to exude the confidence that the young man playing basketball exhibited. Forget it; I can't cover up the truth. The truth is spelled n-e-r-v-o-u-s. I've never taught kids before. Well, once I did teach summer Sunday school to second graders, but that was ages ago. I haven't been to church in months. I don't broadcast this to just anyone, though. Mom would shake her head, certain I am on my way to hell. Dad would try to comfort her, and I'd want to crawl under the carpet and join all the microscopic critters that live there.

Smiling into the mirror, I push my shoulders back and try to show poise, grace, and calmness—everything that teachers are supposed to have.

"Cooking is my passion," I say to my reflection. The words seem to float around in the room, and I grab them and let them rest inside me. If cooking is my passion, then telling someone else about it should be easy, right? Fluffing my hair, I smile into the mirror again, but soon break away because my look of fearful anticipation is making my stomach ache.

At the Presbyterian church, I park in front of the gray-stone annexed building that connects to the main sanctuary by a narrow hallway. Inside The Center's hallway, laminated signs point to the right to indicate where the preschool classes are. These classes, Miriam told me yesterday, are held Monday through Friday from nine until noon. Down a corridor to the left, next to Miriam's office, a sign announces *The Center.*

I swallow three times, using Sally's advice, and grip my Whole Foods bag. As I walk, I note the Bible verses on the walls. In bold black letters, suspended above a large bulletin board, are the words *God is love.* A sign on the wall next to the board reads, *Jesus said: I have not come to call the righteous, but sinners.* By a closed door on the right of the hall, a round plaque declares, *Trust in the Lord with all your heart and lean not on your own understanding. Proverbs 3:5.* At the kitchen door, a poster lists the fruit of the Spirit: love, gentleness, kindness, goodness, faithfulness, patience, self-control, peace, joy.

Hearing voices, I enter the kitchen by swinging open the large brown door. The kitchen is where Miriam told me the class would meet. It's full—children are seated on metal folding chairs. Darren, the boy with the deep brown eyes from yesterday, is absorbed with drawing in a notebook that he steadies on his thigh. His felt pen moves quickly across the page.

Miriam is there, too, standing with her cell phone in her hand. She greets me with a smile and a flash of her blue eyes. Some people are really overly blessed in the good-looks department.

"Everyone, this is Miss Livingston," Miriam says to the waiting group of middle-schoolers. "She has just moved here from Atlanta."

twelve

"I've been to Atlanta."

This is proudly spoken by a girl with a massive amount of curly hair and a Harley Davidson T-shirt. She is seated next to Darren.

"I saw a Braves game," a boy with a buzz cut bellows.

"You did not!" the curly-haired girl squeals. "You are such a liar!"

"Your momma's a liar," says the boy.

Miriam claps her hands twice and the room comes to order. "Let me introduce the children," she says to me. Starting with Darren and going around the room she tells me their names. "Darren. Charlotte. Lisa. Dougy. Bubba. Rainy. Bobby. Joy."

I relax a little. Eight, I think. How hard can teaching eight kids be?

Joy, the curly-haired girl, raises her hand. "Are you related to Mr. Livingston?"

"Yes," I say.

"He died," she tells me.

"Yes."

There is chatter and comments I can't decipher, and then Miriam claps her hands again and the class settles. When her phone rings, she leaves me alone with them.

My stomach feels like a blender on high speed. I try to smile at the assembled group. They all look at me—all but Darren, who is focused on his notebook. Standing straight—how awful to slouch on my first day of teaching—I find my words. "We'll start with the basics."

I found a cloth Whole Foods bag in the cabin and have used it to carry the ingredients for today's lesson. From it, I take a saucepan and place it on the stove. Then I pull out a stick of butter, a small sealed jug of milk, and a bag of white flour. I look into my saucepan, and for a second, I have no clue what to say next. I look out at the students. They're surprisingly silent, just staring back at me. I finally say, "We'll make a white sauce."

"White sauce?" asks the one who I think is named Bobby. He is stocky, and his shirt keeps rising up to show his soft and generous white tummy.

"Why can't we make a brown sauce?" asks the girl named Rainy as she adjusts a pair of sunglasses over her large, round eyes.

"How about French fries? Can we make them?" A girl with long brown hair jumps out of her chair. I think her name is Lisa.

After that everyone talks at once.

"Let's just go get some at Burger King."

"Yeah, their fries are good."

"Duh!"

"No, you have to go to McDonald's. They have the best fries."

"No way!"

"You're making me hungry."

"Kids!" I am amazed at the power of my own voice. I have their attention; now what do I do? "Sit down." I point to the chairs as if they don't know where to sit. My tone is like a tractor leveling the ground on a spring day. "We are going to listen." I measure milk and butter with yellow plastic cups I pull out of the paper bag. I turn the heat on low under the saucepan and add butter, flour, then milk. Suddenly I realize I have brought nothing with which to stir the sauce. I open a drawer and find knives. I slide over to another and find forks. "I need a spoon," I say. The sauce is going to burn if I don't stir it soon.

"Look to your left," says Lisa.

"No, her right, dummy!" Bobby's voice booms across the room.

I look in both directions and find a wooden spoon in a canister filled with utensils. If the canister had been a snake, it would have just had to slither once to make it into the sauce-pan. Quickly, I stir the melted butter and bubbly milk. I lower the heat.

"Can I go to the bathroom?" asks the girl named Charlotte. This is the first time she has spoken. I tell her she may go.

"Are you Mr. Livingston's granddaughter?" Joy asks. Flatly, she adds, "He never told us about you."

"Can we play basketball now?" Bobby asks.

I try not to roll my eyes at the group, or scold them like my mother would. "Please come here and watch this sauce."

"Where do you live? Are you from here?" Joy seems to have a lot of questions.

"Dummy, didn't you hear? She's from Atlanta!" This is from the boy with the buzz cut. I now realize his name is Dougy because I see that DOUGY is printed across his green shirt.

"Please get out of your chairs and come here. Now!" I hope my voice sounds authoritative.

They all leave their seats to form a circle around the stove as I stir the white sauce. "It will thicken soon," I say and just then I notice one child is still seated and shading in some drawing on a notebook page.

"Please come here." I eye Darren, but he refuses to budge.

"Darren never participates during the inside stuff," Lisa tells me.

"He's afraid," says another.

"He's scared of stoves," says Bubba.

Darren looks up. With fire in his eyes he shouts at me, "Cooking is a waste of time! Why did you come here? We don't need you!"

His words slice a part of my heart.

thirteen

Do not cry, I say to myself, which makes it harder not to cry. I am the only adult in the room—I can't let them see me fall apart. I focus on the pan on the stove.

"It does get thick," Lisa observes, chewing on a strand of her brown hair.

"What do you use it for?" Bubba is suddenly interested. I'm not sure why he's called Bubba; he is one of the scrawniest boys I've ever seen, looking no older than a third grader.

"You can add cheese to it and pour it over broccoli or pasta." I work hard to make my voice even and steady.

The kids don't care. They just want to go outside. And find the nearest McDonald's for the best fries.

I wonder what to do next. The clock on the wall says it's 3:14. How long was this lesson supposed to be? "What do you all make at home?" I ask, hoping to take up some time.

"My grandma doesn't like to cook."

"We eat McDonald's!"

"I like onion rings better than fries," Dougy informs us.

Darren just sits and draws. When I ask to see his notebook, he slams it shut.

"Okay," I say as I inhale. "Why don't y'all go outside?"

This is just what they have been waiting for. They race outdoors, and I feel my frustration mount. I should have gone really basic and taught them how to boil an egg. Regret fills me, and to try to shake it off, I begin to wash out the saucepan in the large sink. Flinging open cabinets, I finally find the dish soap—Palmolive, the same kind we use at the restaurant. I squeeze drops onto a scouring pad.

The door swings open, and I glance over my shoulder to see the tall basketball-playing guy from the other day. He gets a drink of water from a plastic container in the fridge.

"You're Deena Livingston, aren't you?"

With the scouring pad still in my hand, I smile. "And you're Zack."

He nods. "Zack Anderson." Placing the water container back into the fridge, he asks, "How did it go?"

"What?" I turn off the water.

"Aren't you the cooking teacher? Didn't you have a class just now?"

I sigh and sink my hands deeper into the suds.

He comes over to the counter where the Tupperware container of white sauce sits. He sniffs. "Butter?"

"White sauce." Don't these mountain folk know anything?

"White sauce?" The way he says it, I am so aware that this was not the item to prepare today. I have made a big mistake. What was I thinking?

He uses one hand to brush back his curly hair. I've always wished my straight hair would one day turn into a head of curls. Sally says for me not to be fooled, that curly-haired people have plenty of coiffure-related troubles. When I see her thick, red hair, full of lively curls, I can never think of one.

Zack asks, "So, did the kids do okay?"

I know we are in church, and I know that telling the truth is important. Even so, I lie. "They were great." My smile is as plastic as the Tupperware.

"Terrific!" He produces dimples in both cheeks and light in his hazel eyes. Yes, some people are way too blessed in the appearance department. I bet he has no scars or moles or flaws whatsoever. I'm certain he models regularly for *GQ*.

"Yeah." I sigh.

"Sorry I missed it." He stands beside me as my fingers work to scrub the last of the white sauce out of the pan. "I wanted to be here to make sure everything went well on your first day, but I got a phone call from social services about another kid, and that took a lot of time."

"Well, thanks for your concern."

"Yep." He grins at me, then leaves the kitchen.

What on earth am I doing? What was I thinking, quitting my job to come here? Why did I leave Atlanta? I left a place where I was wanted and needed and where no one yelled at me.

Closing my eyes, I breathe in, trying to smell the aroma from the kitchen at Palacio del Rey. I see a leg of lamb marinating in basil and mint and a plate of fresh asparagus cooked in butter, garnished with slivered almonds. Next, I conjure the aroma of the light buttercream frosting of my velvet white cake and just the idea of it sends a pang of yearning to my heart. I see each uniformed employee in my mind; all the dishes they will make for dinner tonight whirl before me—perfect and ready to be enjoyed. I try hard to get a whiff of one of them, but all I smell is lemon-scented cleaner and yesterday's popcorn.

I take in another breath. There is one more scent—nostalgia.

fourteen

Lucas was seated in the pew in front of Sally and me. I sat through the whole church service staring at his wavy black hair. The sermon was on David and Bathsheba. That should have been my first clue that he was bad news. If you are seated in a sanctuary and the pastor preaches on sin and greed, do not greedily hope that the cute new guy in front of you will ask you out and not at all be interested in the dozens of other attractive single women in the other pews. Women with four-year degrees, wearing Liz Taylor perfume. Women with 401(k)s and matching leather luggage.

I stuck out my hand, told him my name, was too nervous to remember his, and invited him to the singles Sunday school class. I hoped that the way I said *singles* didn't make it sound like it was a horrible disease. I was twenty-five and often thought I was carrying some deadly flaw or illness that kept me from finding the love of my life.

Lucas smiled and his aqua eyes crinkled at the edges. His black lashes gently swooped down, and when he looked at me again, we both smiled.

Then others approached him and I was literally lost in the swarming crowd.

The next week he appeared in my Sunday school class, making his way toward me. I felt anticipation fill every pore in my body, although, of course, thanks to my upbringing, I knew not to show it. When he chose the chair next to mine, I could feel my pounding heart.

We talked after that class about the simple things that are often discussed at the beginnings of relationships—the best restaurants in town, noisy neighbors, and the Atlanta Braves. Caught up in the moment, we nearly missed the worship service that followed.

When he called me four days later, I thought I was the luckiest girl on the planet. The sensation was even more exciting than baking a three-tier butter cake and icing it with the most perfect pink roses.

―――

"So how was teaching?" Aunt Regena Lorraine asks as she boils water for sassafras tea. She is standing next to me in the kitchen, where I just pulled a white velvet cake from the oven. The aroma is enticing. However, her question quells my cheerful mood.

Funny how at church I lied, but here at home, I choose to be honest. "Tough." Then I let out a sigh. It aches as it leaves my lungs, making me feel tired, as though I have just cooked a five-course meal for dinner guests. I push aside a cardboard box to make room for us at the table. When I sit down, I add, "I don't think it could have gone worse."

I don't tell her that I threw myself into making the cake just to prove that I can still function in some normal way that resembles the me I'm familiar with. I don't tell my aunt that while baking, I had conversations with myself. My reluctant-fearful self was the clear winner of all my arguments.

"Well, well." Sucking in air, she repeats, "Well, well." As she pours the tea into mugs carrying the face of an Indian and the face of a bear, she tells me, "Those kids have been through a lot." She rubs a pudgy hand across the neck of the bright dress she has on this afternoon. The fabric resembles an artist's palette of reds and purples. "Did you meet Darren?"

"Yes," I mutter. "Even his mother."

"His mother?"

"She called him her son when she came to The Center."

"Hair orange or red?"

"Orange."

My aunt nods. "At Christmas it was red. Was she determined to see him?"

"She was yelling."

"She's on probation and there is a restraining order." She turns on the faucet and washes her hands.

"Why?" I ask.

But the question gets lost because Regena Lorraine says, "Looks like Jonas fixed the water pressure." She smiles at me. "Did he come over the other day?"

I think of Jonas waving his wrench and calling me Deirdre. "He did. Is he a little . . . ?"

I'm not sure what the politically correct term is. What do you call someone who repeats phrases, delivers his words like lines from a poorly rehearsed role, and sings verses from the *Eagles' Greatest Hits* as he goes around your house tapping every faucet with the top of a Sharpie?

My great aunt has no concerns about political correctness. "Retarded. Jonas is retarded. He has a little house in Fontana and lives alone." She dries her hands on the linen towel that Grandpa must have bought in Venice. *Venice* is stamped under a lopsided bowl of printed fruit. She joins me at the table, handing the bear mug to me and setting the Indian mug in front of her. A spoon swims in each mug. As she shifts into her chair, her rings picking up the sunlight, she smiles into my eyes. "I bet they love you."

"What?"

"Young and attractive."

I want her to stop right there. Notice the long sleeves, Auntie. I'm not wearing them because I'm cold. I am covering all my bad and ugly that is visible to the human eye. The trouble is, I still know those scars are there.

She wraps her ringed fingers around the mug. "Darren has a beautiful voice. He can sing 'O Holy Night' and make you cry."

"That kid sings?" I don't doubt he can make me cry. He already did that today.

"Wait till the pageant at church. His voice is magnificent." She sips her tea, adds two teaspoons of sugar from the bowl I've placed in the center of the table, and stirs.

"Really?"

"Surprise you?"

"Yes."

She reaches across the table and touches my arm. " 'In youth we learn. In age we understand.' " As I try to decipher what she means, she adds, "Austrian writer Marie von Ebner-Eschenbach." She says the name like this writer is her friend, like she drops in at her house often for sassafras tea and pound cake.

I think of showing my aunt the letter I found from Grandpa and asking her about the raccoon bowl. Perhaps she could even solve the mystery of why he wrote a letter and never mailed it to me.

Rubbing a band of silver etched with swirls of yellow gold and tiny diamonds, she smiles. Looking up from the ring, she says, "Many rings from men, but there is nothing like a sentimental gift."

I wonder if this is another quote from someone important, but she accredits the words to no one. "My mother died when I was still young. Well, younger than my sixty years now. I was only thirty-five." Her eyes turn dark, suddenly, like a cloud that covers a summer sun. "Your dad was only thirty-two."

"So your mother gave you that ring?"

"Oh, no! I found it among her jewelry when she died. Ernest said any necklaces or rings she had could be mine." Her face breaks into a smile that almost glitters like the ring's diamonds. "As long as none of my siblings found out and grew jealous. People can fight viciously over the family gemstones."

I wonder what my sister Andrea and I will fight over when our mom dies. Mom has one sapphire ring, but I've never liked it because it looks like it came out of a gumball machine. Once I asked if the stone was real and she just said, "Deena, Deena."

Solemnly, Regena Lorraine adds, "A lot of forgiving needs to happen in church after a funeral, I think."

Forgiving. The word makes me feel queasy. I grit my teeth and hope that Lucas's face will disappear from my memory.

"Oh, speaking of church," she says, pushing her chair back from the table, "I'll pick you up this Sunday. Ten-twenty."

Giovanni, who is lying on the rug by the sliding door, lets out a woof, and I wonder if my aunt brings him to church, too. If he sits in the passenger seat of her truck, does that mean I have to sit next to him? Does he use a seatbelt?

"Service I go to starts at eleven." My aunt wipes her lips with a tissue. "Not much of an early bird, so I'm still sleeping during the eight-thirty service."

I want to say that I haven't been to church in months, that even before the accident I was neglecting Sunday morning services. Lucas suggested we take drives instead. Then one day he didn't show up for our Sunday morning drive. When he finally returned my frantic calls that evening, he said he'd come down with the flu. I brought chicken soup to his apartment, but when I got there, only his roommate Allen was home, watching a football game on TV.

A wave of sadness starts to spread over me.

"Okay, Shug?" prompts my aunt.

I just nod.

She takes a few more noisy sips of tea and then announces, "Time to go." Abruptly, she stands.

"Going to play Clue?" I ask.

She pulls her tote bag over her shoulder and gives a little tug at her gray hair that is now hanging straight, except for the ends, which curve toward her chin. "Not tonight, Shug. Tonight is Scrabble at Jo-Jen's."

"Who is Jo-Jen?"

She laughs. "Josephine Jennifer. Friend of mine. She saved me once from a deep depression."

Is she serious? I can't imagine my aunt ever being depressed.

"But that's another story. I'll tell you later." She heads toward the door, her rubber-soled sandals flopping against the floor. Over the shoulder without the tote bag, she calls, "It's a good one."

Then she's gone, her dress billowing in the afternoon wind. Giovanni is slobbering and bounding after her.

No wonder people like their dogs so much. They are the most loyal and faithful of all beasts. No dog is going to cheat on you, or make you promises he doesn't intend to keep. Canines don't run off with other humans, even if those other humans happen to be better-looking; they stay loyal to their owners, regardless of how bad they look or smell.

fifteen

I am sipping Belgian coffee from the bear mug and thinking of the kids at The Center when Chef B calls the next morning. In his typical fashion he makes it sound as though he hasn't slept at all since my departure because he's had no idea if I even made it to North Carolina. "You not call me," he scolds. "I worry you end up in hospital in Gainesville."

Well, don't think I wasn't afraid of the same thing.

Chef B asks about the cabin and the state of the kitchen appliances.

"Gas stove," I say, because he, unlike Sally and Jeannie, will care about that.

He doesn't disappoint me. "Ah, gas is good, good. Better control of heat."

I smile at his approval of the stove.

"Are you writing in journal book?"

I tell him I have written in the book; I do not say that I haven't written in it every day as he instructed. He asks what I'm doing with my time. I tell him about my grandfather's plan for me to teach cooking lessons to children.

He clears his throat, and I anticipate that he will say, "How awful!" or "That is beneath your skill!" Instead he says, "Deena, that is perfect for you." With eagerness in his baritone voice he asks, "What did you teach them?"

I mutter that I started with a white sauce.

"White sauce?" His voice is raised, and I have to pull the cell phone away from my ear to save my hearing. "Teach them fun stuff," he tells me. Again I am aware that white sauce was a big mistake.

"Children want to make brownies. Sweets. Things they eat right away. How you say?" He pauses for a few seconds. "Instant gratification."

As I long for the kitchen at the restaurant, he tells a story about how Ashley Judd came to Palacio del Rey for dinner the other night. He wants to tell me what she ordered and who she was with, but all I want to know is if her skin is as flawless as it is on the cover of *Cosmo*. Does she have wrinkles? Does she have scars on her arms?

He doesn't tell me because I don't ask.

———

I carry the ingredients to make brownies in my Whole Foods bag. My prayer is that all the children will be absent today.

The kids are all there when I arrive.

When I say that we will bake brownies and then eat them,

there are a few cheers. Then they all wonder why I have brought sugar, cocoa, and flour.

"Don't you just add water to a brownie box?" Dougy asks innocently.

"You can," I say, "if you have a brownie box or brownie mix. But we are going to make brownies from scratch."

"We get to scratch?" Bubba looks confused.

"No, dummy!" belts out Bobby. "That means . . ." But he doesn't know how to explain what it means, so I tell them.

"When we cook from scratch it means we don't use any mix or box already prepared. We measure our own ingredients."

The class still looks confused until Lisa says, "It means we don't use instant."

"Oh. Oh, yeah," Bubba and Dougy say in unison.

Lisa beams like she is the teacher's pet; at this point, the pickings are slim for that honor, and she is the only one on my "almost good" list.

Darren sits with his notebook, not giving me any eye contact. I am sure he hates me. I should have asked Chef B how to make this kid like me. I think it will take more than brownies.

———

When the class is over and the kids run outside to play basketball, I head to the bathroom before washing the dishes. Making brownies was a good choice, but even so, the kids talked incessantly and fought over who was going to stir the batter next. I asked Darren to chop some walnuts and he refused. Dougy said Darren was afraid of knives. Darren yelled, "Shut up!" It was aimed at Dougy and not at me this time, but it still wasn't appropriate. I told Darren to be considerate of others, and he shot me an evil glare that made me think of his mother, Felicia. So much angry resemblance.

As I come out of the bathroom, I try to conjure courage and to walk with dignity. Courage is a tough thing to conjure. If you don't believe you own it, you almost suffocate from feeling fake. Passing the bulletin board with the array of Bible verses, I pause. *God?* My cry is silent and yet I feel like every bone in my body is shouting for help. What does that quote say? *"Trust in the Lord with all your heart and lean not on your own understanding."* And from Grandpa, I received, *"Put your whole hand in His."*

Yes, but how is that done? My own understanding is that this place is not for me, and I will never understand why my grandpa thought I should teach these children. Obviously, Ernest did not know me at all to place me here, or else he was just cruel, which can't be true. Everybody adored Grandpa. Except for my mother, but that's not my grandfather's fault. Even Mom's own mother told me once that "She was a stubborn child." Dad only sees her soft hair and features, and in college he was mesmerized by her shrewd business skills. She keeps her emotions to herself while keeping the farm in profits. Her good qualities are evident—I know I've gained from them over the years—yet sometimes I do wish she were not a prickly pear but more like a smooth Georgia peach.

When I turn from the bulletin board, Zack is walking toward me. His look holds genuine empathy. It prods me to say, "I'm not a teacher."

His face softens, and he gives me a small smile. "I'm not either."

"I don't even know if I like kids." Surely he will tell Miriam this tidbit and she'll oust me from The Center. I'll be kicked out forever, which, come to think of it, would not be a bad thing. Then I can work totally on establishing my cake-decorating business and eventually turning it into a catering company. No more kids to teach!

Zack says, "I used to think the same thing."

"You used to think you didn't like children?" What in the world? He is a kid magnet.

"They were so young and hopeful, and I didn't want to disappoint them."

Well, those are not my fears at all. I continue spilling out my emotions. "They're so . . . so . . . ." What is wrong with me? I know what I mean.

Zack supplies, "Noisy? Undisciplined? Aggravating?"

Does he agree that they are? Or is he just saying this to appease me? I hate being appeased like I'm a . . . a child. "Yes, yes, yes," I say. I take a breath, and we both smile. His eyes are hazel with a tint of green around the edges.

"I know. But they will grow on you. It takes time."

"Why are you here?" I ask him. My voice is more demanding than I intended.

He looks a bit baffled and then slowly says, "I just wanted to make sure you were okay."

"No, not that. Why are you here at The Center?"

"Oh." His faces relaxes. "I'm a social worker. I'm the case-worker for a bunch of these kids."

"You're a social worker with social services?"

"Yeah. But most of the time I spend here is volunteer. The Center is a really good program."

"Oh." What can I say? He *chose* a profession that deals with children. He even *volunteers* to spend time with children. He could be anything he wanted to be, I think. He's confident and articulate and grows more handsome every time I see him. He could be posing for *Maxim*. Instead he is here in the mountains of North Carolina working with a bunch of kids.

His smile is broad, and I note his dimples.

"You'll be okay," he says.

You'll be okay. How many times have I heard that line in the last three months? If I had a penny for every time a friend, coworker, parent, or doctor said that string of words to me, I'd be rich enough to bribe the lawyer on Main Street so he'd have to let me have the cabin sans teaching cooking to wild children with no manners.

———

After a dinner of steamed broccoli and pasta seasoned with oregano, olive oil, and tomatoes, I take out the Bryson City phone book. I study the local businesses—potential places I can market my cake business. I plan to ask them if they will place my brochures in a strategic location with lots of customer traffic. That should generate some responses so I can start getting orders for custom-made cakes.

What if no one calls? What if no one even allows me to place my brochures in their shop or restaurant? The more I think about my new business, the more discouragement sets in.

Stop it. Don't think like that.

I call Sally, just to hear a familiar voice. After the phone rings five times I leave a message on her answering machine. I hope I sound perky and well-adjusted to my new mountain life. She's probably at a veterinary emergency, but I wish she were home. I just want to laugh with her about anything we think is funny today.

sixteen

T he first thing that appealed
to me about being a chef was the uniform. I wanted to wear
the white smock and the tall white chef hat. Then, I wanted to
make sauces. Cheese sauces for vegetables. Sauces for roasts,
pork tenderloins, and briskets. Growing up on a pig farm gave
me plenty of opportunity to watch pork being prepared. We
seemed to have it every day in one form or another. Sausage
or bacon for breakfast, ham sandwiches for lunch, and pork
roast or tenderloin for dinner.

My mother always made her standard sauce or gravy to
go with each pork dish. No matter which side of the pig she
served for dinner, the gravy accompanying it was the same as
the day before. This flavorless sauce was served in the family
heirloom we called "the gravy bowl," and always placed at
Dad's end of the oak dining room table. The gravy bowl is
the color of mildew. My great-grandmother thought it worthy

of passing down to my maternal grandmother, and then my mother inherited it when her mother died. I have let my sister know that she is welcome to it when our mother passes on. Andrea told me, "I don't need a gravy bowl in Taipei."

They say necessity is the mother of all inventions, and even as a kid, I knew it was necessary to create a new sauce. I was tired of Mom's standard mixture of milk, butter, fat drippings, and salt and pepper, with a few tablespoons of flour to thicken it. I experimented in the kitchen and came up with sauce à la marmalade (a white sauce with a tablespoon of orange marmalade), sauce au garlic (adding minced garlic really spiced up the palate), and sauce au basil—my favorite—which had fresh minced basil and parsley. Andrea liked the marmalade one the best; Dad raved about the garlic. Mom said she couldn't decide between the basil and garlic, but if I wanted to cook dinner one night a week, that would be a great help.

Pretty soon one night a week became two, and then it got so I was cooking every night. Mom was proud of my culinary talent, which delighted me. Dad was proud, too, but I could simply breathe and he'd be proud of me.

When I told my family I wanted to go to Atlanta for culinary school, they weren't surprised. Mother did comment that she wasn't sure I could get a real job with a degree in *cooking*. I showed her an armload of books written by gurus who were skilled in cooking—graduates of culinary institutes all across America and around the world. She then nodded and asked if I could make a dessert for the next night.

"What's tomorrow night?" I asked.

"Friday," she replied. "And the Jeffersons are coming by after dinner to buy Hector."

"Daddy's selling Hector?"

Hector was the largest sow in the history of Georgia, I was sure. She was the size of three hogs. Champion pig—that was Hector. She'd won the blue ribbon at the state fair for four years in a row. When people saw the name, they would assume Hector was a male. When they found out she was female, they'd scratch their heads, let their cotton candy stop bobbing for a moment, and wonder. Dad named the pig. Apparently, he had an uncle Hector who was rather large and pink. When Hector was born, Daddy said the pig reminded him of his uncle. He started to call her Hector, and that was that. People wondered if the real Hector was offended to know that a pig had been named after him, and not even a male pig, but a sow. "Oh, no," my father would say, "Hector is pleased." The truth was, Hector had died long before his namesake squealed into the world.

When my mother didn't reply to my question, I rephrased it. "Why is Daddy selling Hector to the Jeffersons?"

"They're offering a good price."

The first cake I ever made and decorated was for Hector's farewell. I used a recipe from an old Betty Crocker cookbook. I spent the entire evening icing it with a buttercream frosting, staying up till midnight. The Jeffersons made a big deal over the cake, saying it was tasty and moist.

I was sad to see Hector leave us. I patted her good-bye and felt like little Fern in *Charlotte's Web*. It took all the strength Mr. Jefferson and Daddy had to haul Hector onto the Jeffersons' truck. Without Hector to feed, I thought we could probably save enough to build a new barn.

The next time I baked and decorated a cake was the night before Grandpa Ernest visited. "Could you make that same cake you made for the Jeffersons?" my mother asked.

"What's happening tomorrow night?"

"Grandpa Ernest is stopping by on his way home from Greece."

I thought it was funny to use the phrase "stopping by." Tifton, Georgia, is not at all a place on the way to or from anywhere. It is so out of the way that most people can't find it even when looking for and *wanting* to come to the town.

Grandpa Ernest took one look at the frosted two-layered butter cake and gave me a hug. Then he told me that he'd just spent two weeks on Kos, and although beautiful in both scenery and food, nothing he had seen in the cake department came close to my cake. I was so nervous. I wondered if the taste could live up to his compliments. It must have; I found him at two in the morning helping himself to a second slice. "Ah, Deena," he said, "you have a God-given talent."

I smiled twice. Once because I was happy he was my grandfather. Twice because I had just decided I was going to make cakes for the rest of my life.

Of course, I may have had the God-given talent, but pride goeth before a fall, and after those first two cakes, I had a few disaster cakes. Daddy told me disasters in life produce character. I suppose I developed character when I had to rush to the store on three occasions because the cakes I made fell or crumbled. No amount of frosting slathered on could save them.

Later, I learned that every cook has a few failures tucked under her crisp white chef's hat.

———

Grandpa Ernest's deck holds a red canvas chair, two weather-beaten Adirondack chairs, and a gas grill, along with the hot tub I have yet to unveil. When I sit in one of the wooden chairs, I lean my head back and breathe in the delicate mountain air. The sun is coming out from behind a milky cloud, and as it warms my face, I watch a pair of sparrows flit around the limbs of two birch trees. The sloping mountain peaks within my view are brightened by the sun; they're now the color of blueberries. It's the first week of May. *May in the mountains.* That has a nice ring to it. I bet it could be set to some country music tune.

I should tour Bryson City and the surrounding area. When Dad called this morning, he said I could drive to some of the nearby attractions. He suggested a trip to the Cherokee Indian Reservation, or heading into Gatlinburg, Tennessee, via the Smoky Mountain Parkway, for a day trip. "I bet it's real pretty this time of year," he said.

His voice filled my heart with everything I know to be good, and I knew that I should just hop in my Jeep, buckle up, and go.

I rest my arms against the Adirondack chair's flat, smooth arms. One day, I think—one day the thought of driving won't make me nauseous. One day I won't have to deal with all the post-traumatic stuff. One day I won't care about the scars on my body. One day my days will be as beautiful as Neville Marriner's symphony playing selections from Vivaldi. Wherever I go, I will be his "Summer" concerto.

Right now a trek in my Jeep down curvy roads into Bryson City for a stop at Ingle's or The Center is all that I can handle.

A cardinal flies by, and his bright color makes me see only one thing—blood. Blood, fresh and dried, all over the seats of Lucas's Mustang. I try to force away the memory of that rainy night. I wrap my arms around my waist as though to comfort myself from the tragedy.

Standing, I leave the sunny deck to head inside. The accident was three-and-a-half months ago. Surely—surely—it will leave my mind one day.

———

That evening when the owl calls in the nearby tree and I awake, I remember the envelope with my name on it and the letter inside. Searching in the bookcase, I find it again. I sit outside on the canvas chair and read it again. This time a different part jumps out at me. *Sometimes I have wondered why we have to face so much sorrow in this world. Our sorrows often multiply, our disappointments increase, and our hearts are heavy. Perhaps this life is not the one we would have chosen.*

I would have chosen Lucas to be faithful and loyal and to love me forever. I would have made him see only me in my teal dress.

I scan the recipe for Grandpa's peanut soup printed at the end of the letter and think that it sounds worth trying. I jot down the ingredients I'll need to purchase from Ingle's. Slipping the memo paper into the pocket of my bathrobe, I look forward to making something my grandfather enjoyed. It will certainly taste better than my own tears. If all the tears I've cried since the accident were piped chocolate roses, I would be as round as Hector by now.

When I write in the journal, I start with a few lines about growing up on the farm—how pigs are my favorite animals, how exciting it is to watch new piglets squeal into the world. Even my mother, who once hoped to marry a big-name lawyer and take vacations to the south of France, isn't able to conceal her awe when these births take place on the hay-strewn barn floor. In spite of what she tells Andrea and me about her once-upon-a-longings, we know she is married to the wisest and sweetest man in the world. His profession as a farmer only makes him humble.

My mind wanders to what kind of childhood the children who come to The Center for the after-school program have had—and are having—but I push the topic as far away as my mind will let me.

No, Grandpa, this is not the life I would have chosen.

seventeen

Sally and I sit on the deck, grilling trout and catfish as the sun vanishes behind the edge of the mountain closest to the cabin. Sally is a good fisherwoman; she brought two rods, bait, and tackle, and we spent this morning fishing in Deep Creek.

Perhaps she had heard the sorrow in my voice when I told her that my hope to drive to Tifton to visit Dad and Mom and spend four or five days on the farm was not going to be realized.

Whatever the cause, Sally didn't hesitate. She hopped in her Honda Civic and made the winding trip of 152 miles to Bryson City. She left another doctor in charge of all her fuzzy-furred, wet-nosed clients.

"School is out June eighth here, but they want me to teach all summer," I told her as I stood in my kitchen with my cell phone clutched in one hand and stirring buttercream frosting with the other. "Summer school. It starts on Monday."

"They really want these kids to learn to cook, don't they?" Sally sipped from her cup of coffee. I could hear the slurp over the phone. Starbucks Mocha Latte. Two percent milk, a dash of cinnamon. Sally's favorite.

While I longed for my own cup of Starbucks, I said, "They want to keep them occupied and off the streets."

"Well, that's important, I guess."

"Miriam says that the summer program also has this guy named Robert teaching drama and art. I'm sure the kids will like that."

Just art, drama, and basketball would be enough to keep their minds and hands busy, wouldn't it? Are the cooking classes really necessary? When I asked Miriam about it, she said, "Cooking helps them learn about measuring, and ingredients, and how to use them in recipes, but it also teaches children to follow directions in order to obtain a satisfactory result." She shuffled her tennis shoes, reciting the words, and I wondered which cookbook produced this wisdom.

I squeeze some lemon juice on the skins of the fish fillets and tell Sally that I think the money they pay me at The Center comes from some kind of account Grandpa Ernest set up.

"Your grandpa seemed to have loads of money." She lifts a piece of smoky catfish off the grill with Ernest's tongs. "What did he do?"

"You mean besides traveling all over the world after he lost his wife?" I deliberately pause for effect. "He was a surgeon in Pennsylvania. You know, one of those rich doctors."

Sally smiles and pokes me with the end of the tongs. "How's the hot tub?"

"I haven't . . ."

"Don't tell me you haven't been in it yet!"

———

Catfish and trout always taste better when you've caught and cleaned them yourself. We enjoy our meal out on the deck as a tame breeze blows against our faces.

After we wash the dishes, Sally helps me pull the covering from the hot tub and shows me how to heat the water. Sometimes all you need in life to get something done is sheer determination, and Sally is set on enhancing her mountain cabin weekend with time in the hot tub. She's brought her swimsuit, a cute little one-piece that slenderizes her even more than she normally looks. I put my suit on, too. I try not to look at my scars, even though Sally does. "They are healing nicely," she tells me in her most medical tone of voice.

"But they'll never completely fade," I say. I know this for a fact, regardless of Dr. Bland's attempts to encourage me. "Will they?"

She looks at me with empathy; her eyes are full of warmth and understanding. "Deena, they will only cause you as much trouble as you allow them to cause you."

That's a strange thing to say, I think, as I lower myself into the bubbly water. That isn't even an answer to my question.

Later, as we put sheets on the couch's pullout bed, Sally tells me that she ran into Lucas at Starbucks. "He tried to avoid me at first, but I made a great effort to make sure he noticed me."

"How'd you do that?"

"I stood right in front of him as he went over to that little counter to put cream in his coffee."

"What did he say?" I want to hear that he asked about me, that he missed me, that he was oh-so-terribly sorry for cheating on me. I wait, feeling like Giovanni must when my aunt pulls a dog biscuit from her pocket.

Sally tugs at the corner of the fitted sheet and smoothes it onto the mattress. Then she sits on the edge of the bed and glances down. "I lied."

"You didn't see him?"

She's let her hair down from the clip, and now her red curls bounce as she shakes her head. Looking at me, she explains. "I did see him."

"At Starbucks?"

"Yeah."

Okay, I think, this is going around in circles, like Giovanni before he settles onto the rug by the sliding glass door.

Sally bites her lower lip, the familiar Sally gesture that endears her to me. "I told him you were madly in love with a cardiologist and living in London."

Laughter bursts out of me. "Really?"

She peers at me, lets her eyes lock with mine. "Are you mad at me?"

"That you lied? No."

Her sigh, a form of release, fills the living room. She smiles. "It was just time for payback. You should have seen his face."

Lucas once said if we lived in London we could go to a different pub every night and see a play at the theater every Saturday. He was in an artistic mood, and his voice was rich with dreaming. "I'll play polo and then we can eat those tea sandwiches or scones or whatever they eat over there."

I held his hand and told him that I would go anywhere

with him. Now I say to Sally, "He always wanted to live in London."

She nods as her eyes grow wide for emphasis. "That's exactly why I said you were living in London. I wanted him to feel something." She twists a curl around her index finger. "I wanted him to feel jealous."

My thoughts spin. Jealous? Is that what I want him to feel? Is that what I feel? Hatred—that's my little flame I keep throwing sticks into. Keep those fires of hatred burning.

Sally, who has never been able to be serious for any length of time, is ready to get back into her comfort zone. She scans the room as a smile rushes to her mouth. "What's with all these kitchen tools?"

"He collected them, won them, bought them, whenever he traveled."

"He . . . meaning your grandfather?"

"Good ol' Ernest."

She eyes the water buffalo drawing. "This is like being in a museum of sorts."

"Of sorts."

"So when the place becomes yours, do you get to redecorate?"

I think of the few pictures of mine that are stored in my parents' shed. There is a print of a piglet resting in the sun beside a run-down barn. I'm not sure where I'd hang that in this living room. Before I can answer, Sally says, "What's the woman with the fan about? Is she hiding behind it?"

I study the framed drawing of the kimono-clad woman with the fan discretely covering half her face. I still have no idea what she's hiding or why, yet I know that picture, with all its mysteries, belongs on that wall, like marshmallows go with hot chocolate and jackets with spring mornings. I could never replace it with anything else. "I'm not much for redecorating," I tell Sally.

She laughs. "Oh yeah, I remember when you wanted to paint your room orange with yellow dots to look like a sunset."

"Yeah, I'm not a decorator." I smile.

"Only of cakes," she says with admiration. "Those, you do well."

Sally brushes her teeth as I climb the stairs to the loft bedroom where I have grown used to sleeping. When she lies on the couch-bed I hear her turn over a few times until she's comfortable. The cabin is dark when, minutes later, she calls up to me. I'm watching the flickering stars from the windows in the ceiling over my bed and hearing chords of wedding music that will never play for me. Before that, I was realizing that Sally really stepped out on a limb to try to make Lucas jealous.

"Deena?" Her voice sweeps through the cabin.

"Yeah?"

"I think your moving here was the best thing you've done in a long time."

I'm still not sure myself, but it's nice to have her approval.

I turn onto my stomach. Since I can't picture a doctor I would run off to Europe with, I fall asleep thinking about a curly-haired social worker who plays basketball.

———

The next afternoon, as Sally places the rods and fishing gear in her Honda, I want to jump in the passenger seat like Giovanni and head back to Atlanta with her. Instead, I tell her to come back to visit me soon, to have a safe trip, and I smile until I think my face will break. She says she envies my life. I merely swallow and nod.

"Next time I'll bring Jeannie."

"That would be great."

Her car is long gone before I head back inside. I view the mountain peaks, lush and green before me and pale blue in the distance where they kiss the horizon. It's funny how humans are never quite content with what they have. Yet, according to Grandpa, the key to happiness lies in putting your whole hand into God's. I wonder if just holding the hand of the Almighty is enough to cure this sadness inside of me?

eighteen

Charlotte, the quiet girl with long, dark hair and large round eyes, has a face that looks like a doll in the American Girl collection. While she might smile and show rows of bright teeth, she rarely says a word except to ask if she can go to the restroom. Miriam told me that this girl was abandoned by her mother at age five. Her mother, then only twenty-four, ran off with a Native American blackjack dealer. They left secretly in the night while Charlotte and her sister slept in their beds at home. Their maternal grandmother took care of them until her death, and then an aunt. Now twelve-year-old Charlotte lives with her sister, Cindy, who is twenty. Cindy works as a waitress at the Fryemont Inn's restaurant, and rents an apartment on the edge of town.

"Is she always so quiet?" I asked Miriam once about Charlotte.

"Yes," Miriam answered. "She is afraid of people, and

especially of people leaving her." She was in her office sipping from a mug of fresh coffee, taking a break from a hectic morning meeting with The Center's accountant. I watched as she rubbed tension from her neck with one hand, balancing the chipped ceramic mug in the other. "Charlotte thinks, like most of these kids, that it was something she did to cause all those she cared about in life to abandon her."

"Her fault? How could it be her fault?" My voice reached that high-pitched level Mom despises. "I mean, of course it's not."

Miriam found a place for the mug on her crowded desk. "No amount of convincing will make her believe it isn't. The social workers try."

I felt a familiar pain welling inside my chest when I heard that. How many hours had I spent after the accident, while working on my jigsaw puzzles, trying to convince myself that Lucas leaving me was not my fault? I blamed myself for his behavior, until finally, one night I realized that those pieces didn't fit. He had made his own choices.

Just before Miriam headed off to a fundraising meeting, she told me, "Charlotte is quiet, but don't let that make you think she's not taking everything in. She is a smart cookie."

And now in the church kitchen on this Wednesday afternoon, Charlotte is raising her hand in response to my question—"Who wants to volunteer to slice tomatoes for a chef salad?"

Pinch me. I have the urge to dance around the kitchen. I motion for her to get out of her seat and come to the cutting board.

Slowly, she makes her way toward me, her long hair pushed away from her face by a silver headband. I watch as she carefully takes a juicy red tomato from the cluster I purchased and holds it under the running faucet in the sink. Timidly, she places the tomato on the cutting board. I want to help her so I look for a knife, but she has found one and uses it to cut the fruit in half. "This child has been listening!" I want to shout. In spite of all her restroom visits, she's been paying attention.

Rainy lifts her sunglasses from her eyes and echoes my thoughts. "Nice job, Charlotte."

Then Zack enters the room and all form of order is lost. The kids jump up to greet him, their chairs sliding across the linoleum. As he approaches Charlotte, she stops cutting to give him a hug.

Lucky guy. Bubba pounces onto his back, but Zack tells him to behave since this is Miss Livingston's class. I smile and excuse myself, saying I need to get the other ingredients from my Jeep for the salad. I doubt anyone even notices as I leave the kitchen. They have King Zack with them; what more could they need?

Once again, I wish I could be the popular teacher who breathes peace and harmony. Walking toward my Jeep, I think that I could recline in the front seat, take a little siesta, and they'd never miss me. Chef B would be proud of me because I wrote five pages in my journal last night, but that meant I didn't get to sleep until almost one. Which is probably why I left the majority of the ingredients for the salad in my Jeep.

From the trunk of my car, I take out a bag filled with lettuce, radishes, and cucumbers. I anticipate the taste of the salad we are about to prepare. Earlier I placed a jar of my own balsamic vinaigrette dressing in the kitchen's fridge. I made a batch of it a few nights ago as I listened to my Vivaldi CD. Maybe Zack can join us and we can all eat the salad in the fellowship hall and comment on how perfect the dressing is. It occurs to me, then, to wonder if kids like balsamic vinaigrette dressing.

When I get to the glass front door of The Center, I see Bubba race out of the kitchen and down the hallway toward me. He flings open the door and yells, "Hurry!"

"What is it?"

His face is streaked with perspiration. "Charlotte!" he cries.

"What?"

"She cut her finger with the knife!"

We both rush into the kitchen and sure enough, Zack is securing a wet paper towel around Charlotte's index finger.

"Is her finger still attached?" asks Bubba, making attempts to catch his breath. He may be skinny, but apparently he is not used to running.

Charlotte's face is flushed, and I can see that she's trying hard not to cry. She clings to Zack and sinks her teeth into her lower lip like Sally does.

Joy is crying. Massive sobs puff from her lungs.

Bubba repeats, "Is her finger still attached?"

From my purse, I grab a Band-Aid—a wide sterile strip with chocolate cupcakes on it. I found these chocolate cupcake bandages at an outlet store in Atlanta last fall. I peel off the paper cover and wrap it around the tip of Charlotte's finger. Immediately, blood leaks through; I contain my nausea by swallowing a few times. Adding another Band-Aid, I wait to see. There is no sign of blood. "I think that did the trick," I say.

"Wow," says Dougy. "Miss Livingston even has Band-Aids with food on them!"

I smile in spite of the situation. Then I clean up the blood that dots the cutting board and knife. I don't know what else to do. I want to hug Charlotte, but I notice Darren is glaring at me from his perch at the back of the room.

I suppose I should have offered a course in basic knife skills before allowing one of the students to use a knife in the kitchen. What was I thinking? These kids usually eat at McDonalds; they've probably never had cause to use a sharp knife before.

Zack tells the kids to get back in their chairs. Looking at me, he says, "It's going to be fine."

That is his standard reply to everything.

No one wants salad now, so we continue to make sure that Charlotte is going to be fine. She's enjoying all the attention, and I think to myself that she deserves it. She's had a rough day, and from what I've heard, her life's been no slice of apple pie.

nineteen

As I store the salad in the fridge and then fill the sink to wash the dishes after class, I gaze out the kitchen window. Zack, dressed in shorts and a blue T-shirt, plays basketball with the guys and Lisa. Rainy, Charlotte, and Joy are on the sidelines. Charlotte is still getting lots of attention due to her wounded finger. Earlier, I watched Darren open the door for her when the group charged outside.

Lisa grabs the ball Zack gently tosses to her. The other girls cheer. Lisa flies down the court, her long brown hair swaying. Bobby sticks his fleshy abdomen at her, forcing her to stop. She looks for Zack, who is being blocked by Bubba, although it is hard for any five-foot-tall kid weighing approximately ninety-two pounds to really guard a man over six feet tall. As Lisa throws the ball to Zack, Darren tears down the court, snatches it out of the air, and rushes toward the other basket for a shot. The cheering section goes wild. In spite of

Zack's attempts, Darren scores two points. Bobby and Darren slap a high five.

How easy it is for Zack to reach these kids. He's such a natural. Darren smiles when he's with him. Darren has never smiled at me. The kid is like a splinter in my finger. I want to make him carry slop for the pigs until his arms wear out and then see if he'll be too tired to irritate me with his defiant words. Zack must have opened up his own soul and let Jesus pour in the fruits of the spirit—all that patience, kindness, and joy. He oozes with every one of those on the basketball court. I know that he knows about each child's history—how they were bruised or abandoned by their parents. Clearly, he is familiar with every child's likes and dislikes, strengths and weaknesses. It is his job.

Two days ago, when he had to break up a fight between Darren and Dougy, he asked if I'd like to hear more about the children's histories. I sucked in some air and said, "I really couldn't." I didn't explain any more than that.

When they fight with each other, he knows how to command that they stop it and find a better way to resolve their issues. After the fight between Dougy and Darren, he had the boys write an essay on what they could offer to others around them.

"You mean like money?" asked Dougy. "Cuz I don't got none of that." His face was sweaty, and he kept wiping it with the collar of his shirt.

"No," said Zack. "Things money can't buy."

"Ah," said Dougy, as though a lightbulb had flickered on inside his head. "Priceless things. Like on the MasterCard commercial?"

"Exactly. It's about who you are as a person. What can you give others?"

Darren started writing, using the same notebook he uses

for his drawings. Dougy licked the tip of his pen and got to work. The two boys who had been hitting each other minutes earlier were now calmly contained in chairs, adhering to Zack's assignment.

If the word *peace-magnet* appeared in the dictionary, the definition would include Zack's name.

I turn away from the window and pop two Tylenol into my mouth and then realize that the pain is not in my legs or arms. The pain is inside, deeper than any limb. The pain, this time, is in my heart. Sure, I've had pain in my heart before, like when I heard Lucas was going out with Ella. I had pain when my almond butter torte didn't win the Atlanta State Dessert Competition.

This is a different pain.

I'm not exactly sure of its cause.

I feel that if I'm going to have to suffer with pain, I should at least be able to know what's causing it.

———

On my way home I stop by Ingle's and buy the ingredients for Grandpa's Southern Peanut Soup. Strategically, I avoid the magazine rack.

In the cabin's kitchen, I find a large pan and rinse it out well because I don't know how long these pots and pans have sat in these cabinets unused. Grandpa traveled a lot, and in his last years he was away much of the time in Greece and other parts of Europe. What a life. Instead of the cabin, he could have left me a plane ticket to Kos. The pictures sure look inviting with the shimmering blue ocean, white beaches, and graceful palm trees. In one picture stuck to the fridge with a magnet that says *It's all Greek to me*, he stands by a sea that holds more shades of blue than any box of Crayolas.

I read over the recipe and line up all the ingredients needed to make the soup. I like to have everything ready to go and not have to dig around the cupboard for flour or sugar or measuring spoons once I start to create the recipe. I read the end of my grandpa's instructions for serving the soup. *Eat it from the raccoon bowl.* What is a raccoon bowl? I have searched all over for it and have found nothing with a raccoon on it or in the shape of a raccoon. I'll have to ask Aunt Regena Lorraine.

When I cook, there has to be music playing. Vivaldi, of course, is my favorite. I turn up the volume and begin to measure the ingredients using my stainless-steel measuring cups and spoons. These were a gift from Lucas, and I did consider tossing them and buying cheap plastic ones to replace them. Then I drank a cup of coffee and thought, "Am I crazy?" Keep the state-of-the-art measuring cups and spoons, girl. One day you will forget who gave them to you and be glad to have them.

I haven't forgotten who gave them to me yet.

I read over the recipe to make sure I haven't left anything out.

Ingredients:
   1 T butter
   2 T minced white onions
   2 T flour
   6 cups of chicken broth
   ½ cup heavy cream
   ½ cup milk
   1 cup creamy peanut butter
   1 tsp red pepper
   Paprika
   Salt and pepper to taste
   1 cup dry roasted unsalted peanuts, chopped
   Fresh parsley

In a large pot, heat butter and onion over medium heat until tender. Stir in flour. Simmer and stir in chicken broth, cooking until soup thickens. Add other ingredients except the parsley and chopped roasted peanuts. Garnish with parsley and peanuts and serve in individual bowls.

When the soup forms little bubbles along its surface, I ladle two scoops into a small bowl. I sprinkle parsley and peanuts on the top. It looks good, I think. Chef B always told us the appearance of the food we serve at Palacio del Rey is just as important as the taste.

Standing by the stove, I eat. Single people are known for forgoing a sit-down meal so that they can stand in the kitchen and enjoy the solitary experience of eating over the sink or stove. This is how we manage to keep our tablecloths clean.

I stir the soup in my bowl and take another bite, tasting the distinct flavors of cream and peanut butter. I think it needs more salt. Grandpa had high blood pressure, so he probably cut down on the salt when he made this dish. I eat another spoonful. My mouth feels warm. My taste buds are satisfied, grateful. I smile at the picture of Grandpa on the fridge. "Do you get to eat this good in heaven?" I ask.

I hear a noise and, looking out the kitchen window, see a truck pull into the driveway. Jonas steps across the gravel. His large boots bound up the porch steps. The sun is setting behind him; wispy colors of rust and peach swirl along the sky. He taps at the door, and I yell, "Come in." Eagerly, with a wide smile, he does. Maybe I will not have to eat my meal of peanut soup alone.

twenty

"Hi, Deirdre," Jonas says as he shuffles across the kitchen. His bandana is the color of a male cardinal, matching his wrinkled, red button-down shirt. I wonder if he ever irons. Or owns an iron.

"Want some soup?" I ask him.

"Soup?" He fills his lungs with the aroma from the kitchen. "Did I get here in time for dinner?" He produces a wide grin. Then he wants to know, "What's inside?"

Grandpa said to taste all the flavors. I'll let Jonas guess what's in the soup. "You can eat some and then tell me."

"I tell you?"

"Yes."

"Will I like the soup?" He says each word slowly, in monotone. I could pick out his voice in a crowd any day. I have never known anyone who speaks like Jonas. Come to think of it, I have never known another mentally handicapped man.

I recall how, last time he was here, he shifted from foot to foot and said, "Yes siree" in almost every sentence. Could it be that Jonas actually feels comfortable around me now?

I refill my bowl and prepare one for him. He joins me at the dining room table. He eats without saying a word, fingers gripping the spoon, each bite absorbed by his ample mouth. I listen to the violins playing from the CD in the living room as Jonas methodically chews, even though one really doesn't need to chew soup.

"Did you make this?" he asks as he reaches over to the napkin dispenser and pulls out a paper napkin to wipe his lips.

"I did. What do you think?"

Looking into his bowl, he says, "This is good. Lots of tastes in here."

"Like?"

Closing his eyes, he recites his list. "Butter, peanuts, peanut butter, parsley, cream, milk, chicken, paprika, and . . . and . . . oil!"

I smile, amazed by his ability to pick out all those ingredients. I know what's in the soup and yet I'm not certain I can taste each ingredient. "No oil," I tell him. "But everything else is right."

Jonas grins. "Well," he says, "I got 99.9 percent of it right." He seems pleased. "Pretty clever for a retard. Huh?"

I am surprised to hear him call himself this word.

"What is this music?" he asks as he strums his fingers against the top of the table.

"Vivaldi. Do you listen to music?"

His belt buckle says *EAGLES* in bronze letters. Pointing at it, he claims, "Eagles are what I like."

Of course, I know this. People usually hum or sing what

they like, and Jonas sang lines from his favorite Eagles songs as he tapped on the cabin's water pipes during his first visit.

When he's finished wiping his mouth, I ask, "So, Jonas, did you come by to check the pipes?"

"No, no pipes today." He places the napkin by his bowl.

"You knew I was making soup and came by for that?"

"No, no soup."

"No pipes and no soup?"

"A book."

"A book?"

"Ernest let me borrow it. I forgot to give it back. Then he died."

Jonas pushes away from the table, stands, and says, "Wait here, Deirdre." He leaves the cabin, I hear a truck door open and slam, and then Jonas is inside once more. In his hand is a hardback book with a silly cover. *Oh, the Places You'll Go.* Dr. Seuss. "Your grandfather let me borrow it." Jonas hands me the book.

Miriam claimed this book meant a lot to her when she heard Grandpa read it. And now I hold Grandpa's own copy.

"Thank you, Jonas."

Jonas motions toward the bookcase in the living room. "It belongs there."

"I'll put it there, then."

He says he'll do it, and I watch his tall body kneel at the bottom of the bookshelf, where he fits the book between two others. He stands, brushes off his knees with his hands, and gives me another wide smile. "Today is your day, Deirdre!" he sings. "You'll move mountains!"

Could this be another line from an Eagles song?

"Your grandfather told me that I can do whatever I put my mind in."

Grinning, I ask, "And what do you put your mind in?"

"Peace, praiseworthy, excellent, and noble."

This sounds vaguely familiar, like a Bible verse. Perhaps it's one I see every day on the wall at The Center, although I can't place exactly where it hangs. Across the bulletin board in the hallway? By the front door? I'm still pondering as Jonas, humming, shuffles out the front door and jumps into his truck.

After he leaves, I do two things. First, I check the back of the peanut butter jar for its list of ingredients. Reading the fine print, I see the line: *Made with saturated oil*. Jonas was right; he did taste oil in the peanut soup. Next, I find the Dr. Seuss book, sit on the couch, and start to read. *Congratulations! Today is your day*. A smile finds me as I realize that this is where Jonas got his line that he sang to me. The book is written to the reader, telling him or her that she will have good days and bad days, lonely times and happy ones. The end does tell me that I will succeed and move mountains.

The despair that came over me shortly after I was discharged from the hospital starts to creep in again. I feel it in my fingertips as I slip *Oh, the Places You'll Go* back onto the shelf. I make sure to place it exactly where Jonas put it, right between a dark leather-bound book and a book on the Roman Empire. The leather-bound book is a Bible. I ease it from the shelf and recall with sweet nostalgia how I faithfully read my NIV Bible every night when I was about twenty. Then one day, life got busy and I became content with that. Bible reading began to be reserved for church services only. I was dating Lucas and . . .

Forcing thoughts of Lucas from my mind, I consider the

lines in Grandpa's letter. "*Trust God. Put your whole hand in His, not just one finger or two. Get to know the feel of your hand in His.*"

I open the Bible, clearly one my grandfather read often, for many of the verses are underlined with pen. Familiar passages leap out at me, verses my own parents read to me from the family Bible. The pages smell like firewood and damp earth. Soon I'm curled on the couch with the quilt over me, absorbing passages from the New Testament. I read about the withered fig tree in Mark and the feeding of the five thousand. Turning over to Galatians, I read and reread the fruit-of-the-Spirit verses. In Ephesians, I see the command to get rid of malice and anger. My stomach twists, I pull the quilt tighter around my shoulders and then glide over that verse.

Eventually, the stars light up the sky and I lie on the couch, gazing at them through the glass in the A-frame ceiling. Again they seem so close, like I could reach out and latch onto one if I only lifted my arm.

Hungry, I heat up some more soup, look again for the raccoon bowl and, not finding it in any of the cupboards, ladle my dinner into the mug with the bear.

Oil. I can't taste any oil. However, the peanut flavor is pronounced. Complimented by the fresh parsley, it does pique my taste buds.

———

I wake after midnight to the lullaby of the singing owl and feel as though my heart will break from pain. Sally would say that, medically, such a thing is impossible. Yet I wonder, has she ever felt what I am experiencing now? Sally has had men become friends, then boyfriends, and then, it always ends after a few months. She claims she hasn't met that Special One yet. She pictures the scene, though. He'll walk into the clinic with a large German shepherd and smile into her eyes as she asks, "What's wrong with this sweet doggie?" She will examine the dog as Mr. Owner stands nearby. He'll ask her out—eventually. He'll be as much of a dog lover as she is and they will live happily ever after in a secluded house with a fireplace and at least ten pets.

Sally doesn't know this pain I feel. But Jeannie likely does. She's been married, and then disappointed.

All day yesterday I wondered why the ache was so large and pronounced. This isn't just heartache. This is consuming, relentless pounding, even when I don't think it's there. This is the horned monster—anger.

If I want to stop living off Extra Strength Tylenol, I need to learn how to deal with this fierce emotion a lot better than I have been. But how do I do that? Anger has embedded itself into the crevices of my heart. I feel it when I drive, when I cook, when I teach, and, like tonight, when I wake from sleep.

Maybe I'll need surgery in order to get it out.

twenty-one

The brochure for my cake business is finally ready to be printed. It is a tri-fold with a glossy color photo of my famous chocolate swirl cake made with two round tiers of chocolate butter cake and scoops of chocolate ice cream between them on the front.

How Sweet It Is: Cakes by Deena is printed in 22-point Bookman Old Style font. I came up with the name for my business while sitting on the deck last night. The next four lines are in Arial, 16-point, and read:

Buttery custom-made cakes for all of your festive occasions!
Anniversaries, weddings, birthdays, and just any day.
Every day deserves a cake!
Order your cake today.

The following page lists the kinds of cakes available: butter, white velvet, chocolate butter, ice cream swirl, and almond. The sizes are given, and the prices. At the bottom is a short blurb about me and where I studied. The back side has my name and contact information in 10-point font. I've included my cell number because, although this cabin has a phone, I have yet to hear it ring. The brochure also says I need at least twenty-four hours' notice on all cake orders.

Jeannie calls and asks how I'm doing. She is going to meet a blind date for coffee after a long shift at the hospital where she's a pediatric nurse. "Only coffee at seven tonight. You know, in case he's a dweeb."

"And if he is what you've been looking for?" I ask.

"Then, we quickly finish our lattes and head over to Palacio del Rey for scallops. Or would you recommend the parsley-seasoned trout?"

I want to ask how she was set up with this man and what his name is and if she is going to color her hair to get rid of the gray for the evening, but she rushes to her reason for calling me. "Have you found a place to print your brochures?"

I tell her I have proofed the final text and copied the file onto a CD, but I haven't found a printer yet.

"Deena, honey." Jeannie's voice is serene and has my full attention.

"Yes?"

"You have to know you have what it takes. Do you know that? Go for it!" With that, she says she has to hang up and find shoes to go with her dress. She sounds extremely excited about this date.

I fill my mind with thoughts of the Bible passages about love and trust, the story of the feeding of the five thousand with small loaves of bread and a few fish, and the accounts of bodies being healed by the touch of a hand. If Jesus healed people with broken hearts and limbs, consumed with demons and disease, surely He is able to help me.

Holding my completed brochure, I feel the sensation that yes, I am capable. I have not felt this way in months. Not since the accident. Not since Lucas plowed his 1987 Mustang into the Woodruff Arts Center and dumped me for Ella.

————

It was the ninth of January, a cold night by Atlanta standards. We were on our way to a concert by the Atlanta Symphony at the Woodruff Arts Center. Lucas had been late picking me up from my apartment, decided to take a shortcut, and suddenly had no idea where he was. I was fuming because he wouldn't stop and ask for directions. The concert was to start in ten minutes. Lucas raised his voice at me, calling me a nag. I was shocked to hear that word fly off his lips. Never would I put up with that. I told him so, right there, as he cut corners and sailed through yellow traffic lights.

Then it started to rain, the drops mixing with ice and beating against the windshield. Lucas drove faster. He took a turn around Tenth Street and then went through a red light at Peachtree, going so fast I had to close my eyes. When he skidded on the wet pavement, my eyes flew open to see that we were hydroplaning off the street, right toward the Woodruff. I screamed; there was no hope of avoiding the side of the building.

Glass shattered. My seatbelt snapped at the buckle and my head hit the dashboard. My body broke, but something deep inside me broke, too.

twenty-two

The kids want to go camping. Last fall they went for a whole weekend, funding their trip by mowing lawns for church members and holding a bake sale.

They are excited about the bake sale because they know that the more they earn there, the better food they can buy for the camping trip. Bobby wants lots of marshmallows and pancakes. Bubba hopes the hamburgers will taste like Burger King's.

Charlotte seems a little uncertain about the trip. She wasn't able to go last year due to a stomach virus, so while the others camped, she was at home being cared for by her sister. Charlotte doesn't tell me this; Rainy lets me know when Charlotte leaves the kitchen to go to the restroom.

When Charlotte returns, she slinks up to me and asks, "What will cooking be like over a campfire?"

Lisa, with a strand of her brown hair in her mouth, shakes

salt onto the diced potatoes we are preparing and says, "As long as the bears don't get us and eat our food or us, we'll be okay."

Charlotte sinks back into her chair.

Great, I think. She finally comes out of her shell with something besides just asking to use the restroom and Lisa destroys her confidence. I want to shout lines from *Oh, the Places You'll Go.* "Today is your day, Charlotte! Don't let anyone stop you from living and succeeding at what you want to do." But I don't say this because the last thing I want to do is to embarrass her.

Suddenly the kitchen is filled with commotion about bears. Bubba says once he saw a man get his leg chewed off by a bear, and then Rainy says that she sees bears all the time because they live in her foster parents' backyard. Bobby says that's a lie, and then, calmly, I bring the class to order.

"First, we are going to talk about the bake sale," I say. "What would y'all like to make for that?"

"We can make brownies!" Dougy says.

"Duh!" Bubba adds.

"From scratch." Dougy smiles.

"Are you married, Miss Livingston?"

"No, dummy," Dougy cries and hits Bobby's large girth with a spoon.

"Of course she is. She makes white sauce for her husband for dinner every night, don't you, Miss Livingston?" Lisa is at my side stirring the potatoes once before we put them in the oven. She uses her sweet smile.

"If we are going to make foods to sell, we need to work," I say, hoping to change the subject. "What did y'all make last year for the bake sale?" I slide the baking tin into the oven and remove the oven mitt from my hand.

"Blueberry cookies." Rainy offers this.

"Really?" I have never heard of blueberry cookies.

Rainy takes the sunglasses from her eyes and balances them on the top of her head. "They were squishy."

"I liked them," Dougy says. "I like the color blue."

"Last year we didn't have a cooking teacher." Bobby pulls his shirt over his stomach. "Just some church volunteers came in to help us make those cookies."

And after that experience with the kids, I bet they vowed never to set foot in here again.

"What are we making today again?" asks Dougy.

"Crispy potatoes." Joy announces and then looks at the recipe card lying on the counter. "With spices."

Bubba repeats what I stated at the beginning of class this afternoon. "The recipe is from a Spanish chef who has a fancy restaurant in Atlanta."

"That's right," I say, hoping that the potatoes will turn out as good as Chef B's.

"And we are going to *love* them," says Bubba.

"Maybe even better than the fries at McDonald's," adds Dougy.

"Maybe even Burger King." Bubba smiles at me, his round face looking like a potato.

Lisa takes a strand of hair from her mouth. "I just wonder why you aren't married, Miss Livingston."

Rainy pops her sunglasses over her eyes. "Really."

———

Yes, I was once engaged. Engaged in June, with a wedding

scheduled for sometime the following year. I wanted it to be in May, but Lucas hesitated. Now I realize that the hesitation came because of his uncertainty about marrying me, not because he couldn't decide on the best month to wed.

June is now here; this is the month I would have been married. This is the time we would be taking off to California for our honeymoon as Mr. and Mrs. Beckley.

I study the ring he gave me: two carats, gold band. He never asked for it back, and I never offered to give it back.

I'm standing over the sink in the upstairs bathroom and holding the ring as the sun streams through the tiny window and dances off of it. I remember how proud I was to first wear this ring, always adjusting my hand so that I could view it as I created desserts at the restaurant. In the evenings, I liked being at stoplights so I could have time just to watch the diamond catch the city lights. Sometimes it looked red or green or gold, depending on the light reflecting off it.

Suddenly, the ring slips from my hands and hits the inside of the basin. I gasp, reach for it, but I'm too late. The ring has gone down the drain. Gone. The ring is gone, Deena. So much for pawning it off to get money for a trip to Hawaii.

I stand at the sink. What do I care? I'm not engaged. I should have tossed the ring into the sink the minute I landed in this town.

The doorbell rings, and I hear Jonas's voice downstairs as he opens the front door. "Deirdre?"

"I'm upstairs," I say as I rush out of the bathroom and wave to him from the open loft. "Hi."

"Hi. I came to check the pipes." He twirls his wrench and smiles. His bandana is the color of apricots this afternoon.

An idea hits me. "Can you help me?"

Jonas looks perplexed. "Upstairs?" he asks, looking up at me.

"Yes."

"Pipes?" he asks as he starts to climb the loft ladder.

Believe it or not, yes. Just when I need a plumber, along comes Jonas.

My bed is strewn with cotton shirts in all my favorite colors—amber, rust, light blue, pink. I was trying to see which summer shirts I can wear. My plan is to wear shirts that won't make the scars on my arms look hideous. None of these looked right. They're short-sleeved, so of course each one shows the *rivers*. Disgusted, I took off shirt after shirt and wondered if I could get away with long-sleeved shirts all summer. I envisioned teaching in a warm kitchen at The Center, sweat pouring off of me, and the kids asking why I'm wearing long sleeves when it's ninety degrees. Conclusion of my shirt-trying-on: I may need to move to Antarctica. Forget the trip to Hawaii.

Jonas isn't bothered by the mess. He enters the tiny bathroom and asks, "Which pipe?"

"Actually, it's the drain in the sink."

He gives me a confused look.

"I dropped a ring in there."

"Why?"

I sigh. I was distracted, clumsy.

"Why did you do that?"

"It was a mistake." And so, it turns out, was my engagement to Lucas.

"An accident?"

I nod.

After that clarification, Jonas sets to work, getting on the floor, opening the cabinet under the sink, using his wrench.

"Do you think you can find it?" I ask as the top half of his body holed up under the cabinet.

"99.9 percent sure I can," he says, his voice muffled.

I watch his broad back, his shoulders and elbows moving, and then, the next thing I hear is a triumphant, "I got it!" As he backs out from under the sink and out of the cabinet, his head bumps against the cabinet door. "Ouch."

The sight of blood makes me queasy. My friends work in the medical field; they deal well with this kind of thing. I fumble in the medicine cabinet by the mirror and find a chocolate cupcake Band-Aid. I place it on the cut above his left eyebrow, just below the fold of his bandana.

"Are you done?" he asks.

I smile at him. "Yes." I pat the top of his head.

Then he opens his hand. In it is a mass of black slime. From the glob, he picks out a small object. "This it?"

Part of me is grateful he was able to get Lucas's ring out of the drain; the other part of me wishes it was lost forever. I am amazed also at how filthy the drain of a sink can be. That thought actually makes my skin itch. I carefully take the ring from him and then head down the stairs to wash it in the kitchen sink. To keep from losing it again, I place it in a colander and run water over it until it is free from gunk.

I read a story once about a couple going through a divorce. The wife threw a pair of Italian champagne glasses off her deck. They'd been a wedding gift, and I imagined that when she opened the box where they lay, all sparkling and new, she'd been excited. And then, the downfall, and instead of quietly drinking champagne with her adoring husband on their home's deck, she tossed those glasses as far as her strength would let her.

"No," I say to the ring, now clear and bright. "I won't throw you out. I'll pawn you off." I make a note to ask Jonas where the local pawn shop is.

When I return to the upstairs bathroom, he's looking in the mirror. "Chocolate cupcakes," he notes. "Pretty for a Band-Aid."

I ask if he'd like some coffee.

"Do you have sugar?"

"I do."

"You have sugar? Okay."

He washes his hands, puts the drain back together, and comes down to the kitchen, where I'm pouring coffee in the Indian mug for him.

We sit at the table. He takes his coffee with six teaspoons of sugar.

"My brother was to be married, but she died. She died."

This is the first time Jonas has ever mentioned a family member to me. I suppose I just thought he lived alone and had no other commitments, that he just appeared one day in Bryson City the same way he just appeared on my doorstep. "What happened?"

"Sick. She was sick." A shadow looms across his face. "My brother prayed."

"I'm sure he did."

"She died." Jonas lifts his eyes to meet mine. "We don't know why there was no miracle."

"That is so sad, Jonas."

He nods, looks down at his hands. Silence follows, as though he's honoring this woman's memory.

Through the window I watch a blue jay perch on one of

the deck railings. I wonder what it would be like to be free from the tangled emotions of life.

Jonas raises his head. "She was real nice, real nice. Like you."

"Thank you, Jonas."

He takes a gulp of coffee. "Who gave you the ring?"

Some guy, I forget his name. He would take my hand and kiss each fingertip as we sat together on the sofa watching videos in my apartment. We took Sunday drives with stops for coffee, talk of which house we'd buy—I liked brick two-stories and he preferred the ranch homes—and the promise of a future together. Once his loan was approved, he was planning to open a business in DeKalb County, selling home furnishings. Oh, I wish I could forget it all—Lucas, Ella, the accident, the 179 stitches. But each time I get over one hurdle, another one blocks my ability to keep running this race called life.

"The ring is pretty," Jonas says.

I used to think so, too.

Dare I tell Jonas about my past? My fingers crunch into fists as though their tightness will keep me from speaking. Yesterday, when Regena Lorraine came over to bring a bushel of Granny Smith apples, she made a comment about my past and how sorry she was about what I'd gone through. I offered her nothing more than a nod and a slight smile. I know she wanted to know more, wanted me to tell all. I'm not sure what my parents told her when they went up to Pennsylvania for Grandpa's funeral. I don't know if they said much. My mother believes in keeping your problems to yourself. When Andrea got engaged to Mark, she told only me at first. "Do you think Mom will be okay with this?"

"Are you kidding? She thinks Mark is the best around."

"She does?"

I laughed. "No. She doesn't think any man is worthy of you or me."

"Yeah, that's what I remember about Mom." My sister sighed. "Can you tell her, then?"

I shook my head. "Oh, no. I'm not doing your dirty work for you." I liked Mark and knew he was interested in overseas missions, a perfect candidate for Andrea because since she was six and I was four, she had made me listen to her desires to explore the world.

Andrea and I both sat on the sofa in my apartment and looked sad. We realized most girls would be elated when they got engaged, excited to tell their parents. While our dad would be happy for us, Mom scrutinized everything.

But it is Jonas sitting before me. Jonas with his wrench. And he wants to know who I was engaged to. I'll keep it brief. I'll just say Lucas was in love with someone else. "My fiancé was in love with someone else. He wasn't the committing kind."

I expect Jonas to nod, finish his coffee, stand, start humming. I expect to watch him as he picks up his wrench and swings it as he walks around the cabin to check the pipes. I'll wash the dishes, I think. I'll fill the sink with hot soapy water and forget that I ever made the humiliating mistake of telling this man about my heartache.

He does finish his coffee, but then, folding his hands, he looks at me. "What was his name? How old was he? What was his job?"

Twenty minutes later, I am still talking, finished with the answers to all of Jonas's questions, and now focused on my own, explaining the situation. I tell Jonas how Lucas proposed to me and how I bought every bride magazine available to plan our wedding. I tell him how happy I was. Then Lucas rammed his car into the side of the Woodruff Center, and although he sent flowers, he never came to see me in the hospital. I push up my sleeves and show Jonas the scars, my own personal rivers carved on my arms, and tell him about the larger scar on my abdomen and the ones on my thighs.

Jonas looks like he might cry. He runs a hand through his hair. His bandana loosens, slips over the eyebrow near the Band-Aid. He slowly ties it again and then says, "My brother was in love, too."

Jonas tells me his brother is kind and likes to do jigsaw puzzles, too. He tells me his brother raised him after their parents died.

"So he's older than you are?" I ask.

"No. He is younger. He's a young man, not old like me."

I wouldn't call Jonas an old man.

Jonas looks at me through his deep-set eyes. "My brother loved Abby. But she died."

"She died?" I hope this time he might tell me how she died. Yet I can't bring myself to ask what the cause of her illness was—like perhaps it is too private and I have not received the privilege to ask.

Jonas nods. "It was a long time ago. Long time." He brushes his hair back, gently touches the cupcake Band-Aid, acts like he has said enough.

The cabin holds silence; we look at each other.

My eyes roam over to the painting by the couch. The kimono lady still holds her fan across half of her face, continuing to hide what she dares not uncover.

After a few minutes, Jonas says tenderly, "I'm sorry."

"I'm sorry about your brother's girlfriend, too."

He picks up the mock-up for the cake brochure. I've left it on the end of the table.

"What is this?"

I clear my throat. "It's a brochure for my business. I'm calling it 'How Sweet It Is'—what do you think?"

He notes the chocolate ice cream cake on the front of the brochure. "Looks yummy."

"I made that cake."

"Does it taste like the velvet one?"

"Not as good, in my opinion."

Simply, he asks, "What are you going to do, Deirdre?"

I could go on for days about what I would like to do, starting with running my dad's tractor over Lucas's size-eleven feet. "I need to get copies made so I can hand them out to people." I wonder if Jonas will think my plan is silly.

He turns the brochure over and asks, "You print this? Lots of copies?"

"Yes, I hope to find a printer to professionally print it."

"Custom Print on Everett Street. They do good work for a fair price." He sounds like a blurb from a TV commercial.

"They do?" What do mountain folk think constitutes good work?

"I can take it when I go in to town."

Can I trust Jonas with my brochure?

He grins at me; even the lines around his eyes are smiling.

Why not? If he fails to get the CD to Custom Print because it gets stuck somewhere in his truck, I can make another copy.

He is so eager and ready to help. "I can do this for you." His eyes hold an intensity I haven't seen in anyone in a long time.

"Okay." I grab the CD, tuck it in the brochure, and hand it to him.

He flashes his Tennessee smile. "I'll get them to do a superb job for you."

Then, just because I feel relaxed and hopeful, I ask, "Do you read the Bible, Jonas?"

"Oh, yes." He quotes three verses.

All three I recognize from the walls at The Center, especially the one about forgiveness. The forgiveness one will always hit a chord in my heart. "Wow! You've memorized a lot."

"Don't read the letters, Deirdre," he says. "But I hear real good."

I have one more question. "Jonas?"

"Yep."

"Is it hard to forgive people?"

His lips draw together as he squints his eyes. "Forgiveness helps us," he tells me. "Heals the bad feelings so that they don't make us mean."

I don't speak for a minute, and he looks uncomfortable. His feet shuffle and he shifts from side to side. When I do talk, all I can say is, "Jonas, that was very good."

———

That night the owl doesn't wake me, but a memory does. I am standing in the elevator headed to the first floor of the hospital. Sally is bringing the car to the entrance, and I am going home. The elevator door opens and a couple enters with a baby wrapped in a pink blanket. The man holds the bundle, all warm and soft. Neither he nor the woman takes their eyes off their baby. I assume they are going home, too.

I have just spent five days in the hospital because my

fiancé crashed his car. He never visited me during my stay, and through the grapevine I learned he has been dating someone else. My future has crashed and evaporated like a puff of smoke. I think it's uncanny that for a brief time in space, this couple and I share the same elevator, getting off at the first floor—to start new lives. Their happiness, my shock and sorrow, all combined in that tiny square, until the doors let us out, and then we share nothing anymore.

twenty-three

When Jonas delivers the brochures to me four days later, I am astounded. I'm on my deck, looking for the tree the owl cries from. I wonder why I'm so doggedly determined to find and see the owl, the creature whose call I have grown to accept and expect each night.

Impulsively, I hug Jonas.

Sheepishly, he says, "You are happy, Deirdre."

The color brochures are beautiful. They are even on a beige card stock, not just regular twenty-pound computer paper. The photo of the ice cream cake looks clear and tempting.

"How much do I owe you?" I ask. Come to think of it, I have offered him nothing for checking my pipes. Is Aunt Regena Lorraine paying his bill? She told me to hand over any utility bills I get for the cabin because she pays them from a fund my Grandpa set up. Whenever he traveled, she paid his bills for him.

"Zero," replies Jonas. He presses his hands into the pockets of his jeans.

"No, Jonas. I have to pay you."

"The guy at Custom Print owed me money."

"He did? Why?"

"I fixed a leak in his kitchen." Then he laughs, and drawing attention to where he cut his head in my bathroom, he says, "I almost hit my head on a pipe at Custom Print!"

I'm glad to see that his wound from the other day has disappeared. If only all cuts could leave our bodies so quickly and without a trace.

"Let me pay you."

"No." He shoves his hands deeper into his jeans pockets and shakes his head. "Zero."

"I can't do that."

"Well, you will have to."

A moment later he enters my kitchen and bellows, "Got any cake to eat?"

———

I do three loads of laundry after Jonas leaves. As my clothes spin in the dryer, I admire the fancy lettering, the vivid colors, the texture of the card stock, and the way the photo of the chocolate ice cream cake entices. Chef B would not think the cake is regal enough for the intricate decorating I do, but Jeannie was clever in suggesting this cake be the one for the front of the brochure. This cake speaks of people's everyday lives—brownies and chocolate chip cookies. Not tiers of frosted cake layered with unpronounceable orange filling.

I feel a bit foolish for thinking that Jonas wouldn't get the job done. I'm sure I'm not the first one to doubt his capabilities.

Before he left in his truck, I thanked him again. He just smiled and said I should start making cakes.

Giovanni barks as my aunt knocks on the door. I yell for her to come on in, which she and the dog do. Today my aunt has on a bright yellow dress with two big pockets below the waist. But she is not feeling bright today and immediately upon seeing me at the dining room table, cries, "I'm sorry, Deena."

"For what?"

"You'll have to excuse me for coming in here so often. I know you don't need your old aunt barging in every day."

"That's okay. Want me to put water on for tea?" I look at the clock and see I need to leave for my cooking class in ten minutes.

As Giovanni relaxes on the rug by the sliding glass door, Regena Lorraine finds room on the couch. Her face is blotchy; her eyes are rimmed in red. She moistens her lips, starts to speak, and then looks longingly around the living room. "It's just that . . ."

"Yes?" I sit in the chair across from her.

"Well . . ." She takes in a long breath and lets it out like air being released from a bottle of soda. "This cabin is filled with memories."

I join her in glancing from wall to ceiling to floor.

A tear runs down her cheek. "I miss him."

A gentle feeling eases over me. My aunt is missing her daddy. "I wish I'd known him better," I say.

"Yes, well. Well, yes." She considers saying something else, stops. Finally, "Families. They often don't see eye-to-eye. You know, how it can be. Your mother . . ."

"Never liked Dad's relatives?" I complete the sentence for her.

161

She dabs at a tear that rolls from under the bottom rim of her designer leopard-spotted glasses.

"True, right?"

My aunt lets another tear follow the first. "True." Then quickly, "And Ernest traveled a lot. He was often gone to some foreign place, especially after Mother died. So he wasn't around to make those visits that probably made your mother turn up her nose."

I laugh. *Turn up her nose.* Yes, that is what my mother does when she doesn't like or approve of something or someone. My aunt knows her well.

Regena Lorraine blows her nose into a pink tissue she takes from her bosom. "I miss so much about Ernest. He was a good father."

I look at my aunt with her reddened cheeks and sad expression and think she has never looked more endearing.

Suddenly a thought comes to me. "Do you know anything about a raccoon bowl?"

"Raccoon bowl?" Removing her glasses, she wipes both eyes. "Yes. I gave it to Ernest when he was harassed by hungry raccoons a few years ago."

"Where is it?"

This time my aunt laughs.

Although she confuses me, I allow her this indulgence. Anyone who has just cried deserves to laugh.

"I came in and stole it."

Is she telling the truth? "Really?"

"Yes. I'm a regular thief. Shortly after he died, I saw it on the counter. I recalled that time three raccoons surrounded him. That was some story!" She glances at me. "Have I told you?"

"No, you haven't."

Clapping her hands together, she begins. "Well, he was carrying a bag of potatoes and had to lift it over his head so that the raccoons wouldn't be able to reach it. Then he ran inside. I was in my car in the driveway. I laughed so hard. Once the raccoons left, I went into his cabin and we laughed together." She takes a deep breath. "When I eat my bran cereal out of that silly bowl every morning, I can hear his laughter."

I decide then that I will not ask for the bowl so that I can get the best effects from my grandpa's peanut soup. Perhaps I will never be able to taste all the flavors. Yet Jonas tasted every single one and I served the soup to him in a white ceramic bowl. Ordinary people think that the dishes we serve our food in don't matter. However, early on, Chef B taught me that the plates and silverware we use to present our works of art must compliment the food. "Never serve mint curried chicken in dark bowl. See? Its color is dark, so to present it well, place it in a light bowl, white or cream in the color. See?"

I did see. I have tried to follow his instructions. My grandfather Ernest must have realized the importance of serving food in the appropriate dishes, as well. If he were here, I know he and I could have some amusing conversations. Especially if I got the chance to tell him about the family gravy bowl that is so ugly I once considered purposely knocking it off the counter onto the kitchen floor.

My aunt stands, and I catch the scent of her perfume. She makes her way toward the door. "Gotta go." Giovanni stretches, shakes his massive frame, and prepares to leave with her.

Quickly, I say, "No, you don't. I have to get to class. But you take your time sitting here . . . and remembering."

She looks surprised that I would let her stay while I'm out.

Then she sits back on the couch, relaxes, and crosses one heavy ankle over the other.

Again I note the kimono picture hanging on the wall—that half-covered face of the woman, hiding—hiding behind the opened ornate fan. Suddenly, I'm hit with the thought that my aunt has been hiding from me her sorrow over the loss of her own father. How much like me she is. We really are from the same gene pool.

"Help yourself to cake," I tell her, as I load the ingredients I need for today's lesson—blueberry muffins—into my Whole Foods bag. "Jonas ate a slice earlier, but I think there's a little left."

"You're a godsend," she breathes as she rests against the quilt on the couch. "Did I ever tell you about the time Jo-Jen saved me from a depression?"

"No, you haven't done that yet."

She fingers her Minnie Mouse watch. "It was after my mother died. And now, you are helping me, Deena."

"I am?" I can't believe what she's saying. Me? Not too long ago I was in a hospital bed, wishing I would have died in the accident.

"Your being here in this cabin has done wonders for me. You bring life to this place."

At times like these, I'm not sure what to say.

"I was married once," my aunt says as she looks through the sliding glass door, somewhere over and beyond the edge of the visible mountain.

I make my voice soft. "I didn't know that."

"Men are . . . Well. Just make sure you know that no one can possess you."

I do know that. "I know," I say with force. I think of Lucas for a second and suppress the urge to scream.

My aunt glances toward the windows in the ceiling that are letting in an array of light. "Did you know that Katharine Hepburn said that plain women know more about men than beautiful ones do?" she asks the ceiling.

That, I didn't know.

"My husband, Charlie—he appreciated gambling more than he did me."

When she looks at me, I want to say something but no words come.

"He grew up in a home without hope. No one gave him any. I tried. I really gave it my best, Shug, but I guess it wasn't enough."

My sorrow is about to explode in my chest. Now I think I recall Mom saying something about how Regena Lorraine used to be married, but that her husband left one day for Vegas and never came back.

Her smile surprises me. "That which doesn't kill us makes us stronger."

That line I have heard many times since my accident. I wonder if my aunt would have preferred death to becoming a pillar of strength. My guess is that she might have looked around her and wondered why other women's husbands stayed, offering happiness and fulfilling relationships. My guess is that she might have woken on many lonely nights to ask the age-old question, "Why me?!"

She catches me off guard when she comments, "You are like a lemon in the fridge."

A lemon in the where? Could this be another of her entourage of quotes? Who said this one? "What about lemons?"

She lets out a slight laugh. "Ernest always believed that a lemon in the fridge is a good sign. He told me as a little girl that a lemon just sitting on a shelf in a refrigerator is a symbol of hope and contentment. It's a long story. I know you have to go."

I tell her I'll see her later and head out the door.

My mother never cared much for Dad's side of the family—this is true. Growing up, I recall that her parents, her siblings, and her siblings' kids visited us often on our farm. As far as dad's relatives in Pennsylvania and North Carolina, we rarely saw them.

Yet Grandpa Ernest didn't let my mother's coolness stop him from putting me in his will. Sometimes family has to persevere in spite of the obstacles in the way.

My aunt was thoughtful and parked her truck beside my Jeep instead of behind it, leaving me room to back out without much trouble. The driveway, being so close to the edge of the mountain, still makes me nervous, but I am getting a little more used to it and learning how to maneuver in and out.

I drive down the steep road, grateful for my father's father. Sometimes life's biggest blessings come in the wrapped packages that you never expected and didn't choose. They are just there for you with your name on the card, waiting to be opened.

And appreciated.

twenty-four

As I'm in the kitchen washing the tins from the blueberry muffins we made in class earlier, Miriam enters and asks if I'd like to help—the kids want to make posters and flyers to promote the upcoming bake sale.

"They just came in from playing basketball. They're in the fellowship hall." With that, she leaves me, her tennis shoes squeaking in rhythm.

I can hear them; the fellowship hall is the next room over, and no walls can keep out the noise the kids make when they talk.

As I enter the large room lined with metal tables and chairs, Lisa is pouting because she didn't get the anticipated visit with her mom last weekend. She moans that she had to stay with her foster family and all they did was rent a movie.

"A movie sounds good," Zack says to her. He is wearing

jeans and a dark brown T-shirt that brings out the flecks of brown in his hazel eyes.

"What did ya see?" asks Bobby. The group is seated around two rectangular tables—tables Miriam has piled with colorful construction paper, poster board, and markers.

"*Ratatouille*." Lisa makes a face; the others laugh.

"That's a fun movie," says Zack. For some reason, I'm surprised he watches movies. I thought he spent all his time helping the kids. I imagined that when he wasn't with them, he used every available hour to figure out how to make their lives better, maybe poring over his psychology books from grad school.

Lisa's frown doesn't leave her face. "My mom was going to take me to buy clothes at the mall in Asheville and out to dinner at the Fryemont Inn."

"Your mom ain't that rich!" yells Rainy, and her voice bounces off all four walls.

"She is so! She's got more money than all of you!"

"My mom's got two houses," Rainy boasts.

"And one of them's the jailhouse," quips Dougy. "Where she lives all the time."

Rainy rises from her seat. "Just because I'm black, you think my mama's in jail?"

Zack interrupts sternly, "Okay. That's enough." He waits for Rainy to sit down again and then he turns and nods to me.

I'm standing by the wall near the door where I entered. I don't want to intrude on this gathering, which to me feels like a family trying to work things out. I feel like the intruder, the one who doesn't belong.

"Miss Livingston," Joy asks when she sees me, "are we gonna make posters?"

"Can I make them? I'm good at art," says Rainy.

Lisa announces that she is too sad to make anything.

"You can't live on sadness, Lisa," says Zack in a steady voice. "You have to keep on going." He looks from her straight at me. "People suffer broken promises and dreams many times in their lives."

"Duh! We know that," says Bubba.

Then Zack lets me take over the class by stepping aside and gesturing for me to stand before the group.

Broken promises? Why was Zack looking at me when he said that? I feel heat rush to my face. I will not let his comment bother me. I have kids to teach. I march over to the whiteboard and pick up a black dry erase marker. "Why don't we list the ways we can advertise our bake sale?"

"I want to make a poster," says Rainy. "I'm good at art."

"We could put them up on the bulletin board," says Joy.

"We need everyone to see them," says Bobby. He expands his hands to show just how wide he wants this coverage to be.

"Duh!" says Bubba. "We need an airplane to fly in the sky with an announcement."

The class laughs. Except for Darren. He is drawing something in his notebook. With his head lowered, he moves his red pen across the page to make bold lines.

"We can make flyers and pass them out," says Dougy. "Go all over town and hand them out at places like McDonald's."

"And I want to make a poster," Rainy tells us again.

"Okay, Rainy can make a poster." On the whiteboard I write *Poster* and place Rainy's name by the word. As I write, Rainy's eyes brighten.

"Do we need another poster?" I ask. "How about one for

the church's bulletin board?" I've seen the bulletin board in the main building on Sundays when I've attended the eleven o'clock service with Aunt Regena Lorraine.

No one says anything.

"Any takers?" I ask.

You could hear a toothpick drop; this silence is un-believable.

"Darren, you could do that." Zack's voice swells with affirmation.

The kid actually looks up at Zack.

"Okay, I'll make it," he tells Zack, carefully averting his eyes from mine.

I am about to fall down onto the fellowship-hall floor.

———

Zack hot-glued a piece of blue plaid flannel to the bulletin board by the restrooms. The flannel was Joy's idea and both Miriam and Zack agreed it was a fine one. On the bulletin board we will place the poster Rainy made announcing that The Center will hold a bake sale in two weeks. Darren's poster, clearly made by a boy with superb talent, will be tacked to the bulletin board by the sanctuary.

Bubba and Rainy cleaned up the fellowship hall under Miriam's supervision as the other children left the building with their parents and guardians. When Darren's grandmother came to pick him up, she shook my hand and told me that Darren loved The Center and its programs. I wanted to say with sarcasm, "Oh yes, I can see that he loves being here every day." But I didn't.

Rainy's foster dad came to get her just as Rhonda, Bubba's social worker, drove up to take him out to dinner at Burger

King. She is pretty, this Rhonda. I have seen her around The Center before. Her smile makes me think of a river sparkling under a summer sun. I know the kids think she's cute.

"Is Zack still here?" she asked as Bubba fastened his seat belt.

I didn't know if I was bothered by her asking or if it was more the look of longing in her wide eyes.

"He's here." Bubba supplied the answer. "But don't go talking to him like you always do. I'm hungry!"

We all smiled, and Rhonda backed out of the parking lot. I felt something funny deep inside. It was pain, but not the usual kind. Rhonda spends a lot of time talking to Zack?

Now that all the kids are gone and The Center is quiet, I walk over to Zack. "How did you know?"

Questioningly, Zack looks up at me. "Know what?"

"That I was engaged."

"Oh." He studies the tip of the glue gun. I assume he's trying to get out of answering the question. "Did I say that you were?"

"Yes! You talked about broken promises in your little pep talk and looked right at me."

"Did I?"

I let out a sigh of disgust.

He looks at the board, avoiding my eyes. "I can tell."

"You can tell?!" What on earth does that mean? How can you tell that a person has been engaged? Does the air around her smell of post-engagement perfume? I have to know. I edge closer to him, careful to avoid the glue gun. "How can you tell?" Don't I still have my decorative fan covering half my face? Have I exposed too much of myself to this church crowd?

Zack focuses his gaze on me. "Your ring finger is tan except for where your ring used to be."

We both look at my ring finger as I hold my left hand out against the edge of the bulletin board. There is no mark, no untanned area. "Right," I say.

Who told him? Who knows I was engaged? The only people in Bryson City who know are Aunt Regena Lorraine, because she is family and she can't help but know, and Jonas, because he rescued the ring from the drain. Neither would have a reason to talk to Zack about my engagement to Lucas. I give a big sigh and then do what I used to do in grade school, and still do when the occasion calls for it. I walk away.

"Listen, Deena." His voice is sharp and stops me from taking another step.

"What?" I ask without turning around.

"Why is it such a terrible thing for people here to know about you?"

I spin to look at him. My head throbs with puzzlement. "What?"

"We aren't exactly perfect here. We handle our own bad luck, and we've gotten good at handling that of others. You can talk to us, you know."

Bad luck? I am jarred by the two words he has just used to describe my failed engagement. *Bad luck?* Bad luck means having to stop at three red lights in a row when you're late for work. Bad luck is the Atlanta Braves losing two games at the start of the season. Very bad luck is when both the entrée and the salad have raw onions—onions you're allergic to. I am about to turn and walk away again, but then he smiles.

"Deena," he says with clarity.

I like the way my name sounds on his lips. Gosh, I didn't know that my name could sound like that.

"We don't bite. We're not the raccoons or bears that live in the woods."

My eyes narrow as I say, "I know that."

"Do you?" He gives me a peculiar grin and returns to his task, adding another drop of glue to the flannel material.

With his attention no longer fully devoted to me, I feel free to go. Yet, even as I walk down the hall, farther and farther away from him, my shoulders straight, my mind is still with him. I want to understand what he's saying, where he's coming from. I want to believe that he would listen to my story of woe about Lucas and show enough empathy for me to fill all my new stainless-steel cake pans. I want to open up and tell him.

At my car, the realization hits me that he cleverly kept from telling me how he knew that I'd been engaged. He gave away none of his own secrets. Yet he wants me to trust him?

The truth is, I am afraid to find out whether these people bite or not. I know this about myself, and yet I cannot seem to change it. I have already been hurt enough.

I get into my Jeep and gun the engine. I will not be putty in Zack's basketball-playing hands.

twenty-five

At Southern Treats, a little coffee shop beside the railroad tracks, I meet the elderly owner, who introduces herself as Mrs. Dixie. She is dressed in black with a string of milky pearls swaying from her narrow neck.

I have been to Heaven's Railway, the bookstore, and Yum Yum, the Chinese restaurant, to ask if I may display a few of my brochures. The employees behind the counters at both places said the exact same thing: "I don't think that would be a problem." Then they took a dozen brochures, smiled, and continued to wait on customers. I hoped my brochures ended up somewhere where customers could see them, but I did suspect that they very well could end up in the trash bin behind each location.

Mrs. Dixie holds one of the Southern Treats menus toward me until she realizes that I'm not there for coffee and pie. Standing at the front entrance of the store by windows framed in pecan-colored curtains, she opens my cake brochure. She studies it as I watch three patrons inside the tiny shop sip on cappuccino in delicate white cups.

Adjusting her glasses, she looks me over. "So you make cakes?"

"Yes." I attempt to stand straight.

"That's all?"

"For now," I say.

She flips the brochure over, removes her glasses, then looks at me. "Cakes." She has an impish voice, a cross between the squeal of a piglet and the cry of a calf.

"Yes."

"Do you make pies?"

"No."

"Hmmm." She flips her glasses back on and turns the brochure over once more.

"I mean, I can. I have. I studied at the Atlanta School of San Sebastian."

Apparently, she is not impressed by where I went to school. So much for Sally's theory that Atlanta is looked upon as the New York City of the South. "Hmmm." She twists her necklace in her fingers. "I like pie."

"Oh, I do, too." I say this using my gushing tone. Immediately, I feel foolish.

"Chocolate." She raises her eyes to look at me. "That's my favorite."

But of course. It's my least. "Oh."

"I don't eat cake."

I nod.

"Now, my mother made a chocolate cake I ate growing up."

I'm not sure how to comment so I just stand there.

"I didn't like it, though."

I want to go home.

"I sell cake here."

"Yes." I shift from one foot to the other.

"I just don't eat it."

I force a smile.

"What kind of pie do you like?"

"Peach."

"Peach? Hmmmmm. You're from Georgia."

I hope she doesn't say anything corny like I'm a Georgia peach. Or ask if I have seen the huge peach that stands tall near Interstate 85 outside of Gaffney, South Carolina.

"Atlanta? I went there once to hear the symphony at the Woodruff Arts Center. Magnificent music." She smiles broadly as my stomach spins like Lucas's car did the night he crashed into that very place. I would have taken a comment about a Georgia peach over the one she just gave me. She resumes her reading; I take wispy breaths.

Without looking up, she says, "It's a beautiful arts center."

Yes, it used to be to me, too.

Carefully, she fingers my brochure like she's pushing a pie crust into a pan. "How many did you bring?"

"Brochures? I have hundreds."

Waving at the rack by the front door she says, "Put fifty of them there."

She walks away, back toward the coffee-sipping customers and over toward the kitchen.

I gulp. It takes me a while to know what to do. I head outside, open my trunk, and grab a handful of brochures. That looks to be about fifty. I carry them inside. She's nowhere to be seen. I place the brochures in the rack right under postcards for rental property, brochures for Grandfather Mountain, and neon-pink flyers for a weight-loss program.

A train's slowing wheels sound in the near distance. For a moment, I consider jumping aboard and going someplace where life is easy. My next thought is that God's hand should be able to hold me anywhere. Even here in this small town. And, according to Grandpa Ernest, if you have God's hand to hold, what more could you want or need?

Inside my Jeep, I do something I haven't done in a long time. I close my eyes to pray. Right now in this little mountain town, it feels as though God is closer than He's ever been to me—except for maybe my childhood on the farm. I ask God to make people pick up the cake brochures and decide to buy cakes from me. Dozens of orders each week—that's what I want. Then I think to myself that this sounds a little selfish.

I wonder if God would agree.

Opening my eyes, I watch the train heading into the station. I pause and view its shiny colors and see the steam rising from its smokestack or whatever the chimney of a train is called. I feel a tender bond with my father even though he is miles away. There is something about trains that make him happy, especially locomotives. Maybe it is their ability to travel with ease through the valleys and peaks of the land; perhaps they make us hope that our lives can be lived on course, following a track that will take us to wherever we are scheduled to go.

Again, I lower my head, focus on the dusty dashboard, and then let my eyes close. I feel a little uncomfortable, yet natural, all at the same time.

"Help me know how to teach these kids." I wait, nod. That seems right. Then I think of the fruits of the Spirit listed on the kitchen door at The Center. "And please . . . show me patience."

I open my eyes, finished, and place my key in the ignition. Before starting my Jeep, I close my eyes one more time. "Patience, especially for Darren. Help me reach him. Make him not be so bitter," I say, hoping I don't sound like a waitress with a request for the short-order cook. "Please." I make the word sound as soft as I can, as though I want God to realize that I can be grateful in spite of my frustration.

twenty-six

Each time my cell phone rings, I answer with anticipation that it will be someone in town who has picked up my brochure and wants to order a cake. I imagine a baking-challenged mother with a daughter who is getting ready to turn sixteen finding my brochure as she exits Southern Treats. "I can ask this woman Deena to make the cake," she says to the coworker she has just shared a pot of tea with. Her voice contains relief that comes when one realizes she doesn't have to bake. I've heard that voice in my own mother many times. I see this coworker, nodding and adding, as she peers at my brochure, "Wow, what a beautiful cake. I'll have to order one for our anniversary next month."

Instead of cake orders, Jeannie calls to say that Sally told her I'm doing well. I assume Sally's visit brought her to that conclusion. It's a good thing Sally isn't able to read my mind, for I'm still thinking about Lucas and his new girlfriend far too often.

When my phone rings again, I've just dumped ingredients into my blender to make salsa.

Mom asks if I still have a supply of vitamins. She tells me she has been taking Omega-3 supplements in addition to her usual vitamins and it's doing wonders for her.

"What kind of wonders?" I ask as I stare at my KitchenAid blender filled with canned tomatoes.

"I can finish a crossword puzzle in half the time."

I picture her sitting straight—no slouching for her—in the den, working on a puzzle from her book, Dad seated in his navy recliner watching a Braves game, a can of diet Coke in his hand.

"How are you doing?" she asks.

I miss y'all, I miss Atlanta, I want to go home. I think all of that, but only say, "I'm doing really well. Teaching is great." The surprising thing is that she believes me. Then I tell her how wonderful Regena Lorraine is. I wait for her response.

All she comes up with is, "Oh? Well, that's nice."

I want to say that Mom needs to quit talking through her nose about people, especially my aunt. I feel like getting on a soapbox and shouting, "She needs people! She misses her dad. She's normal! And isn't she part of our family?"

Just as I am thinking this, Mom says, "Deena, I'm glad you have someone to look after you."

She is the queen of mixed messages, this Mom of mine.

After we say our good-byes, I turn the KitchenAid to the blend setting and watch it go to work on mixing tomatoes, cilantro, garlic cloves, minced onion, and lime juice. There is something amazing and invaluable about a kitchen tool that can do so much good in such a short amount of time. Chef B once said he's in love with the blender, and I can understand why.

Earlier this week, I told the kids that for our next lesson we would use the blender to make salsa. Their eyes grew wide. "Salsa? In a blender?"

"The blender is one of the most versatile apparatuses," I said, and immediately was overcome with a yearning to be in Chef B's presence. "You can make soups with it, too, and smoothies."

"Soup in a blender?" Bubba squinted up at me. "You're kidding, right?"

"Let's make smoothies," said Rainy.

"I hate smoothies," piped out Joy. "I had an avocado one and it was nasty."

"Why'd you choose that kind?" said Bobby.

"It's all they had."

"Girl, you need to expand your horizons," said Bobby. "Right, Miss Livingston?"

I smiled because when the kids had complained last week about making a broccoli casserole, I told them they needed to get out of their McDonald's and Burger King mode and try something different. "Expand your horizons," I'd said as I stood beside the church stove.

"What the heck?" said Bubba.

"It means," I said slowly and with all the precision my voice could deliver, "you need to open yourself up to try foods that you normally might not. Be adventurous."

The kids looked at each other, frowned. Darren continued with his masterpiece, his pen silently moving across the page.

Now I want to test the recipe before I teach it to the class. I don't want any failures. I've already taken my homemade chips out of the oven. I cut flour tortillas into triangles, coated them with olive oil and a little garlic salt, then baked them for fifteen minutes at 375 degrees.

Chips and salsa—that should make the kids happy. Isn't that supposed to be food kids these days enjoy?

I finger my cell phone, wishing for another call, this time for a cake order. I can't take the waiting. I wonder how my aunt is and decide to call her.

"Hi, Shug. Do you need me for something?" she asks when she answers.

"No, no." I hope we're on terms where I can call her just because. I try to recall if she ever told me not to call her. One woman in my church in Atlanta gave birth to triplets and set the rule that she accepted no calls after eight. Surely, my aunt hasn't adopted this standard, has she? Hesitantly, I say, "I just wanted to see how you are."

Her voice becomes warmer. "Thank you for letting me sit and remember in the cabin the other day." To someone else I hear her say in an excited tone, "I think it's Professor Plum in the conservatory, or is it the billiard room? With . . ." There's a pause. I wonder if she's still on the other end, and then I hear, "The lead pipe!" Her excitement bounds like Giovanni when he's found a squirrel to chase. "I know it has to be the lead pipe." To me, "Thank you, Shug." The other voices in the background muffle hers until I hear her tell the group, "No, no. This is my final observation. I'm changing it to Mrs. White in the billiard room with the lead pipe."

Clearly, she's busy, so I tell her I hope her guess is correct.

"Thanks, Shug. You know I love to win." I bet she's smiling.

When we hang up, I turn my attention to the salsa, which looks and smells enticing. I pour some of the chunky mixture—just the right consistency for scooping up with chips—into a white bowl, dip a tortilla into it, and eat. Adding a little more salt and a dash of pepper, I taste again. Perfect, I think. The cilantro tastes so fresh. Chef B told us, "Always use lots of cilantro. It keeps the taste so flavor." The entire class smiled at that.

I sit on the couch, turn on the TV with the remote, and find a program to watch. By the time the show ends, I've finished the salsa and chips, and have no idea what the story was about. My mind has gone down memory lane again. My skin itches, and I once again feel an overwhelming sense of stupidity for having trusted a man who took advantage of my devotion and spontaneous kisses.

When the front door opens and I hear, "Deirdre, I'm here to frost," I'm a bit perplexed, but very grateful that the voice doesn't belong to Lucas.

Jonas rushes into the living room as I turn off the TV with the remote.

"Jonas, what a surprise!" I'm glad I'm not in my pajamas or just out of the shower, wrapped in a towel, hair dripping, scars showing. I hope it's not obvious to Jonas that I was thinking about Lucas.

"No surprise, Deirdre," he says as he faces me with his hands in his jeans pockets. "You said I was to come over to frost." His smile spreads across his face, like the morning sun in a summer sky.

Up until this point, Jonas and I have communicated well.

I suppose that couldn't last forever. "Jonas, I said you'd have to come over to frost the cakes for the bake sale." I recall telling him just days ago that he could come over to help me prepare for the event.

He nods. "I am here."

"Next week."

"I come next week?" He rubs his temple and produces a frown.

I look at this man who is wearing a bandana the color of Giovanni's fur. Something inside me knows that the misunderstanding between us is not important. Standing, I say, "Let's frost, then." I lead the way to the kitchen. "We can practice."

"Practice makes perfect."

I laugh and it feels as refreshing as a cool drink on a sweltering day on the farm. "Where's the cake?" Jonas asks, his eyes searching the counters.

"I haven't made one," I say.

Jonas looks confused, then blurts, "How can we frost a cake when there is no cake?"

The bake sale is not for another nine days. While the kids and I have made a few items and placed them in the freezer at The Center, I wasn't planning to do my share of the baking until closer to the event. I do have some leftover buttercream icing in the refrigerator. So we can ice . . . something.

Jonas notices the bag of Krispy Kreme donuts on the top of the Kenmore. "I like donuts."

And that's when I decide that we'll create top borders on mini French crullers.

Jonas watches as I open my large plastic box of decorating supplies and take out a four-inch polyester pastry bag. I fold the cuff over and adjust the plastic coupler snuggly into the tip of the inside of the bag, choose a stainless steel star tube because I think that Jonas will appreciate icing his crullers with stars tonight. He edges even closer to me as I screw a white plastic ring over the shiny tube's base. Using a small palette, I scoop buttercream into the bag and then force the icing toward the base, trying to press out any air bubbles. I twist the top of the bag to keep the buttercream inside. To test the contraption, I squeeze a mound of icing onto the counter, forming a sugary star.

"Wow," says Jonas. "You do fast work." Tempted by the icing on the counter, he dabs at it and then lifts his finger to his mouth. He chews methodically.

"Well?"

Like he's talking for a commercial, he states, "Plenty of butter in there." Looking at me intently he asks, "What do I do?"

"You pipe icing onto the top of the donut."

"Pipes?"

"It's a verb, not a noun." As soon as I say this, I shake my head. Whether I've used pipe as a verb or noun means nothing to Jonas. When he hears *pipes*, he automatically feels he needs to swing his wrench and Sharpie. I take the bag from him, realizing that squeezing icing from a bag is not necessarily second nature to everybody. Even if you can operate a wrench. Placing both hands around the filled bag, I lower it to press two star shapes onto the tiny French cruller. "There!"

Jonas claps his hands together the way Miriam does when she wants the children's attention. "My turn?" he asks, reaching for the bag.

He bends at the waist so that his nose closes in on the donut. If he moved two inches closer, his nose would be in the donut hole. Shifting from foot to foot, he squirts two dollops onto the edge of the donut. They run together. He straightens himself and glances at me.

"Good job, Jonas."

"No. They look like a crash, not stars."

A crash? Uh oh. "Just be steady," I tell him, hoping my voice is encouraging. "Slowly let one star out, then move the tip a little and press out another star."

He wipes his palms on his jeans. "Steady?" When I nod, he tries again. He lifts the bag a little lower until the tip touches the surface of the mini cruller, then quickly, he presses the bag to let out a white star of icing.

"You're a natural."

"My brother will love this." He now has two dollops of frosting around the rim of the donut and one star. The top of the donut has no more room for work, so I place another donut on the counter. He adds two stars, both free from any error. He admires his work. "Not bad, huh?"

"You're a pro."

"Can I take this one to my brother?" He points to the second donut, gingerly picks it up, and then quickly makes his way out of the kitchen toward the hallway.

"Sure," I say following him.

"I'll come back another day," he tells me, the frosted donut in one hand, the keys to his truck in the other.

"I'll let you know when," I say, but think to myself that Jonas comes and goes as he pleases; he operates on his own timetable.

"Not tomorrow, because I have to do work at Mrs. Dixie's."

"Southern Treats?" I open the front door for him and the smell of burning wood waltzes from the outside air into my hallway. I should light a fire in the fireplace, I think. Although, the last time I tried, I forgot to open the flue and had to sleep with the windows open to let out the haze of smoke.

"Mrs. Dixie makes good pie."

"I took my brochures there," I tell him.

"Did she tell you she wanted them? Did she take fifty?"

How does he know? "She did. She told me to put fifty on the rack by the front door."

He smiles and his teeth glisten under my porch light. "I knew she is a good person. I told her she should take fifty."

When he leaves, I spend several minutes feeling that contentment and satisfaction that oozes over you when you know you've done something right. I hope Jonas feels it, too. I smile, thinking of how he looked pressing frosting onto the donut and how the simple task made his face radiant. Then my thoughts change gears. So much for thinking that I could break into this small mountain community on my own. Jonas must have asked Mrs. Dixie to display my brochures at her restaurant. That's why she took fifty of them. And the other stores, too. Obviously, Jonas is looking out for me.

He is a good person.

twenty-seven

Although there are probably a lot of monumental events happening all over the world on this Saturday, The Center's bake sale feels like the most important to me. The children are eager and excited. Bubba and Lisa race over to greet me when I enter the fellowship hall. Dougy and Rainy let me know about all the baked goods that have arrived so far. They want to know where my cake is. Darren cowers in the corner at a table laden with paper plates of cookies wrapped in cellophane. I smile at him and he produces a small nod. Charlotte is seated behind a table. Joy and Bobby haven't arrived yet.

My making a cake to be auctioned off was Zack's idea. I was reluctant, but the kids said that was a good idea, especially if some rich people came to the sale like they did last year.

"Where's your cake?" Bubba asks, sounding like he hopes I haven't forgotten it.

"It's in my Jeep." I pray it's all in one piece.

The children, Miriam, Zack, several church members, and I had placed advertisements about the sale in the *Smoky Mountain Times*, at shops, restaurants, the Swain County Chamber of Commerce, the Fryemont Inn, Harrah's Cherokee Casino and Hotel, and the library. I baked all week. I taught my classes, baked cookies and cakes with the kids, and then baked at home. My two favorite items are the cranberry bread and the banana muffins.

Last evening I baked the cake to be auctioned, and then when Jonas came over to help frost it, I made him a cup of coffee with sugar. He watched me mix shortening, confectioner's sugar, vanilla extract, and butter as he drank the coffee. Eager to help, he kept exclaiming how large the cake was. He asked if I had any donuts that needed frosting. "They are easy," he told me. He started to hum "Take It Easy."

Then he said, "My brother liked the donut I brought him. He said you were society's finest."

"What?" I lifted my head from the three-tiered cake to note Jonas's expression. Was he teasing me?

"Yep. My brother said, 'That woman who taught you how to frost a donut has got to be one of society's finest.' "

Jonas squeezed a few beaded dots where I told him to, admired the cake, and circled around the living room. I could see he had lost interest. I sent him home, telling him what a help he'd been. He grinned like the kids at The Center do when they know they deserve praise. I didn't finish the final touches on the cake until long after the owl had started his solo cries in his tree.

As he enters The Center, Zack greets me with a smile, large and warm. The whites of his eyes look especially clear, like he's had a good night's sleep. He's dressed in a pair of jeans and a forest-green shirt.

I smile, too. I hope it's a decent smile; my body is sore from lack of sleep.

Bubba walks with me to my Jeep to help carry the cake. Two cars pull into the driveway, and from one steps Bobby and from the other Joy jumps out. Both drivers wave at the children and me.

"Are we late?" asks Bobby.

"No," says Bubba. "Man, you should see all the food on the tables!"

"I hope nobody made anything gross this year." Joy runs a comb through her curls. "Does my hair look puffy? I didn't have time to wash it this morning. I hate it."

I unlock the trunk of my Jeep. The cake should be fine, I think. I didn't drive more than twenty miles per hour the whole way down here.

Bubba peers at the cream-colored cake, beaded with frosting and crowned with two candy roses. "Just beautiful," he says.

Joy thinks he is talking about her hair. "Thanks, Bubba," she says with a smile that makes her eyes glow.

"Thanks, Bubba." I lift the cake from the Jeep and, ever so slowly, with the guidance of the children, walk it into the building.

———

Before the doors open to the public at eight, Zack assigns a task to each child. He reminds the kids to be polite, to nicely encourage folks to buy, and then adds that each child should make sure to thank people for buying.

Miriam has been at The Center since seven, making coffee. Robert, who teaches drama and art in the afternoon to the kids, has covered each table in the fellowship hall with a white linen tablecloth and an arrangement of daisies and lilies. Rhonda, Bubba's social worker, also has come to help.

Charlotte accepts her post behind the table loaded with assorted cookies. As she sits in a folding chair, she asks if Miriam would like some oatmeal cookies. There are two packaged in cellophane with *$1.00* written on the sticky label. The children and I made these cookies last week in class. After they'd cooled and we'd sampled a few, we wrapped three dozen and then placed them in The Center's kitchen freezer. Yesterday, we took them out and decided on the price. Bubba thought they should cost seven dollars for two. He said they were "the bomb."

Now Charlotte smiles shyly at Miriam.

"Yes," says the director. She hands Charlotte a one-dollar bill.

Charlotte takes the money, places it in a metal box on the table, and then gives the cookies to Miriam. "Thank you," she says with a small smile.

"You do that well," Zack compliments Charlotte.

Charlotte shakes her head, says she's no good.

Zack tells her only insecure people can't handle compliments, remember? He must have taught them this when I wasn't around because this is the first time I've heard that line. Insecure people can't handle compliments? I wonder which one of his psychology books holds that tidbit.

When the doors open for business, I think the whole town must be here. The fellowship hall is filled with crying babies, men, women, and adolescents. I see two men in police uniforms and three firefighters.

I look up from the money box where I've just placed ten dollars from a woman who purchased six cups of coffee and five plates of cookies. She told me to keep the change. There stands Marble Gray, wearing pink curlers underneath a violet scarf. She picks up one of my cake brochures, which have been placed at the table where my decorated cake proudly sits. She stuffs another brochure into her large black purse and then heads over to the food tables. She tries to get two chocolate chip cookies for the price of one. Then she picks up a sugar cookie, claiming that it's for Sinatra. I can tell Charlotte wants to tell her to pay for it, but I shake my head and mouth, "Let it go."

Marble meanders around the room, smiling at a few people, but no one seems interested in talking with her. Perhaps she's cheated them all out of something at one time or another.

Jonas enters the fellowship hall; I can hear his shoes even though he is surrounded by groups of people. He shuffles in his style over to the tables covered in the sweet-smelling baked goods. "Hi," he says to me, and then to Zack he bellows, "Hi, Buddy!" He waves his wrench.

"Hi, Jonas. Working today?" asks Zack, noting the wrench.

"No, not working. Eating."

Jonas picks up a chocolate pie that Robert's wife made for the sale. It is carefully wrapped in cellophane with the ingredients listed on a white label. Robert's wife is allergic to nuts and peanut butter and feels food items should always be marked. Apparently she had a bad reaction to a cake a few years ago and ended up at Swain County Medical Center. Of course, if you can't read too well, a label indicating that the pie has no nuts does you little good. Jonas says, "Looks yummy," and turns to me. "Where is your cake, Deirdre?"

"Deirdre?" Rainy snorts. "He calls you that?"

Zack points to the table along the edge of the opposite wall that holds my cake and the pile of brochures next to it.

Jonas says, "I helped with decorating that." To Zack he asks, "Do you know that putting frosting on top of a cake takes lots of being steady?"

Zack smiles. "I imagine it does."

Jonas winks at me. "You pipe it," he says.

"And you love pipes," Bobby says.

"Yes, I love pipes."

Zack grins, and Jonas turns back to me and says, "Ah, I haven't introduced Zack to you, Deirdre. This is my brother." He places his arm around Zack's shoulders. "I want some chocolate pie," he tells Bubba, who is standing by the pies. "I have money today." He fishes out a worn ten-dollar bill from his jeans.

Zack and Jonas are brothers? No, they can't be. This is some sort of prank. Bubba and Dougy are probably behind it.

I look at the boys and see no smirks on their faces. While Zack talks with Jonas, I note the men's features, and when they both smile, I see it. Something about the laugh lines around their eyes is identical. Other than those lines, Jonas's mouth is wider, and Zack is not as muscular or broad in the shoulders. Yet, they are about the same height.

After I finish looking them over with all the discretion I can manage, I am hit like a tornado whips the side of a barn. All the things Jonas has told me about his brother fly at me. His brother was in love with a woman who died. He likes jazz; his favorite pie is lemon meringue. His brother is the best.

Immediately, I feel a blanket of embarrassment spread over me, tucking me in at every side. If they are brothers, and right now they appear to be close, then how much of what I've told Jonas has he shared with Zack?

I watch Jonas now; surely he wouldn't have told Zack everything? Yet the comment Zack made about knowing I was engaged . . . So Jonas did tell his brother. I feel like suddenly the cloud has been lifted and I am seeing with 20/20 vision.

It is hard to concentrate on chocolate cookies and coffee when you're trying to come to grips with the fact that two people you respect in very different ways share the same mother and father.

Marble Gray stops by my table and asks if Sinatra can have another cookie. She tells me that he just had surgery and almost died and oh, please, just one sugar cookie?

Rainy is about to tell her she needs to pay for the baked goods, I can feel it.

Quickly, I hand Marble an oatmeal cookie, and as she smiles and walks away, Rainy protests.

"Maybe she'll go home soon," I tell Rainy.

"She better," says the girl as she forces air from her mouth. "I'm tired of her cheating people."

twenty-eight

Night has fallen, and the church is nearly empty. Miriam went home, congratulating me on an excellent bake sale. Jonas sailed off in his truck, waving good-bye to his brother and saying he'd be by Zack's later to check the pipes. My tiered cake was auctioned by Zack and made $80. Marble Gray wanted it, but the pink-curlered cheapskate was only willing to bid $11.50. Darren's grandma offered $32 and Charlotte's sister, Cindy, went up to $40. Aunt Regena Lorraine said she'd pay $50 and then someone yelled out $60 and before I could catch my breath, the bidding ended at $80. A couple about to celebrate their forty-fifth wedding anniversary carried it off in their silver sedan, looking almost as happy as the day they were married.

I'm in the kitchen washing out the coffeepots and thermoses we used for the coffee we sold. It was a good day, I think. The kids were on their best behavior and remembered to thank people for buying. Miriam counted the money and said we made $265.75. That'll be enough to pay for the campsite and buy firewood and food for all the meals. There is also other money that has come in because Bubba and Bobby mowed lawns and pulled weeds for a few church members last weekend.

Zack enters the kitchen and places a pitcher that held cream on the counter. Then he sees me at the sink. Sometimes it feels like I spend my life at the kitchen sink.

"You could get the kids to wash the dishes," he tells me.

I could, I think. But the question is, would they? Sometimes if you want a job done well and without complaints, the easiest way is to do it yourself.

Zack grins. "Things went smoothly today."

"I think the world of Jonas," I say. I smile as I think of how much he has added to my life. How he sings entire verses of Eagles songs to me, not just a line or two. His voice isn't bad. He sang the other day, " 'Don't let the sound of your own wheels drive you crazy,' " which made me think, was that song penned for me? He's always eager to try a new recipe I come up with, even the one that was more or less a failure the other night—squash biscotti.

Zack picks up a towel from the counter and a bowl from the drainer. "I'm sorry about Lucas."

I hate hearing that name from Zack's lips. Dismissing the subject, I say, "Oh, that's all over." Mom always said to act like nothing bothers you, that a real woman is an expert at covering her emotions with a slight lowering of her eyes. I focus on the dishwater, all the filmy suds.

"It hasn't been that much time." His words filter through the kitchen and grapple with my heart.

I want to say in a nonchalant tone, "Time? Who needs time?

I'm a picture of health and happiness right now." Instead, I mumble, "I'm sorry about Abby."

When I look up from the sink I see that his eyes hold pain—like two dark corridors that I will never be able to enter or bring any sunshine to. She must have been his moon and stars. Jonas said she was kind. The dead always seem larger than life; we forget their shortcomings, we honor their greatness.

"I had no idea it was you Jonas was talking about . . . at first." Zack places the bowl in the cupboard with dozens just like it. He's draped the towel over one shoulder, which makes me think of how my dad does the same thing when he dries dishes.

"What did he say about me?" How much does Zack know about me, my past?

Zack avoids my question; he's deep in thought. At last he says, "It was the cupcake Band-Aid. He came over for dinner with that Band-Aid on his forehead. You gave Charlotte a Band-Aid that looked just like that when she cut her finger. And then I knew all that he was telling me about this nice woman named Deirdre was really you."

I guess I have no secrets anymore. I bet Jonas has told his brother everything about me. I suppose the whole town will know all about me by morning. Marble Gray will be gossiping about me to the cashier at Ingle's.

After a pause, Zack says, "He was proud of that donut the two of you decorated."

"Oh, he did all the work."

"Did he tell you what I said when he brought it to me that night?"

"Yeah." I start to recite what I remember Jonas telling me

his brother had said. "My brother liked the donut. He said that the woman who helped you is . . ."

When I hesitate, Zack completes my sentence. "The woman who taught you how to frost a donut has got to be one of society's finest."

I can feel heat rising from my face, like it does when I open an oven door to take out a nicely-browned cake. *Society's finest?*

Zack softly says, "I know about your accident. Jonas said that—"

"That I have awful scars?" I realize that everything I've told Jonas over these last months has probably been shared with his brother over coffee with lots of sugar.

"No." Zack looks uncomfortable. "He didn't say anything about any scars."

The next thing I know I am showing my arms to Zack. I even lift my shirt a little so that he can see the deep scar on my abdomen. Bet you've never had anyone show you her scars before, I think as I look up at him. That will shock up your life a bit. I bet you'll never speak to me with eyes shining and a smile again. I sigh. I don't care. And I'm not even sure why I don't care.

"Actually," Zack says calmly, in his typical manner, "Jonas said you are a Vivaldi fan."

"He did?" So, nothing about my accident, nothing about my scars? "Well, I am." I feel foolish now for showing the Tigris and Euphrates to Zack. And especially for lifting my shirt and exposing the wound along my stomach. In church!

"I guess I should go," he says.

Yeah, right, go. Don't mind me. I'm just a little weird. A darkness has spread over me and I can't find my way out. I suppose that, in Zack's book, I am no longer one of society's finest. I resume my coffeepot washing. Why was I suddenly so eager to show him the scars that I otherwise keep hidden even from my own eyes? I lift a soapy hand to my forehead to check for a fever.

"Deena?"

I give a slight nod.

"The kids like you."

I am too tired to argue.

"They just have a little bit of difficulty with new people sometimes . . ." His voice meanders away like a winding mountain road. However, his next sentence is firm. "Your scars aren't going to make them like you any less."

Where is he going with this?

"In fact, most of them have their own set of scars. Physically or figuratively speaking."

I nod again. I hope he won't give me a speech about these poor children. Because the way I see it, maybe if they shaped up, their lives wouldn't be so hard.

I silently berate myself for even thinking that.

You better let somebody love you, before it's too late. I add more Palmolive to the sink water, hoping that the force of squirting the liquid from the bottle will push aside the words to one of Jonas's favorite songs.

"Everyone here is damaged." Zack's words hit me sharply because they are words I can take as my own. Damaged. That's me. He continues, "But that's not our main focus."

"What is your main focus?" I ask, only because I am irritated. I was in a good mood right after the bake sale, but now he bothers me. I want to know what he is really made of. I want to pick at him to find out he isn't all he appears to be. Yet, most of all, at this moment, I want to keep him here, talking to me.

"Love's the main focus," he says.

"Love?" Well, that's about as vast and hard to come by as world peace. Love isn't like a gift you can wrap up and place under the Christmas tree.

"Everybody needs love."

Well, as the kids would say, *duh.*

"Even those who don't know how to give it."

Uh oh. Is he going to make a comment about my inability to show love to my fellow man? Because if he does I won't be able to deny it. Gripping the edge of the sink, I wait.

"Like Darren."

Darren does know how to show love, I think. He shows it to Zack. To the rest of us he just acts like we aren't worthy. He's selective and he's chosen Zack. And Zack, of course, thinks he's a terrific kid. His client. Social worker and patient. What a team. The two of them, leaving the rest of us out of their behavioral management plan. Softly I say, "Yeah."

"Darren was burned as a child." Zack's voice is very soft and emotional.

"Burned? What do you mean?"

Zack's solemn expression lets me know that this is not going to be an easy story. "When he was little, his mom got mad whenever he cried. Darren cried a lot. When he did, his mom would burn the bottoms of his feet on the kitchen stove."

I feel my lunch rising to my throat. "They didn't let her get away with it, did they?"

"She's been in and out of jail. There was a restraining order against her, and now she is supposed to call before she expects to see Darren."

My head swirls and I take little breaths.

"Darren has a hard time with authority. He'll come around, though. He will."

I may not last until he does.

"You have to give these kids a bunch of chances."

I don't like his tone because it makes me feel like I am the one with the problem. And, the truth is, I have so many. I'm just glad that Zack hasn't read my journal.

He heads to the fridge, opens the door, and pours some cold water from a plastic container into a glass. "Would you like some water?"

Why does he have to be so . . . nice? I wish he'd just go. Leave me alone in the kitchen to wash the dishes. To ponder on how good a friend his brother is to me. To wonder why Jonas is so easy to be with, while Zack only brings out the insecurities I hold inside. "No, thanks."

He stands closer to me. My heart begins to feel like bread dough being kneaded with tiny warm caresses. I watch as he takes another sip. His eyelashes flicker. "Sometimes the very people who want to be loved the most don't know how to ask for love."

"And why is that?" I concentrate on scrubbing the lid of the pot. I don't dare look him in the eyes.

"They've been hurt." He places the empty glass on the counter.

His know-it-all tone makes me wish he'd just leave me alone. He's crossed the line, and the thing is, I'm certain that was his intention. Go, I want to shout. Go! My eyes fill with hot tears and that scares me.

Zack starts to dry a spoon. I had no idea there was a spoon in need of drying.

I feel my nose start to drip into the steamy sink of hot water. I sniff, once, twice. With a soapy finger, I wipe my nose.

"Are you—?"

Quickly, I toss out, "I'm fine."

I can feel his eyes on me, boring into my soul. I thought I was ironclad and am not quite sure how he managed to find a gap.

The room feels warm. Maybe the air-conditioner, along with my humility and compassion, has stopped working.

Zack dries the same spoon over and over. "Deena?"

"What?"

"There is nothing wrong with admitting you're hurt."

"I am fine," I repeat, emphasizing each word.

He's silent for a moment, then he moves and I think he's going to leave the kitchen. But he only opens a drawer and places the spoon inside. He starts to dry a knife.

To play the devil's advocate I say, "So, do you admit you're hurting?" There! I feel like a kid who has pulled a prank the teacher can't catch.

His reply is spoken from his heart, and his honesty surprises me. "I'm getting better. After she died, I didn't want to live at first."

I nod a few times. Oh yes, I do know just how you felt.

"Jonas was strong for me."

"Jonas is gold."

And then I realize Zack has those same golden characteristics. He's so gentle, so patient, so kind. His tenderness is ripping up my insides as though he were slicing each part of my anger and bitterness with that knife he has in his hands. I want him to put the knife down and let me fall against his chest, let the barrier collapse between us. I stare at the suds, feel my hands grow wrinkled like prunes. He is going to leave. He's looking for a way out of the kitchen. He'll exit my life after making me wish for things I cannot have.

I wait.

Instead of leaving, he says, "Is that coffeepot clean yet?"

"What? Uh . . . why?"

"So I can dry it."

This time I let myself view his face, his smile, those two dimples wasted on a man. I grin, or try to. When I rinse the pot that has never had such a good bath in its life and hand it to him, he says, "You are not so different from the rest of us."

Suddenly Lucas seems very far away, like a fog you drive through, and when the sun comes out, beaming and hot, you forget what the fog looked like, or how it felt to be surrounded by the mist. All you can feel is the warmth of the sun, and the sun is the only place you want to be.

I'm not sure which is more remarkable—that Zack is drying dishes next to me or that I don't mind that my sleeves are pulled up so that parts of my scars are visible and that what caused them doesn't seem so horrendous anymore.

When I smile at Zack this time, his eyes hold familiarity, like he knows what is going on in my mind and heart right now. Like I am not alone; he has traveled this winding, steep, narrow path, as well.

And in fact he is still trekking on it. Determined to get through, without losing himself. Without losing me.

twenty-nine

I've burned my fingers in the oven many times—by accident, of course. When Chef B or any other employee at the restaurant heard my yelp, the ice pack kept in the freezer for just such an occasion was handed my way. "Be the more careful," Chef B would say as he watched me wince with pain. "You must to use the hot pads. See? I buy new ones last Tuesday."

I cannot imagine what it would feel like to have my feet burned on a hot stove. There are things in life I want to thrust into the Do Not Open drawer, and after doing so, conveniently forget that such a drawer exists.

I can't push the haunting truth of what happened to Darren out of my mind.

I see him clearly in my thoughts tonight as I clean the upstairs bathroom. Darren slouched over his notebook, drawing things he never lets me see, refusing to participate. Does he draw happy pictures? I know that the poster he created for the bake sale had a fancy border and lettering that was curvy and bold. He used red, purple, and green and even drew a picture of a slice of cherry pie and a large carrot cake in one of the corners.

He's a child, I think as I scrub the sink. Bad things have happened to him—things no child should have to face. He's been seriously damaged. The scars on his feet are only the tip of the iceberg of what he's really suffered.

Exhaustion covers me, and I yearn to sleep. Instead, I spray Windex on the mirror and wipe off the streaks with a paper towel. What kind of person would burn a child's feet? I ball up the towel and throw it into the copper-colored waste can. I see Felicia with her vibrant orange hair and push down the nausea filling my throat.

I slip into bed, grateful for the soft sheets. But my mind is full and sleep doesn't come for a long while. Eventually, I get up, sit outside on the deck; against the *wooohooo* of the owl, I write about Darren in my journal until, at last, I can welcome sleep.

———

"If only Zack didn't affect me like he does," I whisper to the mirror in the loft bedroom as I prepare to head over to The Center for my Wednesday afternoon class. I brush my hair, put on lip gloss, and hope I can convince at least part of me that Zack doesn't mean anything to me. I want to push him away. If he were a recipe, I'd cut him out of the book. My reluctant-fearful side wants to drape a quilt over my head and run as far from Bryson City as Beijing, China.

Monday I avoided him as much as I could get away with. I

didn't want to make it obvious to the children; if they started to notice my lack of conversation with Zack, they'd be sure to question it. I simply didn't engage in any talk with him except to say, "Hi" upon seeing him and to answer his question with a polite, "Yeah, my class went well today." I smiled as often as I could; a good smile covers a multitude of insecurities. Mom taught me that.

At the end of my class yesterday, when I was listening to Bubba tell me about how he and Rhonda had a picnic on the Parkway, my eyes locked with Zack's. Zack was helping Lisa put away some dishes and he looked over at me with a smile I can't get out of my mind. Somehow I don't think his action had anything to do with Lisa, or Bubba's detailed account of the large size of the hamburgers he and Rhonda ate for lunch.

Jeannie always says that there are times when a smile seems like more than just a friendly expression. "You know, when he smiles and you feel like the sky just bursts with fireworks," she told me.

I'm probably reading too much into this. But then, why do I try to avoid him as much as I can? Fear of what he is starting to mean to me? The lyrics to another one of Jonas's favorite pipe-checking songs runs circles in my mind. *There ain't no way to hide your lyin' eyes.* Well, as long as I can keep Zack from knowing how he's beginning to take root in my heart, I'll be all right.

My cell phone plays Vivaldi into my thoughts.

"Hello?" says a woman's voice.

"Yes, hello?" I don't recognize this person.

"Is this Deena Livingston?"

"It is."

"Then I want to order two cakes."

I hear a dog barking with vigor in the background. I press the phone closer to my ear.

"I want the cakes for this Saturday."

My heart is doing flips of joy. "Great, and what is your name and phone number?" I scan my desk for a pad and pen.

"My name is Mrs. Marble Angelica Gray."

"Hello, Mrs. Gray," I say. My first cake order and it is from the town's cheapskate. I remember seeing her pick up several brochures at the bake sale. Maybe she thought they were coupons for dog food. "How is Sinatra?"

"Oh." She giggles and I imagine her pink curlers bouncing. "You are good with names. He's running around in the backyard now."

The next thing I know I hear the panting of a beast right in my ear.

"Say hello, Sinatra," croons the woman.

Sinatra merely yelps.

My ear will never be the same.

"So you want two cakes?" I ask over the yelps.

"Sinatra, go play," she commands. With a clearing of her throat, she says, "Yes, I would like one chocolate and one white velvet."

"What sizes?"

"Eight inches is fifteen dollars?" I suppose she is reading from my brochure.

"That's right." Will she actually pay me? I wonder. This woman is known as the one who will cheat you out of your underwear. Suddenly, my enthusiasm for getting my first cake order falls like a cake without baking powder.

"So two cakes is thirty dollars?"

"That's right."

After a moment of hesitation she asks, "Do I pay you when I get the cakes?"

Delivery! What's the mountain air doing to me? I forgot about that. Am I going to cart my custom-made cakes all over the mountainside to people's homes? Quickly, I make a decision. "These cakes will be ready for you to pick up on Saturday at nine in the morning."

Silence on the other end.

"Hello?"

Impatiently, "Well, then, where do you live?"

I think of Jonas and the first time he gave directions to this cabin. Will those work or do I need actual street names? All these mountain bends called roads, do they have real names? I give her the best directions I can, adding that I am near Memorial Methodist Church.

"I'll be there," she says.

"I take cash or checks."

"I'm sure you do."

And no expired coupons, I want to add, but resist.

I'm ready to hang up, but Mrs. Marble Angelica Gray isn't. "One more question."

"Yes?"

"How will I carry my cakes home?"

What does she mean? She'll be driving, won't she? She can put them in her car like other people do. Confused, I ask, "What do you mean?"

"Won't they slide all over the seats? I don't want my leather seats covered with icing!"

"Boxes," I say quickly. "I have cake boxes, and they'll keep the cakes safe."

Grunting, sounding like a pig rooting in the trough for a corncob, she says, "Are they those white boxes?"

I go over to a large box by the desk in my room that is half filled with the pastry boxes. They are flat and can be opened and assembled to hold any size cake, round or square. I look at the box on the top, as though viewing it will help me with my answer. "Yes, they're white."

"Do they cost more?"

"No, Mrs. Gray. The boxes come with your cake order."

"Well. That sounds nice."

Downstairs I hear the front door opening and the bark of another dog. "Deena! Where are you? We need to go!"

"What?" I end my conversation with Marble Gray and look over the banister at my distraught aunt and a slobbery Giovanni.

"Jonas fell off the church roof!"

"Jonas?"

"He's been taken to the hospital."

I grab my purse and sail down the stairs. My first cake order now seems insignificant.

"I tried to call your cell, but I just got your voicemail," my aunt says, her voice heavy with urgency.

At the bake sale I learned that Jonas is the church plumber and sometimes spends time at the church on weekday mornings long before my classes start. But what was he doing on the roof? As we get into my aunt's truck I ask her what happened. I sit in the back of the cab; Giovanni never gives up his cushy passenger seat for me.

She backs out of the driveway with the ease of a woman who has lived in these mountains for a long, long time. "He was getting a badminton birdie."

"From the roof? Why did he go up there?"

"The preschool girls got the birdie stuck on the roof and asked him to get it down today. He was busy. You know Jonas. He had to check some pipes first." She speeds down the looping road as I close my eyes. "He was admitted over an hour ago after first being in the ER. Jo-Jen got the phone call while we were playing Scrabble."

I can't bear to think of Jonas being in the hospital. As we pass homes, I note their roofs and think that the distance between a roof and the ground is a long one.

The next thing I know, my aunt is asking if I know how her dog got his name.

Perhaps this is a trick question, or something that has to do with Jonas? Softly, I say, "No."

"Ah, I never told you." She puts on her brakes when we reach the end of the road and takes a right into the heart of the town.

"I guess not."

"Well, about six years ago, one fall, I was driving on the Parkway in my truck."

I want to laugh at how bizarre this is. Jonas's life could hang in the balance and my aunt uses this moment to tell me about her dog.

Regena Lorraine continues, "Mozart's *Don Giovanni* was playing in my CD player. I was enjoying the day but feeling a bit lonely. Out of the woods came this bounding mass of fur. I stopped my truck in time, or I might have hit the happy critter. Then he walked over to my window, which was down, and licked my hands. Just jumped up and gave me a kiss. His tail was wagging, Mozart's opera was blaring. I parked my truck, saw that there was no collar on him. I took him home, and the rest is history."

Giovanni lets out two happy barks.

We are now at the hospital's parking lot. "Nice story." Then I sneeze; I am still allergic to dog fur, yet my aunt hasn't seemed to catch on after all these months. Some dog lovers, as well as parents, just can't grasp that not everyone adores their babies.

My aunt is still clueless about why I'm sneezing. With all the excitement of a parade, she gushes, "His name is so appropriate, Shug. The opera about Giovanni combines comedy, drama, and the supernatural. That was how that day was for me, that day I met my own Giovanni."

———

Jonas lies sleeping on a sterile bed of white, his heart monitored by a green humming machine. Where his bandana is usually tied, is a large gauze bandage. His face is pale; an IV feeds into his arm.

Regena Lorraine pats his other arm and says, "Jonas, this is no place for you."

I suppose she hopes this line will cause him to pop open his eyes and jump off the bed. He does neither.

I watch the squiggly lines move across the machine. I never know what to call this piece of equipment, although Sally has supplied me with the proper term many times.

Flashbacks of my days at the Atlanta Medical Center come to me. I woke up alone in my hospital room and for a second felt nothing but calm. I thought I must have died and that this was heaven. Then a nurse entered and suddenly the horror of what had happened crept in around me. I asked if Lucas was all right; I was so naïve.

The door swings open; Zack enters the room. In his typical style, he smiles at my aunt and me.

"How is he?" Regena Lorraine whispers. I don't think I've ever heard her whisper before.

"Still unconscious."

"Has he been conscious any since he fell?"

Zack shakes his head.

I know Zack must be thinking of the girlfriend he lost. His parents died within months of each other when he was nineteen. His father was in a logging accident and then his mother had a massive heart attack. In this whole world, Zack's only close relative is his brother. I want to wrap my arms around Zack and give him a hug. Me—the one who lately has made it a priority to avoid him.

Zack says, "Dr. Martin said they should have the results of the MRI soon. I was just talking with him."

"What are they afraid of?" My aunt is bold to ask.

Zack speaks from dry lips. His words come out shaky. "Bleeding on his brain."

We stand in silence, and then my aunt says she must go. She promised to bring dinner over to Butterfly Ormandy, a woman who just had knee surgery. "I hate to leave," she tells us apologetically as she places her tote bag over her shoulder. "But I promised I'd help out with a meal, and this woman was a dear friend of Ernest's."

We tell her that we understand. Zack offers to drive me home later.

"Butterfly was there for me when I went through a cold, lonely time," my aunt says.

I nod and think how nice it is that my aunt has such good friends, even if they do have the most peculiar names.

thirty

A tall nurse with stunning features enters Jonas's room. I bet every man loves to have her as his nurse. I note her blue eyes and the thick blond hair dangling over her back. She even smells good, like the roses on our farm in Tifton after a rainstorm. Jonas needs to wake up so that he can admire her, maybe even sing her a few lines from the Eagles. If only he knew what an opportunity he's missing.

The door flies open; a young doctor bounds into the room with the vivaciousness of Giovanni, a chart under his arm. I sense Zack's discomfort as the nurse and doctor talk quietly and briefly, hovering at the foot of Jonas's bed.

The doctor looks over Jonas's chart and then turns to Zack. "Your brother's test results should be back soon." With a pat to Zack's shoulder, the doctor leaves as energetically as he entered. I wonder what kind of vitamins he takes.

When the nurse finishes taking Jonas's temperature, Zack pulls over a stool for me to sit on. He sits on a matching stool close to the head of his brother's bed. He takes his eyes away from Jonas to look at me. "Thanks for coming."

"He is going to be okay." I hope I sound certain, but my shaking knees belie the words.

"He would do anything for anyone." There is admiration in Zack's voice.

"He's a lot like you, then," I say with feeling. Here I am, the Queen of Avoidance, vowing to keep away from this man, and suddenly, I am letting my heart speak for me.

Zack says, "I don't know if that's always true."

"Oh, it is."

"I balk at being inconvenienced as much as the next person."

"You're always there for the kids."

"Yeah, but if you look at me real close, you'll see that I'm ready to spit nails when they have an emergency when it's time to go home. I'm hungry and tired and just want to get to my house, turn on the TV, and watch something mindless while I eat dinner. Then comes the phone call from some officer or therapist to let me know I have to come pick up somebody somewhere."

"So you're admitting the kids can aggravate you?"

"You knew that," he tells me with a slight smile. "I told you they could one of the first times we talked."

That's true; I recall that conversation now. That was the afternoon I was ready to never set foot in The Center again.

A murky voice whispers, "You two?"

Zack and I both turn to see that Jonas has opened his eyes.

Zack's smile fills the whole room. "Hi."

"Hey, Buddy." Jonas manages a lopsided grin.

"Hi, Jonas," I say, and touch one of his fingers.

He eyes his brother and then me. "You two need to get together one of these nights." His speech is slurred, but his smile is abundant.

Zack ignores the suggestion, clearly relieved to see that Jonas is alert. He adjusts the stool so that he is closer to his brother's face. Gently, Zack says, "You doing okay?"

"Yes. Are you doing okay?"

Zack smiles again. "I'm fine. I'm worried about you."

"I've been sleeping, Buddy. Real comfortable."

"Really?"

"Don't worry about me, Buddy. I'm not working today."

"I can see that. Next time you don't feel like working, take a sick day."

"A sick day?" Jonas pauses, considers the advice. "I'll take a sick day."

"Don't go jumping off roofs," Zack warns, his voice laced with warmth.

"I'll just choose a day that is sick."

"That's right."

After a moment, he asks, "Which one?"

"What?"

"Monday is a sick day? Tuesday is a sick day?"

"No, Jonas."

Jonas continues as Zack rolls his eyes and smiles at me. "Wednesday is a sick day? Thursday is a sick day? Friday is a sick day? Saturday is a sick day?"

We wait and then Zack says, "How about Sunday?"

"Sunday is the Lord's day. Not a sick day."

"That's right."

"Read," Jonas tells his brother.

I wonder what he means. Zack opens the drawer of the bedside table and pulls out a navy blue Bible with the Gideons logo stamped on the cover. I watch as Zack flips through the pages, going from Old Testament to New. He stops turning pages and then in a clear voice reads, " 'Finally, brothers, whatever is true, whatever is noble, whatever is right, whatever is pure, whatever is lovely, whatever is admirable—if anything is excellent or praiseworthy—think about such things. Whatever you have learned or received or heard from me, or seen in me—put it into practice. And the God of peace will be with you.' " When he finishes, Jonas closes his eyes and I recognize that this passage is the one Jonas tells me to live by, the one he claims he fills his mind with.

We are wrapped in a beautiful silence except for the noise in the hallways, doctors being paged and carts rolling. This is life, I think. The beauty of a meal, a word, a moment—and then reality kicks in and you realize you've still got to deal with dirty dishes or heartache or fear. Maybe reality is those brief moments, and the larger blocks of time are just insignificant inconveniences.

Zack returns the Bible to the drawer.

"You're gentle with the kids," I say softly. "But with Jonas you're something else."

He looks at me. "What am I?"

Genuine, terrific, a hero, someone to swoon over. *You better let somebody love you, before it's too late.* "You're the best you."

"The best me?" He starts to laugh and I hold up my hand.

"People who laugh at compliments are insecure, remember?"

"Yeah, I remember." He tucks the sheet around his brother, then shifts his gaze to me.

"So?"

"Say thank you," Jonas instructs him, his eyes still shut. "You're supposed to say thank you to Deirdre."

We listen to a voice paging a doctor over the PA.

Zack whispers, "Thank you."

"You're welcome."

I think Jonas is smiling, too. I touch his shoulder. "Jonas?"

He is smiling, but his snoring lets me know that it is his dreams that are making him smile.

———

Suddenly, I am aware that it is still Monday afternoon and I have a cooking class to teach. I walk into the hallway so I won't disturb Jonas. Then I dial Miriam's number from my cell phone. I explain why I'll be late.

Of course, she already knows about Jonas's fall and says that the kids are in the fellowship hall making cards for him, and not to worry.

"Are you there alone with them?" I ask. Being alone with those eight kids is a challenge no human should ever have to endure. Even if you do own a pair of green tennis shoes.

"Robert and Rhonda are here. I called them to come over since I knew Zack would be at the hospital. They got here just a few minutes ago."

Jonas is important to me, but I also have a responsibility to The Center and to Miriam. "I'll be there soon," I say.

"No," says Miriam. Firmly she adds, "You need to stay there."

"I do?"

"Zack needs someone." Then she says she has to go. The kids have run out of red construction paper. "They all want to make red cards since red is Jonas's favorite color."

"It is?" I ask, but she has already hung up.

Red? I never knew.

thirty-one

The kids from The Center come to see Jonas, one by one, escorted by Miriam and Robert into Jonas's room. They are allowed only to enter his room, drop off their card, and then exit. This could be a disaster, I think, but the kids are well-behaved. Lisa gives Zack a hug, and Dougy says that he is sure Jonas is going to be back fixing leaks by tomorrow.

Jonas sleeps through their visit, which is a shame. He would have reveled in the attention. The cards the children made rest on the window ledge, a row of bright red. Miriam says she found a few more sheets of Jonas's favorite color stored at the bottom of a cabinet in one of the preschool rooms.

Next, Simon Gibbons, the pastor of the church, steps in for a visit. He tells Zack that Jonas is "a breath of fresh air." Just before he leaves, Jonas's neighbor arrives. A mousy woman with a French manicure, she says that Jonas is the best neighbor anyone could ever have. "He takes good care of my plumbing," she says as she places a vase of pink lilies and yellow snap-dragons on the window sill.

When the visitors are gone, the room's only noise is the soft murmur of the machines.

Zack looks at the clock on the wall and says that we could go to the lobby and get something to eat. It's five after seven.

I sit on a cushy chair while Zack gets us coffee and sandwiches from a vending machine. The hospital has no cafeteria. The Atlanta Medical Center it is not.

I press my fingers to my temples, trying to come to grips with Jonas's fall. What was he doing on the roof of the church? He looks so much older lying in the hospital bed. How old is he? Forty? How old is Zack? I feel about ninety right now, and tired.

Beyond where I sit, there is a painting on the wall of a cluster of fruit displayed on a wooden table. I see a bunch of yellow bananas, Muscatine grapes, three Granny Smith apples, four figs, and over to the edge, a lemon. The lemon reminds me that Aunt Regena Lorraine still owes me the story behind the lemon in the fridge.

When Zack sets the Styrofoam cups of coffee and the sandwiches on the small table in front of us, I note his worried eyes.

I peel the cellophane away from the ham sandwich. My hands feel too heavy to lift the bread to my mouth. "I'm not hungry."

Zack adds sugar to his coffee. He pauses and looks at me. "You know? I don't think I am either."

Just for something to say, I toss out, "Jonas told you a lot about me."

"Apparently he told you about me, too. The clever thing is he never mentioned our names to each other."

"Were you engaged to Abby?" I surprise myself by asking this.

Zack looks at his shoes, then up at me. "No. We weren't at that stage yet."

I can tell there is still pain piercing his heart when he thinks of her. She was lucky to have known him, I think, lucky to have held his heart in her hands.

Zack says, "We were both in grad school. Both twenty-four." He sips his coffee. Looks into it. "She died a month before graduation. She had leukemia. That was eight years ago, but I still . . ."

"Miss her," I offer.

When he sighs, his face holds a vulnerability I haven't seen before.

We let the silence spread itself between us until I feel the need for conversation.

"So no one has come close to being as wonderful as her?" I regret the question the second it leaves my lips. What am I aiming for? Zack to suddenly sweep me in his arms and tell me that he loved her, but he now has found another love, and that love is, my goodness—me?

He says, "I have Jonas. Not everyone understands that he isn't just my brother."

"You raised him when your parents died."

Zack lets out a low laugh. "Is that what he told you?"

"He said that even though he's older than you are, you raised him."

"He raised me. It might look like I have to do all the taking care of, but Jonas takes care of me." Softly he adds, "If it weren't for Jonas, I wouldn't be grounded. He keeps me balanced."

My eyes fill with tears, the sudden ones that come on

unexpectedly. I try to blink them away. What is happening to me? Ever since I've been in Bryson City, I've given in to tears. Don't my eyes remember that I don't cry easily? I wipe away a tear that has made its way down my cheek and hope Zack doesn't ask me if I'm crying. If he does, I may be tempted to be like Bubba and say, "Duh!"

He doesn't ask, but his face holds a rich kindness in between the lines of worry that stretch across his temples. "Not everyone understands Jonas."

I sniff again. "What is there not to understand? He's priceless."

Zack grins and, to show his satisfaction with my statement, gently touches my arm.

His action sends warm flutters throughout my body. Even my toes curl in my Reeboks. I could easily—oh, so easily—rest my head against his chest right now. As though in protest of my affectionate thoughts, I quickly cross my legs and sit up straight. Mom would be proud.

We listen to doctors being paged, which makes us aware of our institutional surroundings.

Zack stretches his legs, and then looking into his coffee cup says, "I was thinking that hospitals are difficult places."

No piece of cake, that's for sure.

"I'm sure it's hard to be back in one after your accident."

I am not expecting this from Zack. I don't know why; he's always been considerate, the model citizen for thinking of others and their feelings. "I'm okay."

"You're strong, Deena."

Strong? Strength never has been one of my outstanding characteristics. When I was nine years old and had to have a tooth pulled, I moaned for three days, and those were the three days *before* the tooth came out. After surgery, I complained of a sore mouth for at least a week, allowing Mom to make me special foods to sip through a straw. Andrea, if I remember correctly, called me a *little baby*.

Zack smiles. How many colors are dancing in those eyes?

Glancing at the painting of the fruit, I ask, "Did you know that my grandfather kept a lemon in his refrigerator at all times?" I bring this up just to make conversation, to use this as a way to distract me from falling completely in love with this wonderful man seated across from me.

"Yeah, I knew that."

"Really? He told you?"

"We had lots of conversations. Your grandfather and I went hiking together in the park. Jonas came with us a few times."

"So?"

"What?"

"What's the story behind the lemon in the fridge?"

Zack grins. "He didn't tell you?"

"My aunt was going to, but she hasn't yet." I'm sure she will, at some wonderfully inappropriate time, like when she told me about finding Giovanni.

"Well." Zack stuffs the empty paper containers of sugar into his coffee cup. "It signifies contentment."

When Zack stops there, I cry, "That's all? Regena Lorraine told me that. There's supposed to be some story that goes with it."

"There is." He stands, walks toward a metal trash can by a row of chairs, and tosses in the items from his hand. He reaches for my empty coffee cup, takes it, and throws it away. When he sits again, he rests his elbows on the arms of the chair and gives me a long look. "You really don't know the story?"

"No." I never got to go on a hike with my grandpa, either. Seems I missed out on a lot. I did get the letter left for me. I think about the meaningful words my grandfather printed on the paper, the page I have read many times and yet shared with no one, not even Regena Lorraine. Some words are more intimate when they are kept secret.

"So I'm going to tell you about your own grandfather?"

"That's right." I smile. "Hurry, before the suspense kills me."

His eyes show flecks of green, and something inside me wants to stare into them. I don't stare; I look at my hands, wait.

"When Ernest was little, the family didn't have much money. The kids wore hand-me-down clothes and ate oatmeal for every meal. The winters were bitter in Erie. Sometimes there wasn't any coal to light the fire in the house. All their shoes had holes they patched by shoving plastic into them. He really did walk a mile to school every day. His parents were poor and sick a lot." When Zack stops, I look up at him. "You want me to continue?" he asks.

"Why wouldn't I?"

"You really have never heard this? Any of it?"

I think of telling him that my mother is not one for hard-luck stories. She probably convinced Dad over the years that keeping a happy profile is the way to live, without focusing on a sad past. So that's most likely why my father never shared this story with me. "I want you to continue. I haven't ever heard this before."

Zack looks tenderly at me, a look identical to one I saw him give his brother in the hospital room. He moistens his lips and says, "One day a woman from their church brought them a basket of fruit. The basket had apples, oranges, grapes, and lemons. Ernest took one of the lemons, smelled it, and carried it to school in his pocket. It was durable and didn't spoil quickly like the other fruits. He kept that lemon for weeks. He asked God to heal his sick parents and make it so that he could be smart enough to finish high school and go on to college and med school. He wanted a chance to change the world. He wanted to give his parents a better life in their old age. He prayed to God a lot after that." Zack pauses, and I realize this is the first time I've heard him say so much at one time.

"What else?" I ask.

"He bought lemons by the crate. Everywhere he went he always bought lemons. Truman said he wanted a chicken in every pot. Ernest wanted a lemon in every refrigerator."

"That's amazing."

"Ernest said that for him a lemon signified three things: prosperity, contentment, and memories. Even after becoming a doctor, he never forgot those who had less than he did. He loved to gift people with fruit baskets. In fact, every Christmas, that's what each of the kids at The Center received from him. His method of operation." Zack smiles at me.

I wish I could hug my grandfather right now. I want to call my father and tell him that I've heard the story of his dad and that I love his dad so much. Mom needs to hear this story. Why didn't she like my grandfather? How could anyone not adore a man who loved lemons and gave them away?

We head back to Jonas's room, where a nurse has just taken his vitals. "He's fine," she whispers to us as Jonas falls asleep once more.

"Jonas is always fine," says Zack.

Just like his brother, I think.

———

As the owl cries in the treetops, a solo of evening peace, I open my journal and write about my concern for Jonas's health. After two paragraphs, I close the book. Something isn't complete, though, and I know that there is no way I can go to sleep unless I write a little more. Opening to a clean page, I write *Zack*. I'm not sure what else to put on the page. So I pretend I'm in sixth grade and draw little hearts around his name. Then bits and pieces of conversations we have had come to me like little appetizers on a silver platter. No one will ever read this, so just write from the heart, I tell myself. Hurry, write so you can go to sleep.

He is cute, but there is more to him than that. He has depth. He cares about those who are less fortunate with a passion and love that is so rewarding just to watch. Where do I fit in? I am unfortunate, that's for sure. Perhaps he just feels sorry for me. But that's not how he operates. He holds empathy, but he doesn't feel sorry for any of us. He accepts us where we are and seems to see the potential we hold to become better people. When he told me that I am a strong person, I felt I needed that reminder. I spent too much time thinking of how much Lucas ruined my future. But when Zack takes the time to tell me something I need to hear, I see that he looks beyond what individuals try to convey. He tells me to open up and not be afraid.

I am afraid.
I am terribly frightened to feel something besides pain.

thirty-two

At the end of a warm August, school starts again. The kids now spend only part of the afternoon at The Center, getting dropped off by the school bus a little after three. When they enter the building I am usually there. I find it easier to already be standing in the kitchen, equipped to start my class. I guess it gives me more control. Another thing I've learned is to ask the kids to tell me what they'd like to make. If they suggest it, chances are they'll be more eager to actually prepare the dish. Charlotte raises her hand today and says she'd like to make a pie.

"What kind?" I ask.

"Peach."

"That's my favorite!" I gush. "We can make that next week."

"I hate peaches," says Joy. She sticks her tongue out for

emphasis. It's blue from the flavored lollipop she ate on the bus ride over.

"Joy," I breathe, "you have a lovely name. It's one of the fruits of the Spirit."

"Duh," says Bubba. "We see the sign every day."

I look at Joy, her round, soft face so often contorted by morbidity. "Be joyful, Joy." Then I smile. My motivating side inwardly cheers.

I think I see Darren lift his head and give a grin, but I could be wrong.

Thanks to Zack's suggestion, I have told the children that they need to take turns cleaning up the kitchen after class. A few moaned that they didn't want their fingers to get "pruney" from the dishwater. Bubba said he was allergic to doing dishes. I stood with my shoulders back and said, "Doing dishes makes you more handsome and more beautiful." I don't know why I chose to say this; it just came out.

Bobby ran his fingers down his wide torso. "I'm already so handsome," he announced to the class. "But if I do the dishes, I'll be a regular ladies' man."

While Charlotte and Lisa are in the kitchen washing out cake pans, Miriam invites me into her office. She has a carafe of coffee and some half-and-half on her desk and asks if I'd like a cup of coffee. Then she closes the door to the room.

Nervously, I pour a little of the beverage into a mug, add three drops of half-and-half, and then sit on a leather chair next to her desk.

She sits on her swivel chair and tells me she can't talk long because of a board meeting in twenty minutes.

I hope this is not about the receipts for my class's ingredients. She probably thinks I spend too much on them and is going to remind me that The Center is a nonprofit organization. I sip the coffee, wish it were Starbucks, and wait.

Her blue eyes flash. Clasping her hands together, she says, "The kids want you to go camping with them."

What?

"The other day we were talking about chaperones for the camping trip in October, and they said they want you."

"Camping?" My voice doesn't sound like it belongs to me. Is this what she brought me in here for?

She opens a drawer and stuffs a few loose papers into it. "First weekend in October. Smoky Mountain National Park."

The kids said they wanted me? I clear my throat. "How long do they camp?"

"Two nights, Friday and Saturday. We have permission slips for guardians to sign. We document the medications the kids with prescriptions need, bring a first-aid kit, cell phones, and that takes care of it."

She says a few others things, but I don't hear them because my mind is so heavily wrapped around this request. The kids want *me* to go camping. "Who else is coming?"

"Rhonda. Have you met her? She's Bubba's caseworker."

Oh yes, I've seen her around The Center many times, and we conversed a little at the bake sale. She's shorter than I am, blond hair, plenty of cleavage, no noticeable scars. She talks to Zack all the time. Bubba clearly loves her. I'm not sure if Zack does or not.

Miriam opens a binder, takes a page from it, and closes it. "Oh, and Robert. He went last year and enjoyed it."

I can't fathom that Robert enjoys camping with the kids. He's married and has two kids of his own. Why would he want to spend time away from his family with these wayward children?

When Miriam answers her ringing desk phone, I gaze out her office window at a cluster of lopsided pinecones and ponder the situation. The kids want to go camping in the Smoky Mountains National Park. They've asked Miriam if I will join them. I don't have to, do I? Grandpa Ernest didn't put in his will that I have to go on the camping event, did he? I went camping once with Sally's parents and brother. I remember waking up to wetness. It had rained, the ground was mushy, and my sleeping bag was soggy.

Miriam ends the phone conversation and continues to riffle through her desk, looking for something. I look at her green tennis shoes and decide she wears them for comfort, and in case she has to run fast away from some angry parent like Darren's mother.

I hear Zack telling the kids good-bye outside of the office as the parents and guardians pick up each child. I overhear Darren saying, "I hope I don't have to see my mom this weekend," to which Zack replies, "Don't worry. She's not supposed to come to your grandma's unless she calls me first." Then I hear Rhonda's soprano voice, talking to Zack, giggling. I hear their footsteps as they walk down the hall away from Miriam's office.

When all is quiet, Miriam says, "Oh, Zack usually comes, too. We try to have two men and two women. More, if we can get them."

Zack goes camping with the kids. Of course. No surprise there.

"Think about it," Miriam says as she crams a folder into her briefcase. "Oh." She notices the pitcher of half-and-half on the edge of her desk. "Would you take this cream back to the fridge for me?" She hands me the pitcher.

"I'll take the coffeepot, too," I say. "And wash it out."

"That would be nice. Thank you." Quickly, she stands and lifts her briefcase. "I hope this board meeting is a good one. I hope all the financing comes through for The Center."

I tell her that I hope that is the case, too.

As she leaves, she says, "Thanks, Deena. And please do consider the camping trip." Then she's gone, her tennis shoes making squishy sounds along the narrow hallway.

I am thinking about tents and saturated sleeping bags as I enter the kitchen with the pitcher and coffeepot in my hands. When I swing open the door with my shoulder, I see Zack. He's standing in the arms of Rhonda. Her arms are snuggly placed around his neck. Their faces are inches from each other.

"Excuse me," is all I can say. Balancing the coffeepot and pitcher in one hand, I open the fridge with the other.

The two pull away from each other and awkwardly look at me in silence. I shove the pitcher and the coffeepot onto a shelf in the fridge and exit as quickly as I entered.

As fast as I can, I walk to the bathroom so that I can be alone. *No, no, no,* my mind says over and over. I stand in front of the mirror and see my sad eyes, eyes that had looked so hopeful after the day I spent in the hospital with Zack. Of course he cares about someone else, I almost say aloud. Of course.

All those smiles at me, I took them the wrong way. All those conversations about me opening up my heart and sharing myself with the kids and with him. Those were just bullet points to pep talks he probably gives everyone. He only cares about the kids . . . and Rhonda.

I am faced with the reality that I am not special to anyone.

Not Lucas.

Not Zack.

thirty-three

I bake a cinnamon breakfast cake just because I know this buttery delicacy will help brush away my fears. At least while I'm eating it. I can't guarantee that it will erase all my insecurities. It's not that big of a cake. I use the nine-inch pan from my good-bye party at the restaurant, and as I grease the inside, my mind wanders to the restaurant. I wonder what dishes are being prepared for tonight's specialty. What I wouldn't give for a plate of braised duck in orange sauce with a side of pasta drenched in tomato and roasted garlic.

I turn Vivaldi on high. If I were in my apartment in Atlanta, surrounding tenants would be banging on the walls, begging me to turn down the volume. Here, in the mountains, on my own little steep winding road, one advantage is that I will bother no one with my music. Except perhaps the owl.

While the coffee cake fills the cabin with the aroma of cinnamon and sugar, I brew some French roast coffee. Yolanda used to say that I knew how to make the apartment *muy magnifico* with my cooking, music, and coffee. I pick up my journal, sit on the lone bar stool by the counter, and write.

Grandpa Ernest's cabin. August 30th. 6:10 P.M.

It's okay, really. I let my heart out of its cage for a short time against my better judgment. I got stung, but hey, I'm still living. I'm making coffee cake and coffee, and the kids want me to go on a camping trip. So I've lost whatever it was I thought I had with Zack. So I'm not where I hoped I was in his sky. But Darren smiled at me today when I asked if he'd put the orange-raspberry glaze on the cake we made in class. Then he took the glaze and evenly dribbled it over the top of the cake, just like I'd demonstrated. Bubba told me I am a good teacher and Joy said I look like Grandpa, not old or anything, but kind. Charlotte (she is like a gorgeous doll, but very scared, I wish she'd talk more) suggested we make a peach pie—my favorite! Bobby told the class that, with all the food they have learned to make, we should open a restaurant, and we could become more popular than the Fryemont Inn.

I see prayers being answered.

It's all okay. Really. Zack can be a friend. If he's happy with Rhonda, then I just have to be happy for him. Who knows, maybe one day someone will come along for me. I probably still need time to heal, anyway. My legs and arms don't hurt as much anymore, so my Extra Strength Tylenol bottle is still half full.

When I eat the coffee cake, I enjoy each comforting morsel. I can taste the butter, the cream, the vanilla, and the brown sugar—all are parts of an orchestra in my mouth.

240

Then I decide to make some peanut soup because I have a feeling I'll be able to pick out all the flavors tonight.

After all that food, I'll need to walk a few laps around the cabin.

thirty-four

Rhonda spends time at The Center every afternoon. Although she's assigned to Bubba, I note that Bubba is not her main concern.

Believe me, I am not in the business of stealing anyone from anybody. I have had that happen to me and don't wish that pain on anyone. Besides, I'm allergic to men who break hearts, and I'm getting the feeling that that sums up every man.

I look at Jonas. He is checking the drain under my kitchen sink. I recall the time he retrieved the engagement ring for me. "Jonas? Have you ever broken anyone's heart?"

He slithers his head from the drain and sits up to look at me. I wonder what he'll say. He might ask for an explanation of what I mean. He adjusts his crimson bandana. "Oh, I carry superglue."

I doubt he heard me correctly and get ready to repeat the

question. Before I can, he says, "Superglue will fix anything. Superglue is durable." His words sound like a commercial.

My smile breaks into a laugh. Jonas joins me. We laugh at what he just said, and then we laugh from hearing ourselves laugh.

I am relieved that he is feeling better. Everyone was concerned about his head injury from the fall off the church roof. Zack went to see him every day while he was in the hospital. They discharged Jonas with the warning to stay away from roofs. Zack told him to stick to pipes and drains, things that require only cupcake Band-Aids, not MRIs. Jonas said he'd miss the hospital, especially the kind nurses and the strawberry gelatin with whipped cream served at lunch.

Jonas eyes my camping gear, spread all over the living room floor. Although the trip is not for three days, I am slowly gathering the items I'll need. That sure beats last minute running around. Jonas stands in front of the assortment of piles and asks, "Do you have a sleeping bag?"

"I do." I bought it three years ago after I realized I needed something to replace the pink threadbare one of my childhood—Snow White and the Seven Dwarfs. The last time I used it I was at my apartment, preparing to leave Atlanta and venture to this unknown land. I breathe in and wonder what Yolanda is up to today. I could go for a succulent fried banana.

Jonas observes a large brown bag filled with groceries. "Marshmallows?"

"I went shopping for the trip and got eight bags. I hope those are enough."

"Eight bags should be good." He tugs at his bandana. The Sharpie he sometimes keeps secured in the folds of the material falls onto the floor. "Eight bags is too much!" he cries as he bends down to retrieve his pen.

I laugh. "Well, at least we won't run out."

He continues to toss out the questions. "Flashlight? Pillow? Earplugs?"

"Do you want to join us, Jonas?"

He grins as he sticks his hands into the pockets of his jeans. "No, no. Need a soft bed to sleep on. Doctor's orders. Rest and relaxation."

"Rest and relaxation, huh?"

"Yes." He eyes me. "Is that funny?"

"No, I am sure it's what you need." I hope to get some upon returning from this camping trip. I doubt I'll be able to get comfortable enough in a tent with others to get anything remotely close to sleep. Perhaps earplugs would be helpful.

" 'Take it e*eee*asy,' " Jonas starts to sing. " 'Don't let the sound of your own wheels drive you crazy.' " When he finishes he breaks out with, " 'You better let somebody love you before it's too late.' "

Only a few notes are off-key. He wants me to join him, but I shake my head. I don't even sing in church. But I can appreciate how others have voices that stay on pitch.

Jonas belts out a few more lines, and I clap for him. He bows, bumps into the chair, and shakes his head. "I drop my pen. I trip. I am one clumsy dude."

And charming and endearing.

"Deirdre, what do you think of my brother?"

"Everyone thinks Zack is great," I say, an automatic reflex.

" 'You better let somebody love you.' "

I feel discomfort settling around me. I know where this is headed.

Jonas wastes no time in expressing his feelings. "You and my brother need to get married."

"Whoa, Jonas! I don't think we are ready for that." Zack hugged Rhonda in the kitchen. I don't tell this to Jonas though. I don't want to burst his bubble. He loves his brother, and he sees something good in me.

"Well, you can go out on a date first, I guess." Then he sings another line from one of his favorite Eagles songs. "'We may lose and we may win.'"

I am not ready to lose again. With certainty in my voice, I say, "If he asks."

"You can ask."

No, no, Jonas. I don't chase guys. I protect my heart.

"You can invite him here for some soup."

"Dinner here?" I think the fall off the church roof has done something to Jonas's brain.

He notes my surprised reaction and says, "Or just the oil soup."

"I don't know . . ."

"He likes cake. Make cake for dessert."

"What kind?"

"The soft one."

Soft one? He must mean the velvet butter. "Velvet?"

"Make sure the soup is hot. You can taste the flavors. Taste all the flavors." He gives me a wink. "Even the oil you thought the soup doesn't have."

I've never been one to try to find the way to a man's heart by satisfying his stomach. Even though I am a chef, it seems too juvenile for me.

"And make sure you have music," says Jonas.

"The Eagles?"

Jonas grins. "You got the picture."

I know I shouldn't but I say, "Jonas, I think your brother is interested in someone else."

His reply is quick. "Rhonda? No, no." He waves his hands in front of him as if to remove any such notion. "They went out to talk things over. Zack is like that. Zack cares about everyone."

I know. Everybody knows that.

" 'Desperado,' " sings Jonas as he heads outside to check some pipes underneath the cabin, " 'why don't you come to your senses? You've been out ridin' fences for so long now.' "

A few minutes pass, and then he swings open the front door. "Deirdre?"

"Yes?"

"Your name is Deena."

I smile. "That's right."

"My brother told me."

He leaves and then opens the door again to add, "I guess I'm just not too smart."

"Oh, not true," I want to say, but he has already bounded out the door once more. Yes, you are smart, Jonas. You are smarter than over half of the people I know and your perspective on life is healthier than 99.9 percent of the population.

thirty-five

I'm late to work. Blame it on my aunt, who called to tell me about "seventy-seven things that make a woman beautiful"—some tips written by three massage therapists and an owner of a used car lot. I didn't get the connection between the four compilers of the list, or even how they came up with the tips, but nevertheless I listened as Regena Lorraine read every single one over the phone. When she got to number sixty-three, I looked at the clock and, cradling my cell phone on my shoulder, managed to get my shoes tied.

When I enter The Center's kitchen, I hear whispering. The squeak of chairs against the floor is loud. Then there is a rush to sit down, followed by an eerie silence. If the sink were still a dripping one, it would be making the only sound. Jonas repaired the leaky faucet sometime in July, long before I knew he was the church plumber and way before I knew he was Zack's older brother.

The children pass looks to each other. Charlotte tries to hide a smile.

I ignore whatever it is that has gone on before my arrival and begin to take ingredients from my brown bag. "Today we are making chicken," I say. The chicken breast fillets are at the bottom of my bag in a round plastic bowl.

No one says a word. Bubba sits on the edge of his chair. Bobby looks like he will explode with excitement.

The silence is killing me. "Do you remember what kind of chicken we decided on?"

Do they hear me? I try to encourage a response by adding, "We talked about it yesterday, and what did we say we would make today?"

They are all attentive; my gut tells me something is wrong. Was there a fight? Did Darren's mom come barging into the kitchen demanding to see her boy? I search their faces. Darren even lifts his head from his notebook so that I can peer into his dark eyes. Could they be upset that I'm late? "I'm sorry," I tell the group. "I know I was late to class. I know we stress how important it is to be on time."

That must not be it; they continue to eye each other, mouths shut tightly.

I suppose I should just continue on, and be grateful that they are so quiet. I pull Ziploc bags of basil and oregano and a pint container of sour cream from the bag. I produce the recipe for this chicken dish and, holding the card, ask for a volunteer to come forward to read the ingredients and directions to the class.

There is noise at the kitchen door. Shuffling of feet. Then the door springs open and the kids all boom, "Surprise!"

In walk Miriam and Zack. Miriam holds an aluminum

plate, and as she comes closer, I see that it contains a pie. Lit candles are inserted in the top crust. She starts to sing and the group joins her. "Happy Birthday to you . . ."

Darren even sings; Regena Lorraine is right—his voice is good. It rings out over the other off-key voices.

How did they know?

"It's peach pie, Miss Livingston!" shouts Lisa as Miriam presents the pie to me to blow out the candles.

"Your favorite," says Bubba.

"Looks delicious." Bobby stands next to me, eyeing the pie. His tummy is exposed; he pats it. "Oh, don't worry. We didn't make it. We could never make anything good without you helping us, Miss Livingston."

I have never seen such a large peach pie. I wonder who baked it. Chef B would be delighted.

"Make a wish, a good one," says Lisa.

Zack smiles; I blow out the candles.

The kids cheer, and then we all have a slice of peach pie. I can tell that everyone is on his or her best behavior, and this makes me feel honored. Bobby even uses a napkin to wipe his hands.

Zack tells me that Jonas suggested we get the pie from Southern Treats. "Jonas picked it up this morning on his way to a job in Dillsboro."

I am about to ask how Jonas knew that it was my birthday. We never discussed birthdays, just age. But before I can form the question, Rainy hands me a glass of iced tea with a slice of lemon on the rim of the glass.

When I finish my piece of pie, Joy says, "Did you like it? I hate peach pie."

"Well," I quickly say, as Miriam arches her back, ready to

reprimand the girl, "when it's your birthday, we will be sure not to have peach pie."

Miriam relaxes, pleased with my reply.

"That," says Zack, as he places his empty paper plate in the trash, "was excellent."

This time I smile. He likes my kind of pie; surely this is all the indication we need to know we're meant to be.

"How old are you?" Lisa looks into my face, no trace of embarrassment about asking a woman her age.

"Is today really your birthday?" Flakes of pie crust cover Dougy's lips.

"Yes, today is my birthday. I'm twenty-eight."

"Zack is thirty-two," says Dougy. His smile leaves his face as he notes Miriam's strict glare. Correcting himself, he says, "I mean Mr. Anderson is thirty-two."

This is the first time I've heard any child call Zack by his last name.

From the edge of the room, Charlotte moves toward me, her hands behind her back. When she reaches me, she displays a colorfully wrapped gift. Her smile is dazzling, and she says with clear intonation, "This is from all of us."

The children are eager for me to open the present. I tear off the paper and hold a box made of cherrywood, with a little latch. Inside the box are small pads of paper, a pen, and a receipt book. I take each item and look it over, smiling the whole time.

"You have to have business things," says Rainy as she pushes her sunglasses higher on her head. "If you're going to have a cake business and make your cakes, you need supplies."

"Ya gotta be professional," Bubba adds.

"And polite!" Bobby digs into his second slice of pie.

"Thank you." My throat fills. I would say more, but I can't risk it.

Funny, I must be the crying type, after all.

———

Aunt Regena Lorraine takes me to dinner at the Fryemont Inn. Her main reason for calling earlier today was to say she wanted to treat me to a birthday dinner. After I said I'd love that, she proceeded to read the list of seventy-seven things that make a woman beautiful. One of them was growing older with flair and grace, so I guess the list was sort of appropriate for this day.

I wear a black skirt and gray sweater—my two pieces of clothing that actually have designer names—and I even put on my gold bracelet and earrings. My aunt wears an orange dress with deep front pockets and shoes that match. I don't think I've ever seen orange shoes before. This must be part of her way to grow old with grace and flair.

We drive to the restaurant in her truck, and for this event Giovanni is not with us. "I'll bring him a doggie bag," Regena Lorriane tells me when I ask where her canine is this evening. "He'll like that," she says as she steers the bouncy truck down the road.

People talk about the Fryemont even in Atlanta. Some have spent the night in the inn, and others have only eaten in the dining room. When we arrive and my aunt parks, I realize that my excitement at the opportunity to be here is rising like yeasty dough.

Cindy, Charlotte's sister, is working, and we ask the hostess if we can be seated at one of her tables.

"My sister likes you so much. She talks about you all the

time," Cindy tells me. And I recall the bake sale when Charlotte urged her sister to bid on my tiered cake. Cindy looks a little like her younger sister with her long hair but doesn't have that American Girl doll quality. Maybe one doll per family is all the quota allows.

We are seated at a small table to the right of the large stone fireplace. A fire has been lit, and its light shines across the glossy hardwood floors. Sally would love this place.

"Order whatever you want," Regena Lorraine says as we open menus.

I order rainbow trout, and, from the five ways it can be prepared, choose the crunchy almond topping. My aunt decides on the baked Virginia ham. She thinks Giovanni will like the leftovers. This is the first time I've been with someone who orders according to what her pet will like.

Before our food comes, as we sip from glasses of iced tea, I ask her, "Did you tell them it's my birthday?"

"Here? Oh, I should. They'll bring some dessert and sing to you. Good idea, Shug."

"No." I don't want anyone singing to me here. "I meant at The Center."

"Tell them what?"

"That it's my birthday."

"Oh yes, I did." She places her glass on the table and fingers her own eyeglasses. "They did ask me at the bake sale. Bubba asked."

I smile, still warmed by the thoughtfulness of the children's gift to me. I placed the little box on top of the desk in my bedroom right when I returned home from teaching this afternoon. My own cake-order box. Chef B will have to hear about this.

"How has your day been?" asks my aunt, as I admire the crackling fire and note the restaurant's decor. The plum-and-white linens add a warm touch. I wonder if I could create this shade of plum to use for icing. A lemon cake with bold swirls of plum would make a great centerpiece for some festive occasion.

Gradually, I turn my attention to my aunt. "My day's been good," I say. This morning Jeannie called to wish me a happy birthday. Then Mom and Dad took turns talking to me. Mom wanted to make sure that UPS had done its job and delivered her gift to me.

"A jar of pickled pig's feet?" I said to Mom. "It arrived."

Before my aunt came to pick me up for dinner, Sally called. She told me that she and Jeannie were coming to visit me in two weeks.

As the logs glow in the fireplace beside our table, I feel cozy and relaxed. "It's nice to be here," I tell my aunt, and she admits that this is one of her favorite places.

I feel a tug at my heart and am about to recall my birthday last year and what Lucas gave me. The memory is there, waiting; I push it aside. Instead I say, "Guess what. I got another cake order for Friday, so I'll need to squeeze making it in before the camping trip."

"Are you excited?"

"I love getting orders."

"About camping?"

I wrinkle my nose.

"Shug." She laughs. "You are just like me. I'm not a camper, but Ernest was. He saw the beauty in every experience."

I imagine he did. Anyone who believes that a lemon holds deep significance and that the right disposition is what it's all about must have been able to handle everything. And I suppose his ability to enjoy life came from knowing whose hand held his.

After we finish our salads, Cindy brings us our entrees. My aunt immediately asks her for a small doggie bag. "This way I will put Giovanni's portion aside and won't be tempted to eat it."

Cindy just nods, and I smile.

"Shug," Regena Lorraine says as she cuts her slice of ham in half and secures one half in the Styrofoam box for her dog, "I am so glad it's your birthday."

The wait staff sings to me at dessert. Accompanied by Cindy, they bring a piece of chocolate cake with a single yellow lit candle. Cindy places it in front of me.

"You told them," I say to my aunt, a tone of scolding to my voice.

"No, I didn't."

"Charlotte told me," whispers Cindy. "She told me all about today."

"Make a wish," my aunt says.

The candle flickers as though it is winking at me.

I make the same wish I did earlier today at The Center. Perhaps wishing it two times in one day will better the chances of it coming true.

———

I sit in my bed with two pillows behind me and flip open my journal. I'm almost at the end of the book; there are only six crisp pages left. I can't believe it. As I read a few of the earlier entries, I wonder who would have ever thought I'd end up wanting to write in this book so often?

Smiling to myself, I list all of the children's names on a clean page, one line per child. Then I come up with a few descriptive words about each kid. Interesting that although the kids can be hellions, I have found something positive to put down for every one of them. This must be my grandfather's influence. For Charlotte I write *angelic*. Bubba has *friendly* written by his name. I even come up with something positive for Darren. By Darren's name, I write *never too noisy*.

thirty-six

We take my Jeep, Zack's silver Ford truck, and Robert's emerald Dodge minivan. Rhonda, Charlotte, and Lisa ride with me. The food and cooking gear, along with the large plastic first-aid kit, have been loaded into the back of the Jeep. The sleeping bags and tents are in the bed of Zack's truck.

We asked the church for donations of sleeping bags and tents. There were several announcements about the need in the Sunday bulletin. Apparently last year people were also asked to either lend or donate. The kids were told to bring their own pillows and flashlights. Darren's grandmother bought him a new mega-flashlight. He turned it on while we were packing up the vehicles at The Center and blinded us all.

Bubba wanted to bring his camping chair, a blue vinyl fold-up one. Zack asked him what he was going to do when others wanted a chair. "Huh?" Bubba's mouth stayed open.

"How many kids are going on this trip, Bubba?" the social worker asked.

"I dunno. Seven, eight. Is this a trick question?"

Zack explained, "If there are eight kids and only one chair, what do you think is going to happen?"

"Aw, Zack . . . I mean Mr. Anderson." He smiled.

"Do you want to share your camping chair this weekend?"

"You mean let other kids sit in it? Like Dougy?"

"Yes."

Bubba's smile faded and the chair was left behind in the church. Shortly after that, we were ready to leave.

I've told myself that this trip will be about the kids, their having fun. I don't want to let whatever it is that Zack and Rhonda have or don't have going on take away from the children. *Concentrate, concentrate,* my positive self repeats as I drive, following Zack's truck that leads our caravan to the Smoky Mountains.

We are to camp at Smokemont, which has an elevation of 2,198 feet and is near the Cherokee reservation. Miriam reserved two side-by-side campsites where we'll pitch our four tents.

I am wearing a short-sleeved shirt the color of berries. All summer I've covered my arms, and now on this camping trip, I've decided it is time to expose my scars and just deal with whatever comments come my way. The afternoon air still holds warmth, so I don't feel chilly.

I drive cautiously, but soon realize that I'm more relaxed about being in a vehicle on these mountain roads than I've ever been. Perhaps having the excited girls in the back seat helps. Lisa has a packet of Skittles she shares with Charlotte. Rhonda says little but does find us a radio station with jazz music.

"Do you like jazz?" I ask her as we creep farther up the mountain through the park.

"I love it." She leans back in the passenger seat. Dreamily, she adds, "So does Zack."

I wonder if anyone has packed Tums. We curve around a scenic overlook; a few cars are parked, and tourists are admiring the hues of autumn colors under a shiny blue sky. The day is too nice to let jealousy get the best of you, I tell myself.

When we reach the campsite, the kids from Zack and Robert's vehicles are darting across the fallen leaves and laughing loudly. Where do they get all their energy?

"I'm going to jump in the Bradley River," yells Dougy.

I'd heard that the river runs through the camping area. Hopefully, it will be too cool for anyone to be tempted by its waters. I enjoy swimming but have never had to rescue anyone. I look at Zack, who is starting to set up a tent. He's the one in good shape. If Dougy makes a dive into the river, I'll let Zack help him out.

The boys want to assist Zack with the tents. He lets them help until Dougy uses a rope and pair of pliers to lasso Bubba. Then all of us feel it works better if we have two people setting up each tent, and the selected two are Zack and Robert. Rainy and Charlotte watch closely, and when the boys start to toss a Frisbee and become too occupied to protest, the girls help the men hammer the pins through the rings to keep the tents secure. Zack says he is impressed by Rainy's skill with a hammer.

I call the boys over to help the rest of us unload our food supplies. The food is piled in old cardboard boxes I used to move to Bryson City. Bubba ceremoniously flexes arm muscles he does not have, grins when I tell him I think he has actually put on some weight, and helps me carry the boxes needed for tonight to the picnic tables by the two campsites.

One box contains jars of condiments, cans of baked beans, potato chips, and fruit juice boxes. Hamburger and hot dog buns, chocolate bars, graham crackers, and marshmallows fill another. The third holds paper plates, cups, napkins, and plastic utensils. My Coleman cooler is stocked with ground beef, hot dogs, cheese, sausages, and two cartons of eggs. Some of this is breakfast food. Darren takes two pans of brownies out of the trunk of my Jeep as Joy places a bag of charcoal by the fire pit. Rhonda opens another cooler, one I borrowed from Miriam. From it, she takes out a bottle of Aquafina and unscrews the cap. She pauses to take a few sips and then takes a jug of drinking water from the back of Zack's truck. She sets it on one of the picnic tables.

"Maybe," she says, her eyes glancing across both of the tables, "we should let one of these tables be for storing food and the other the one we eat at."

"Storing food on a table!" yells Bubba, his little body lifting a box. "If you keep food outside, the bears will be sure to find us."

"Bears!" Joy looks like she just saw one. "I hate bears."

"You're right, Bubba." Zack threads the end of a rope through a grommet. "After we eat, we'll have to put all the leftovers back inside the cars."

Rhonda frowns. "I wasn't suggesting we leave food out all night," she snaps.

Zack keeps his attention on the rope.

Robert glances over at me.

Then Joy says, "Will y'all please pray that no bears attack us tonight?"

"Or snakes," says Lisa.

"I'll pray," Rainy tells her. "I'm good at praying."

———

Joy and Bubba help Robert with the burgers and hot dogs. Rainy and Charlotte stir the baked beans cooking on a grate by the fire as I supervise. Rhonda slices tomatoes and onions, because after Charlotte's episode with the kitchen knife, everyone's afraid of cutting themselves. They won't admit it to any of us, but we know. Rhonda opens two store-bought containers of coleslaw and places them on the table. Zack sets the table with the napkins, plates, and forks. Rhonda edges close to whisper a few things to Zack. I try to control my emotions. If I named them, they would be jealousy, jealousy, jealousy. You have to give that up, I tell myself as I watch Bobby, Lisa, and Darren place juice boxes at each place setting. You are not in the business of jealousy. You must protect your heart from everything. Haven't you learned that yet?

At last, Robert announces that the grilled food is done, and with a holler, Bobby rushes to his place at the table, lifting his fork for emphasis. "Bring it on!" he shouts. "I'm starving."

After Robert offers the blessing, we eat in silence, except for the children's noisy manners. I am tempted to smack my lips like Bubba, but I know that as an adult, I have to set a good example. Zack sits beside me, although there is a vacancy by Rhonda. Charlotte fills it after she returns from the restroom.

"This is good food," Bubba says, as bits of bread fly from his lips. "But do you know what would make it better?"

I think we are all expecting to hear some reference to McDonald's. I know I am.

"What, Bubba?" asks Zack.

"Crispy potatoes like we made in class. Ms. Livingston, those were sweet!"

I smile; a tiny quiver of happiness runs into my veins.

"I like cooking," says Rainy. "Of course, I am good at it." She smiles at Dougy, who groans and crams half a hotdog into his mouth.

———

After dinner and a few guesses at charades, we sit around a glowing bed of red coals and roast marshmallows for s'mores. Squares of Hershey's chocolate and graham crackers line a flat, wide stone. The children build their own creations.

Bubba licks the last of his gooey chocolate-marshmallow-graham-cracker treat and cries, "Where's Charlotte?"

The adults do a head count, and not seeing the girl, Zack starts to get up.

I quickly stand. "I'll go look," I say with a firmness I'm not used to. I suppose my trying-to-motivate self is springing forward in this campsite. I hear Dr. Seuss's words in my memory: *Today is your day!*

"Hope a grizzly didn't get her," whispers Bobby.

"Hope a hawk didn't carry her into the river," Dougy teases.

"She's probably in her tent," Lisa says.

Joy has jumped up to scout out the tents. She unzips the door to one, pokes her head and flashlight inside, and calls, "Not in here."

"Remember not to go in the boys' tents," yells Bobby. "Remember them rules."

Earlier, before dinner, Zack laid down the ground rules: "Boys stay in their tents, and no going in the girls'."

Lisa twirled a strand of hair. Batting her long eyelashes and turning her head to look toward Dougy, she asked, "Is it okay for girls to go in boys' tents?"

Zack stood facing the group. "What do you think?"

She mumbled, "I don't know."

Zack set her straight. "There will be no going in the boys' tents if you are a girl. Is that understood?"

"What if my asthma starts acting all crazy and I need help?" Bobby asked.

"Then we'll help you. Did you bring your inhaler?"

Bobby nodded at Zack. "I'm hungry," he announced, his voice echoing across the wooded site. "Let's get this party started!"

After getting all the rules laid out, we ate dinner.

Obviously, Charlotte is not in any of the tents now.

I start out on my search. Immediately, I feel the coolness of the air. Earlier, I took my jacket off because by the fire, it was warm. I wish I'd thought to put it on before heading out to who knows where.

I'm not sure where to look for Charlotte. Last I noticed her, she was seated by Bubba, and then she went to the restroom. With my flashlight lighting the way, I walk along a path lined with crisp autumn leaves. Suddenly, the darkness scares me; the boldness I mustered just a while ago seems lost. How will I find her in this place void of bright lights? I enter the damp, sour-smelling washroom, call her name, open each stall door, watch a spider scurry across a roll of toilet paper, call her name again, and panic.

Dear God, I hope a bear hasn't chewed her in two. How

will I ever tell Cindy? I envision her standing with a pen and pad at the Fryemont, all ready for an evening of waiting on tables, and instead learning that her sister has disappeared.

I leave the restroom and stand under a florescent light, wondering which way to go. The tall pines loom thick around me, their shadows dancing against the crooked paths strewn with pine needles and cones. I consider calling out her name; perhaps then Charlotte will come out from wherever she's hiding. Or it could have the opposite effect. Realizing I've come to find her, she could hear my voice and run farther away. I know one thing: I am not about to fail at this. Determined to find her, I breathe, "God, please help me."

A breeze picks up, rattling oak leaves across the path. I squint and wonder if my eyes are getting worse. Regena Lorraine once said that she could get me a discount on her leopard-spotted glasses. I wonder how long the kids would laugh if I appeared one day in those. But what I wouldn't give to be able to have some help in finding Charlotte now, and if it meant wearing goofy glasses, I'd gladly put them on. Sighing, I look around and hope the rumors of bears really are rumors. Coldness covers me. I want to go back to the warmth of the campfire and to Zack's smile. But I am so worried for Charlotte.

It is then that I hear a rustling sound coming from the left side of the restrooms. I listen; if I were a dog, my ears would be pointed and alert. Guided by the light from my flashlight, I carefully make my way toward the noise.

Seated at a picnic table behind the restrooms is Charlotte. Of course she wouldn't go far. Why did I worry? She's more timid than I am.

Approaching her, I whisper, "Charlotte."

Her head is on top of the wooden table, her arms flung over her hair.

I sit beside her on the damp bench, turn off my flashlight. "What's wrong?"

She moves a little but says nothing.

Okay, I think. We don't have to talk. At least I have found her and she isn't in the clutches of a bear or hawk. Cindy will be able to carry on with being a waitress tonight.

"They laughed at me." Charlotte's voice is muffled, yet it doesn't sound like she's been crying. "When I did the charade, they thought I was stupid."

"They laugh at everyone." They laughed at me as I tried to act out Little Bo Peep. Bobby was literally rolling on the ground, pine needles sticking to his jeans and jacket. I played the game. I could have refused like Joy did. She said she was too tired and then threw in her feelings about the game. When she used the word *hate*, Zack asked her to come up with a different word.

"I don't know any other word," she pouted.

"Try *dislike* or *don't care for.*"

She frowned and said, "The game stinks."

He wouldn't let her get away with that, even though Bubba and Dougy were insisting we get the game started.

She gave in. "I don't care for charades."

Zack told her that was an improvement, and then we began the game.

"You played, at least," I tell Charlotte now. "That's what counts." *It isn't whether you win or lose, but if you play.* The words come to me with a bold profundity, and I wonder if they're stitched on Regena Lorraine's tote bag.

Shivering, I rub my hands over my arms and shake my

legs to get the blood circulating. I'm tempted to get up and head back to my jacket and make Charlotte come with me. *Take it easy.* The words to one of Jonas's favorite songs ring in my mind.

I let my body relax just when Charlotte pleads, "You will never leave me, will you, Miss Livingston?"

What does she mean? Leave her alone at this picnic table? Leave The Center? Leave town?

"You're nice." She reaches out and strokes my arm, her fingers evenly gliding over my scars. "I think you're an angel."

"Well, most people don't feel that way," I say. *Like Darren.*

"You never know about people. People are good at pretending."

"Pretending what?"

She stops touching my arm and flips her legs around so that she has her back to the table. "Showing how they really feel. You know, what's inside. The part only God sees."

I feel a warmth slither over me like a big quilt tucking me in at every side. The air is not so cold anymore.

"Have you noticed the stars?" I ask, because I don't know what else to say.

We lift our heads to see the wide sky of flickering lights. The moon has risen—round but not yet full, and tinted with a yellow glossy glow—just over the treetops.

"I like to think that all those stars are my prayers," whispers Charlotte. "God thinks they are so pretty he chooses to string them in the sky."

I consider her words. "That's beautiful, Charlotte."

"You think so?"

"Yes, I do."

"Well, don't tell Rainy or anyone that I said that."

"Why not?"

"They'll laugh at me some more."

I take her hand between my fingers and gently squeeze it. "You are beautiful," I say.

Quickly, she says, "No, I'm not."

"Oh yes, you are. Don't tell anyone, but when I first came to The Center, I thought you were the most gorgeous. And I mean on the outside *and* the inside."

"You did?"

"Yeah. I even wrote about you in my journal."

She takes a long look at me, and even in the darkness I see her eyes dance. "I have a journal, too."

"That's great."

"It's the only place I can be myself."

I know all about that, I think as I picture my own journal with the apple pie cover. Me, the one who hated my writing class; me, becoming close friends with a journal and a pen!

"You can talk to me," I say. "I'm good at keeping secrets."

Her eyes peer into mine as though she wants to believe me. And I want her to.

We sit for a few silent moments, and then I convince Charlotte that together we can go back to the group and face whatever awaits. My confidence surprises Charlotte and makes me jumpy in my own skin.

Back at the campsite, Charlotte sits close to me by the fire. Earlier, Bubba and Bobby found sturdy logs and stones to place around the fire as chairs.

Zack smiles at us. Even when I look away from him at the others, I can sense his gaze in my direction.

"Charlotte is back," Dougy says. "Did you miss us?" He

hands her a thin stick, which she reluctantly takes. "We're getting ready to cook up more marshmallows."

"We were waiting for you," says Joy. "You two took forever." She emphasizes *forever* like it's a disease.

If you would learn to be more pleasant . . . I stop myself from completing the thought. I look up to see Zack smiling at me. I smile back.

"Bedtime," he announces after everyone has roasted a few dozen more marshmallows and eaten just as many without toasting. Eight bags wasn't too much, after all.

I volunteer to walk with the kids to the restrooms to brush their teeth and use the bathroom before bed. I am like the Bionic Woman—try and stop me. I feel I can do anything. This time I put on my jacket.

As I escort the kids along the path through the woods, everyone shining his or her flashlight, some aiming their beams in the pine trees, Darren switches his to high beam. The next thing I know he is in step beside me.

The girls rush into their side of the building, giggling about something Dougy said. Charlotte is with them, and I am glad to see she's included. No one better laugh at my girl, I think. Or they'll be messing with me.

Darren, still by my side, says, "I got scars, too."

I feel like I've just come out of the cold and entered a room that's warm. Who is he talking to? Certainly not me.

The boys have all entered the building. Only Darren and I are on the path.

"Mine are on the bottom of my feet." His face, lit by the single bulb shining from the front of the washhouse, holds a sincerity I have never seen from any of the children thus far. His dark eyes are glued to mine. This child who has refused to answer my questions and help in the kitchen, this kid who told me that cooking was a waste of time, has voluntarily spoken to me.

Once when I was seven, my teacher gave me a snowflake ornament crafted from the thinnest glass I have ever held. While the gift was an honor to receive, I was so afraid of dropping and breaking it that the ornament made me nervous. I feel like I did then right now. I don't want to drop and break Darren's new trust in me.

He doesn't seem fearful of me or angry at me. He continues to keep his face toward mine and says, "My scars are usually covered up so no one sees them." Then he gives me a look that transcends anything I can describe. It is as though he can see into my heart and knows everything about my scars even though he is only twelve years old.

I start to say something, but if I did I would be talking to myself. He has dashed into the boys' bathroom.

Rubbing my arms, I stand on the dirt path with my mouth hanging open.

When the girls come out of the building, their giggles echo across the campground. Soon the boys join them, and like a stampede, they take off toward our campsite, beams of flashlights bouncing off the trees and each other.

Rainy stops and turns toward me. "Aren't you coming back with us?"

I am still trying to catch my breath.

———

At eleven o'clock, the adults make sure the children are all accounted for. Robert, who has better luck with wood and matches than Zack or the rest of us, sits on a log by the edge of the fire pit and adds kindling to the dying fire. The kids have been sent off to their tents. There are two boys' tents and two girls' tents and a counselor in each tent with the kids.

"Settle down," Zack commands. "Get some sleep so you can wake up for breakfast and a hike tomorrow."

"What's for breakfast?" asks Bobby from inside the tent he is sharing with Bubba.

"Pancakes and sausage."

"Did we bring syrup?" asks the boy.

Zack looks over at me.

I say, "Yes, and butter. The real kind." I also packed the jar of pig's feet Mom sent me. You never know—perhaps I can get someone to try it, eat it up. I certainly won't be ingesting any.

"Don't start without me!" Bobby shouts. Then he tells Bubba to move over, and we hear the zip of his sleeping bag. "Don't snore, Bubba, okay, okay?"

To which Bubba mutters, "I'm trying to sleep."

There is a last cry from Bobby. "When will it be breakfast? Why can't it be morning already?"

thirty-seven

W hat's wrong with Rhonda?"
I ask.

Robert glances back at the area behind us where the tents are and says, "She'll be all right."

"Did the talk about God upset her?"

When the children were finally settled in their tents, Robert, Zack, Rhonda, and I had circled around the campfire with mugs of decaf coffee. I'd supplied the coffee—Starbucks Hazelnut. I even provided a small carton of half-and-half. We boiled the beans in a pan with water until the water was the color of charcoal. Then we filtered the dark liquid into our mugs. The taste wasn't Starbucks, but it was hot and strong.

Our discussion centered on God and building the kids' faith in Him despite all the hardships the children had been through and continued to deal with.

Zack said he had solid hope that showing God's love to each

of the kids would result in something positive. He said he felt every child who attended The Center had showed improvement.

Rhonda disagreed. "They can't experience love," she said as her eyes reflected the fire. "They've been too scarred."

Zack asked if she thought they were a lost cause.

She said, "No, but I don't expect any miracles anytime soon." Her tone was melancholy. Her shoulders slouched, and I wanted to tell her to sit up straight, but I'm glad I didn't. After all, talk of Lavonna Dewanna and her hunchback isn't welcomed at every event.

Zack said, "Don't give up."

"On what, Zack?" she demanded.

If ever there was an undercurrent, that was it. Clearly, she was no longer referring to the kids at The Center, or the other children she and Zack worked with at Social Services. She was jabbing at something else.

He looked over at her, across the flames. In a steady voice, he said, "Only on the kids."

She left after that, heading to the tent she shared with Lisa and Charlotte.

Now, after pouring another cup of coffee and adding cream to it, I try again. "Is Rhonda okay?"

Robert eyes Zack.

Zack tosses a stick into the fire. "She's mad at me."

"Oh." I understand the feeling. I've been mad at him, too. I guess we're all taking turns. Except Zack and Rhonda went out on a date so this is probably some sort of lovers' quarrel. I'm glad I don't have to deal with love anymore. I think of Jonas's words: "No, no. They went out to talk things over. Zack is like that." Well, I don't know if Jonas knows what is really going on. I sure don't.

The fire crackles, and we hear the boys talking in their tent. I wonder if any of the kids is capable of being quiet for any length of time. I see the beams of flashlights dart across the tops of the tents from inside. I hear Rainy say, "Let's tell ghost stories now."

Darren calls from his tent for Zack, and Zack leaves the fire.

Robert edges closer to me. "You know Rhonda has been trying to get Zack's attention for months."

Well, I would say so. I recall their embrace in the kitchen when I walked in on them at the end of August.

"Zack thinks he has to be nice to everybody. I tell him that he has to learn when it comes to being chased by someone you aren't interested in, you have to show some character."

"You told him that?"

"I sure did. He has to tell her where she stands."

In his arms in the kitchen is what I think, but I say nothing.

"I had this woman chase me once." He looks up at a sky of piercingly bright stars and a moon partially covered by a wispy cloud. "I can't say I didn't enjoy it."

I try to remember if anyone has ever hounded me for a date, or for my attention. Nope—unless you count Lester Hurman, and that was back in sixth grade, when I had braces and wore a training bra.

Robert is about to say more, but Zack returns and eases his lean body onto a stone planted across from me. The fire illuminates the features of his face as I wonder if he really doesn't care for Rhonda. Then I shift on the flat stone where I am seated, draw my knees to my chest, and think, Give it up, Deena. You have sworn off all men. You don't need any more confusion in your life. Let it go. Let Zack go.

"Is everything okay?" Robert poses the question to Zack.

"Darren needed his medication."

"He asked for it?"

"Yeah. Two points for him, huh?"

"That's a good sign."

"An improvement over two weeks ago when he refused to take it at school and called the teacher a 'spineless mutation with freakishly large elbows.' "

"That got him detention, I heard."

Zack nods. "That mistake cost him a week."

I never recall calling a teacher any name. I never had detention, either. I couldn't; my mother would have disowned me and then fried me up at the annual barbeque. At least I had a mother who cared about me. And a father. Darren has never known his dad, and over the years, his mother has been charged with and imprisoned for child abuse and neglect. Darren has a good grandma, though. A senior saint.

Robert excuses himself and heads toward the restroom, and now Zack and I are alone.

I sigh and watch the embers glowing against my arms. I've taken off my jacket again, because by the fire—it's warm. My scars don't look as pronounced in the darkness; in fact the fire almost softens them. Maybe if I lived the rest of my life in the evening at campsites, I'd feel more comfortable with my body. Jeannie says when she goes out on dates, she likes to eat at restaurants with candlelight. "I have fewer wrinkles by candlelight," she told me once, as I watched her put on makeup before her dentist-date arrived. Turning to me she said, "But you don't have to worry about wrinkles now, Deena. Wait till you hit thirty-two."

"Thirty-two? That's not that old, Jeannie."

I used to think that by age thirty-two, I'd be pregnant with my youngest child—that is, if Lucas and I stuck to our plan of having two children, two years apart. He wanted a boy first and I wanted a girl. Then I told him it didn't matter which gender arrived first.

Suddenly I realize it has been a while since I've wondered what Lucas is doing. The good thing about being in North Carolina is that I can't run into him like I could in Atlanta. I can shop at Ingle's without worrying that as I decide how much chicken I need for dinner's pot pie, he'll be next to me, looking at steaks to grill.

"A cupcake for your thoughts."

I look over at Zack, who is roasting a marshmallow on a large stick. Coming from anyone else, that line would sound corny. Coming from Zack, it just makes me feel content. I think of the chocolate cupcake Band-Aid on Jonas's forehead and the identical bandage I placed on Charlotte's finger. That was what caused Zack to realize that the woman who put the bandage on his brother was the same one who bandaged Charlotte. Then his mind put two and two together, and he knew all the things about Deirdre his brother had shared with him were really things about Deena at The Center. Which means, he knows so much about me. And I still know very little about him.

"Are you thinking of Atlanta?" Zack asks with a smile.

"How'd you guess?" I can't tell him that I was actually thinking about him and Jonas.

"You have that city-lights glow to your face."

"Is that a good thing?"

"The city is nice."

"Have you ever lived in one?"

"Visited plenty of them. And once those trips were over, I was always glad to be back in the mountains."

"So would you ever do a jigsaw puzzle of a city?"

Zack laughs lightly. "Jonas must have told you that I did a one-thousand-piece puzzle of Boston."

I smile, nod. "He said it took you only six days. He is so proud of you."

We are silent for a while as the crickets and cicadas sing in the woods around us—an orchestra of nature's finest elegance. Instinctively, I listen for the owl. He must be too tired to join in tonight.

Zack leans toward the fire and whispers, "I like your face."

It comes out so naturally, not forced, not asked for, just there, like a hostess offering hors d'oeuvres without any fanfare.

I'm glad it's dark so he can't see me blushing.

"It's nicest when you smile."

"Thanks."

"You should do that more."

It takes me a moment to come up with a response. "Really, why?"

"We deserve to see you happy, don't we?"

Ah, happiness. What is it? Does it exist? Words from Grandpa Ernest's letter come back to me. *"The greater part of our happiness or misery depends on our dispositions and not on our circumstances."*

"I mean, we all want you to like us here. You know, feel comfortable in these mountains."

"I like y'all," I say into the fire. I keep my eyes on the coals because I am too scared to look Zack in the face. I am afraid that I would get lost somewhere in his hazel-green eyes and not be able to find my breath.

He's not for me. He is these kids' hero. Yet . . . I glance over at him. He seems kind and trustworthy and—

No! He's a man. He's capable of breaking my heart. Bending it, pulling it apart like silly putty . . .

There are some things in life the heart is not willing to risk.

Abruptly, I stand and put on my jacket. "Good night, Zack," I say. Then I leave him alone. I would like to think he has a surprised expression on his face, similar to the one Chef B had when I said I was leaving Atlanta. One that would clearly convey disappointment at my sudden decision to get up and leave.

I would like to think that.

I don't wait to see.

———

As I lie awake in my sleeping bag in the girls' tent with Rainy and Joy softly breathing beside me, my heart won't let me sleep. It reminds me of a pot on the stove, boiling water raging down the sides, splashing against the flames. If I could just turn off the flame, the boiling would subside and I could close my eyes.

I recall the nights I slept in my sleeping bag in my apartment in Atlanta—the nights before I made my trip to Grandpa's cabin. That final night before my move up north was lonely, one where I hoped that Vivaldi's music would summon sleep. I kept looking at the clock and watching the numbers bring in a new day, frustrated that I couldn't close my eyes, shut off my mind, and drift off. Now I sniff the sleeping bag to see if it has any aroma that reminds me of my apartment life. Perhaps a faint odor of fried calamari, cinnamon from a candle I often burned, or simply nostalgia.

I can't get comfortable, and the ground is hard. Turning, I

see the outline of Joy's sleeping frame to the left of me and Rainy next to her. Rainy opens her mouth and lets out a snore. I think she'd be mortified if she found out she snores in her sleep.

Massaging my arms, I'm still able to feel Charlotte's fingers as they played against my scars. I think of her view of the stars—how she imagines that God takes each of her uttered prayers and displays them in the sky. Each prayer, a shining light, worthy to be strung in the heavens. I would like to peer into her journal and read what some of those hopes are in her young life. Miriam told me that while the children hope to be connected to their despondent parents, they wish for other things, too. Kids are kids. Charlotte probably wants to grow up to be a ballerina like I wanted to when I was small. Or maybe she dreams of something more lofty—being a physician or an astronaut. I should have asked her, I think. I need to ask more and assume less.

I turn over again, draw my knees to my chest, which I find is hard to do in the constraints of a sleeping bag. I unzip the bag and try again. Now when I breathe, there is no scent of calamari but only of the smoky night. My hair and skin are fragrant from the campfire. Listening, I hear no voices, only the sounds from nature.

I suppose even Zack has gone to his tent. I go over each detail of the brief but comfortable time spent talking with him as the fire blazed. I smile at how we connected. Even though we said little, there was this feeling between us. Jeannie would call it chemistry, but I'm not ready to name it.

He's not what I wished for.

The most remarkable part of the evening was one of the briefest moments. Darren talked to me. He did not yell or curse but actually acknowledged my scars and told me of his own. Sullen and angry Darren opened a little crack in his armor and let me see a hidden part, a section of himself. Tomorrow I'll probably wonder if I dreamed his words to me.

I study Rainy's sunglasses by the light of the moon. She's placed them on top of her backpack at the foot of her sleeping bag. Now they look just like a small object, but when she wears them and chews her gum, those glasses seem larger than life. Maybe that's one of the reasons sleep is so nourishing. When we sleep we remove all the masks we wear by day.

Zack is not what I wished for.

I rise up onto my elbows and watch the girls. Joy's curly hair looks like a halo around her pillow. Amazing that when we sleep, all of us look so vulnerable, like we can't help but be totally and completely lovable. Just like a photo taken in one second of time, an image captured on film that can be contained, held, and even framed. A smiling face locked in place so that it can't talk back, rant, confess, or lie. There were times I longed to be just a happy image in a photograph with Lucas.

On my birthday, I didn't watch the candles on my peach pie and chocolate cake and hope for something to happen between Zack and me. I wished for something else.

Peace. The word is there; it has always been there, in the Bible or on a sign posted to a kitchen door. Peace. I want peace deep inside my heart, lodged so deeply and firmly that no one can ever take it away. How sweet that would be.

But peace and anger can't coexist. One day I will let the anger go. One day I will no longer care about my scars. One day I will stop letting Lucas control me, because even though we are more than one hundred and fifty miles apart, I'm still drenched in anger at him.

I wonder how Jonas can understand the value of forgiveness and operate in it, while I, with my undergraduate degree and normally functioning brain, have not found out how to do it. Jonas, I think, you are lucky. In so many ways.

If I'd brought my journal along, I would turn on my flashlight and write. But I didn't dare pack my journal for fear the kids would confiscate it and read it aloud. I would never live that down. If that happened, I would have to leave town.

The crickets sing over the stillness of the mountain. Then I hear the familiar soothing voice—the sound I have grown accustomed to over these six months in the mountains. This owl's cry is loud and steady, like a heartbeat. I listen over all the other noises around me and imagine which tree he might be in. I wonder what he looks like, how his feathers ruffle as his voice plays out over the breezes—his symphony of evening peace. Does he know the owl from the woods around my cabin? Do they get together and share a rodent or two for dinner, or give each other high fives as they fly from treetop to treetop over the Smokies?

Just before I drift into sleep, I form a prayer to God. It is one of gratitude, the kind my own dad gives. I smile in the darkness, a smile only God sees. Somehow, here, far from my hometown, far away from the life I carefully created for myself in Atlanta, God has given me a gift, and its name is richer and sweeter than any frosted cake. I have been presented with hope.

And I have realized that hope is the necessary beginning. With it, I can hope to one day jump into that river pastors preach and write about. It has a short name, and yet it takes a lifetime to truly navigate this river we call Forgiveness. Why is it so hard, sometimes, to put your hand in God's?

thirty-eight

"Do you want to see, Miss Livingston?" Bubba asks as the sunlight filters through his hair.

"Or are you afraid?" Bobby laughs and pokes the base of the oak tree with a narrow, curvy branch he insists on carrying. He has brushed everyone's skin with it even though Zack has told him to put it away.

We are on a hike on a woodsy trail. The morning is clear, with cirrus clouds moving across the blue sky. I can almost taste the sky—delicate and pleasing, like an almond butter strudel with a hint of nutmeg.

Earlier our hike took us to an opening that overlooked the gentle slope of the mountain range. The mountains were an array of scarlet, gold, and amber. As I breathed in the warm air and turned my face to the sun, I thought I could stay there all day. A hawk cast his wings before us and soared across two mountain peaks.

"It's just beautiful," Rainy said, removing her sunglasses, and she was right.

Now the kids say they have found the hole where an owl lives. With the help of three stones resting against each other to form a stair, each child takes a turn looking into an opened notch in the trunk of a gnarled oak tree.

Dougy peers into the hole, which is the size of a watermelon, and quickly jumps down. "He's in there!" His voice sounds like steam from a teakettle.

"Duh!" Bubba cries. "We told you. We don't lie."

"What does he look like?" asks Joy, who is still too fearful to stand on the rocks and have a turn.

Bubba makes scary sounds, and Bobby jabs Joy on her arm with his stick.

Joy jumps into Zack's arms while everyone else laughs.

Again, I am asked, "Do you want to see him, Miss Livingston?" I look at the child who has just spoken. His dark eyes and hair seem tranquil today, the first time I have ever felt this way about him. He says, "He's sleeping. He won't hurt you."

I am not worried. I would not miss an opportunity to view an owl nestled in a tree. The kids don't know how long I have searched for this nighttime musician. "Yeah," I reply to Darren. "I'd like to see him."

I step onto the wobbling stones and adjust my eyes to the dark hole. All I see is a mass of brown feathers, a few tainted with gray. Cautiously, I edge forward to get a closer look, grasping the trunk of the tree with one hand. I am determined to see this owl, even if I trip and fall into his sleeping place. I focus, squint, and observe the huddled dark figure. I see his body moving ever so slightly. He's alive, I think, real and breathing. He's resting up so that he can serenade the forest again tonight. He is a perfect picture of peace.

"Did you get a good look?" asks Joy, able to speak once more.

"There isn't much to see," I say as I step down from the stones.

"He's a tawny owl," Darren tells us. "Those are the ones who sing the best." Coming from a good singer, I guess he would know.

"Where's his poop?" asks Bobby circling the tree trunk with his stick.

"Yuck." Rainy pops her sunglasses back over her eyes.

"We had to study owl's vomit once," says Bobby. "Remember? In fourth grade?"

"Duh, I remember. It was filled with tiny mice bones." Bubba is enjoying this conversation too much.

I might just throw up today.

Charlotte speaks into the boys' cackling. "They toss it out of their mouths. Did you know that?"

"Toss? Toss what?" Rainy eyes her suspiciously.

"The things they can't digest, like bones, feathers, and claws." Her voice is mellow even when she is relaying something as disgusting as owl vomit.

"Yeah." Bubba stretches the word out long and loud. "You're right. It comes out of their beaks." He uses his scrawny arms to pantomime a regurgitating animal.

Charlotte is so happy to have everyone's attention she looks like she just won the spelling bee, not shared information on the digestive patterns of owls.

"Is that right, Miss Livingston?" Dougy asks as he watches Bubba's gestures.

"I never got to study owls," I say.

Soon we are back on the trail, ambling on top of damp leaves, pine needles, and pine cones, the tall North Carolina pines shielding the sun. Zack and Robert are in the lead, Rhonda is next to Bubba, and Charlotte and I are at the end. The others are scattered across the path, laughing about the most disgusting things they can think of.

"Let's talk about something else," Zack suggests as he runs a hand through his curly hair.

"Like what?" asks Lisa.

"How about food?" Bobby volunteers. "Breakfast was a long time ago." He pats his stomach and announces, "I vote we head back to the campsite and eat lunch!"

"It's only ten thirty," Rhonda says as she looks at the time on her cell phone.

Bobby inserts his blue inhaler into his mouth and takes a couple puffs. He fills his lungs with air and then coughs. "Ah," he says, "but I can't breathe, and I need nourishment."

"You'll be fine," I tell him with a smile. "Think of your favorite things."

"Owl throw-up," whispers Bubba, and then we are all laughing.

"You like owls, Miss Livington?" asks Joy as she paces her strides to mine.

I think of how the one in my backyard calls throughout the night, how it kept me awake early on. Then one night the noise that had been so disturbing became a welcomed lullaby.

"Because I hate them." Spontaneously, Joy covers her hand to her mouth. "I mean," she says with careful intonation, "I don't care for them."

"They sing me to sleep at night," I tell her. "So I guess I do like them."

Her response to my answer consists of sticking her tongue out and grimacing.

I've *learned* to like the owl, I could say. Just like I've had to *learn* to like each one of these kids. Instead I add, "An owl's song can grow on you, and before you know it, you actually look forward to hearing it."

Darren, walking a few steps in front of us, turns his head to give me a smile. Like he knows exactly what I mean.

———

So often it is the small moments that bring the assurance of contentment. These can come in tiny waves, standing out from the rest of the minutes and hours of a day, and as swiftly as they arrive, they leave, slipping into an ordinary moment. You have to be on your toes; you have to be ready to embrace them.

My talk with Charlotte and later with Darren last night are two of the most recent waves of reassurance. I must be doing something right. I recall my prayer for patience. Humans always want to get the glory, but without God to rely on, I'd have given a series of high-pitched sermons to these children. Instead, I asked for patience, and God presented it, working it deep into the fibers of my heart.

And forgiveness? The sparse leaves still clinging to tree limbs rustle as though they are begging me to remove the poison of bitterness and anger I harbor for Lucas. When you forgive, you are really doing yourself a favor—that is what I have heard pastors preach. Forgiveness is the gift you receive in order to freely give it to others.

Lucas never asked for my forgiveness, I want to remind the forest breezes.

Much of the day has passed; dusk settles over the campsite. The picnic table has been set; even the juice boxes have been placed at each setting. A bowl of soft rolls sits in the center.

With a large wooden spoon, one of Grandpa's utensils, I stir the iron pot of Brunswick stew over the grate. Earlier, Robert started the fire and supplied a pile of sticks for me to add to it. Then he and Rhonda took the kids to a clearing to play kickball.

Zack unloads two bundles of firewood from the bed of his truck and places them near where I am standing. He didn't join the others; I'm not sure why. He set the table as I opened the six cans of stew and poured them into the cast-iron pot. He seems preoccupied as I stir the carrots, potatoes, and cubes of beef. He's got something on his mind.

The silence between us is fine by me. Having lived alone the last few years, I'm not used to the constant conversation we've had with the children during this weekend. In fact, the quiet right now is a refreshing and sought-after change. I don't mind listening to my own thoughts for a while.

Once, back when I went to Sunday school classes, the teacher said that Jesus holds whatever we need in life. "If it's patience, he has enough to supply you. If it's love you need, he has that, too. Ask."

I close my eyes.

And am startled when I sense Zack standing beside me. "Rhonda . . ."

I am about to tell him that my name isn't Rhonda, when I realize he is going to say something about her. I look up from the cooking pot into his eyes. They are solemn this evening.

"I just wanted to say that . . ." He fumbles for the right words. "I'm sorry for the tension."

"Tension?" I'm confused by his word choice.

"Between Rhonda and me." His voice is low, sincere.

"Well, it's none of my business," I am tempted to blurt out. But on the other hand, maybe it is. He wants to apologize. If it will help him feel better, then I should let him do just that. "She really likes you." The moment I finish my sentence, I feel like we're no older than these kids. I'm back in middle school, telling my friend that somebody likes her. Girls are putting lipstick on in the restroom and whispering that Lester Hurman is chasing me.

"Rhonda and I have a lot in common," Zack says. "I guess since we work together we've thought that maybe something could happen."

Office romance? We had one of those at Palacio del Rey. When the waitress and bus boy broke up, the strife between them could have been cut with any sharpened kitchen knife. Working anywhere near either of them had been a test of everyone's sanity. We went home weary those nights.

As the children leap over the path toward us, Zack's last words to me are, "It isn't going to happen. It just won't."

Poor Rhonda.

I, who was seething with jealousy yesterday, am now over-come with sorrow for Rhonda. At the same time, I feel like shouting while doing a handstand. But I haven't been able to do a decent handstand since second grade, and besides, my mother's warning about a woman not exposing her emo-tions keeps me from doing anything. I give the stew two good stirs.

When Rhonda approaches me, she looks sweaty from the game of kickball. I offer her a juice box and then a smile.

Humans are the most fickle of God's creations. Also the most hardhearted. Dogs are forgiving; they only know how to pump pureness through their arteries. Maybe I should rethink my opinion about dogs.

I cast a look toward Zack, who is on his way to the restrooms, Bubba and Dougy protesting behind him, "Why do we have to wash our hands again?"

Something about the way Zack is distraught over his relationship with Rhonda brushes against me like a soft sheet drying on the clothesline on a spring afternoon. He really cares about the feelings of others. He hates the uneasiness between Rhonda and him. Mom used to dry our clothes on a wire line strung between two cedar trees. Growing up, she told us that clothes hung on a line were the most sanitary, a claim I have since found to be odd. Probably because as the sheets and towels hung on warm afternoons, I would often come by and hold the ends of the cotton sheets in my hands and press my nose into the fabric, letting the aroma of sun and soap fill my lungs. My hands, after playing around the barn, were less than sanitary.

———

When I am asked to offer the blessing over our meal, I look at Robert as if he's made a mistake. "Me?" I want to say. "You want me to pray? Are you out of your mind? I am clearly the most selfish, jealous, angry person at this gathering, and you want me to talk to God? Aloud? In front of everyone?"

Then I look at Darren seated to my left and think of his burns. I glance at Charlotte and think of how she's been abandoned again and again. All of us here are just mere hope-less creatures—except that we are loved by God. His love is saturated with an equal amount of consistency for everyone.

They are all waiting for me. Zack gives an encouraging nod, lowers his head.

I take in a breath and wish the earth would open and swallow me right now. I have no idea what I'm going to say. When was the last time I prayed audibly in front of a group? Then the answer comes to me. I fold my hands and close my eyes. "Dear God, thank you for each person here. Help us to grow in the love, patience, joy, peace, and forgiveness that you freely give to us. Thank you for this food and this time together. Amen." As I say the word *forgiveness,* my heart feels a rapid tug. I blink back tears.

"Amen!" says Bobby. "Let's eat!"

I stand to fill plastic bowls with stew, sniff a few times. No crying, not here, I tell myself.

As we eat, I realize that praying wasn't hard. I just put into practice what I've learned while living in these rugged Smoky Mountains. I opened my heart and let it out. As Chef B would say, "She write her heart onto the pages of her journal."

"Miss Livingston loves those fruits," says Bubba as he reaches for a roll.

I smile at him.

Rainy says, "Miss Livingston taught us to make some really good things this year, and we're eating soup from a can?"

"Dummy," says Bobby. "At least it's food. Pass me a roll. Or two. Please."

As Zack hangs a lantern on a pole so that we can eat with light, I am starting to feel like I am surrounded by family.

291

If this were a musical, here's where I would break into song. But I still can't carry a tune.

———

Zack and the kids take the heavy pot to a water faucet by the path to wash it. I enter my tent to put on my jacket. It is then that my mind turns to the kimono-clad woman in the drawing at Ernest's cabin. As many times as I have wondered what exactly she is covering with her ornate fan, now I think I know. The woman has lifted her fan to conceal a tear. She is not the crying type and doesn't want to blow her cover. But sometimes the heart overpowers the eyes, and tears somehow manage to escape. The dampness a tear produces is like the dew layering the earth of the mountain—moist and needed for cleansing, growth, and above all else, survival.

"Are you all right?" The familiar voice comes from behind me.

I know I'm supposed to say, "Of course, I'm fine." Mother has told me over and over that no one wants to hear your woes; it's best to smile, and the world smiles with you. Conceal; use that fan. Show no one who you really are, because then they might think less of you, assuming they ever thought highly of you at all.

Zack notes the tear that has made its way down my cheek. I see his eyes observing it like it's a rare gem—or a piece of trash. As he draws closer, he surprises me by moving a finger gently over its trail. "You aren't okay, are you?"

The desire to take his hand in mine overwhelms me. Stepping back, I simply admit, "The mountains don't give you room to hide, do they?"

He tilts his head and looks into my eyes. "We don't

hide here in these parts, Miss Livingston. Every one of us is exposed."

"Are there professionally documented charts on all of us?"

"In your case, all I have is memory."

"What does that mean?" I ask.

"I can recall what Ernest told me about you."

My grandfather told Zack about me? "What did he tell you?"

Zack's smile lights his face. "He said you were stubborn." He pauses. I sure hope my grandfather had more to say about me than just that. Zack lets his smile widen. "He also told me that you're a great cook, and the cakes you decorate are works of art. Right after your accident, he told me his granddaughter needed to come to North Carolina."

"After my accident? You knew about it before I told you?"

"Like I said, we have no secrets here." My desire to reach up and touch one of his dimples catches me off guard.

After a pause, I say, "I guess not. Between Jonas and Ernest, you've probably heard more about me than you want to."

Zack laughs. It's a gentle laugh that seems to clear the air around us. "Actually, it only made me want to learn more."

I hear the others calling to and teasing each other and know that this time with just Zack is coming to an end very soon. "Ernest was a smart man," I say, because it seems like that is certainly worth noting.

Zack agrees. "He knew his granddaughter needed us."

The wind breathes over the campsite as Zack adds, "And that we needed her."

In a wild dash, Bubba comes running from behind a tree, jumps onto Zack's back, and claims with a loud cry, "Gotcha this time!"

Zack playfully wrestles the boy to the ground as Robert, Darren, Charlotte, and Rainy crowd around them to observe. When Zack tickles Bubba, the whole group laughs along with him.

"Are you all right, Miss Livingston?" Charlotte asks in her soft tone, barely audible over the noise. She stands near my elbow.

I realize I am the only one not laughing.

Zipping up my jacket, I nod, paste on a smile, and then purposely step back a few feet. I would like to borrow Rainy's sunglasses right now because I need to cover the look on my face.

This curly-haired, basketball-playing social worker has dodged past all the barriers I so carefully set up and taken up residence in my heart.

Maybe I am not allergic to men, after all.

thirty-nine

I await my dinner guests. I have to be ready. Once the guests arrive, I will not have time to finish up any last-minute details that have gone unnoticed. That's because the doorbell won't ring; my guests—well, one of them, at least—will just open the door and storm through. He thinks he owns the place, or at least the pipes.

As I'm stirring the soup, watching it thicken, I hear a truck door slam and footsteps outside the cabin. Then, sure enough, in comes Jonas, a green bandana secured to his head. He's carrying a wrench. Zack follows. He's dressed in khakis and a blue cotton shirt.

"What's cooking?" asks Jonas. "I'm hungry as a bear."

I smile at the brothers and tell Jonas, "You know what it is. Take a breath."

He smiles his widest smile. "Oil soup." Then he nods, as though he approves and is grateful that I have listened to him when he suggested I make this soup and invite Zack over for dinner. When I included him in the invite, he shook his head. I told him that he'd brought Zack and me together; without Jonas we would never have learned so much about each other. At that, Jonas said, "I guess I could come along. You never know."

"Know what?"

"A pipe might need repair."

I don't believe I have had two guests I care more about. Well, maybe Jeannie and Sally. They visited last weekend and we took in the local tourist attractions, including a drive over the Parkway to Gatlinburg on Saturday afternoon. Sally said my driving had improved; I suppose she was right since my fingers were flexible once we arrived in the buzzing Tennessee town. No knuckles of concrete.

Jonas pops his Eagles CD into the player. Zack protests because he's not sure that his older brother should be acting so familiar in someone else's home.

"Jonas, don't you need to ask Deena?" he prods. He does this with the kids at The Center, too.

"No," says Jonas as the first line to "One of These Nights" starts to play. "She knows me." Then he announces he's going to check the pipes.

"But, Jonas." I am the one protesting this time. I enter the living room. "This is Saturday night. You don't work on Saturday."

"Don't work on Sunday, the Lord's Day. I have worked Saturday before. No sick day." He smiles, his teeth glistening like the first day I met him. It feels as if I have known him for years.

He swings his wrench and hums to "One of These Nights."

Then he winks at me. With his wrench swinging, he heads toward the downstairs bathroom.

Zack faces me.

Suddenly, I feel very awkward. Why are things so easy around Jonas and so difficult around Zack?

"Do you need me to help you in the kitchen?" he asks.

"Are you able to make a fire in the fireplace?"

He gathers some logs from the pile outside on the porch and starts a fire.

I stir the soup and see that the loaf of herb bread is almost done. I open the fridge, smile at the new lone lemon I bought the other day, and take out a bowl of salad. I add spinach leaves to the romaine lettuce and dried cranberries. Then I toss it all with almond slivers and my homemade poppy-seed dressing.

Preoccupied, I am startled when I notice Zack has been standing by the kitchen door, watching me.

I smile and place the salad bowl in the fridge again. "Seems we're always ending up in some kitchen."

"I've enjoyed our kitchen talks."

Well, they've certainly made me think—and be on my toes.

"Deena?" His voice is soft, hesitant.

"Yeah?" I move from the counter.

"Jonas thinks we should—"

"Get together one of these nights?" I surprise myself by my boldness.

"Yeah."

"Well, I don't know, Zack."

"Why?"

"Seems you've hugged lots of people in the kitchen."

"Like?" His face is puzzled.

I give him a knowing look.

The lines on his face ease as he says, "I mean, besides Rhonda. Lots of people?"

"Charlotte. Darren. Lisa. You even managed to give Bobby a hug, one that at least covered half of him."

He looks down and then slowly lifts his face to mine. "You're jealous?"

I swallow. Why is he standing so close to me when we are having this conversation? My knees feel weak, but I will not back down. I have to say how I feel. I mean, this is what he wants, right? I find my words. "I am. Just a little." I'm not smiling, because it is true. Zack seems to be part of everyone's life, and I have had so little time with just him.

"What do you want, Deena?" His smile has faded from his lips.

More time with just you. Would that be too forward of me to say? Mom would turn up her nose. "What do *you* want?"

"I'd like to be in a relationship . . . with you." He speaks slowly, like each word is coming from someplace deep.

I've heard of being honest, but this takes the cake. I swallow and mumble, "You would?"

"How about you?"

I don't know what to say. I look down at his shoes, then at my shoes. All I can see is Rhonda and him standing in the kitchen together. As though reading my mind—and I guess he can do this because he went to grad school for social work—he says, "Rhonda and I aren't together. We never were."

Jonas has let me know this, and so has Robert. Once again, Zack is assuring me that he and Rhonda are not, as the kids say, going out. Yet, there is so much more than just knowing where another woman stands in his life. There are many other components . . . time, truth, trust. These are small words, but each holds great significance for me.

When I look up, his face is right in front of me. I feel unsure, and yet sweet anticipation floods over me at the same time.

"I know it hasn't been long." His fingers encircle my arm just above my wrist; I feel warmth touch my scars.

"I want the three Ts," I tell him.

He gives me a pensive look. "The three Ts?"

"Yeah."

"What are they?"

His face is so close to mine.

"Something to do with cooking?"

I am glad for the opportunity to laugh. "Yeah, they stand for Teflon, tablespoon, and tarragon."

"Tarragon?"

"It's an herb." There's a French-grown variety and a Russian-grown one, and French is usually thought to be best in the kitchen. It's funny how studies at the culinary school can filter through my mind at the most unexpected times.

"I just wondered why there would be an herb when the other two are objects."

I note the tongs hanging by the stove and say, "Okay, Teflon, tablespoon, and tongs. Does that sound better?"

He looks into my eyes.

I'm not able to catch the harsh pain I once felt his eyes encompassed. All I see now is tenderness.

His hands move to my shoulder. His touch is so light, yet strong enough to make me take one step closer to him. As I put my head against his chest, his arms slip around me.

I let him finger my hair, slowly, caressing away pain, distrust, loneliness. Even the scars on my arms, legs, and stomach seem not to matter right now.

I could stay like this all night.

We hear Jonas over the music. He enters the living room and then the kitchen. I expect Zack to pull away from me like he did when Rhonda was clutching him.

"Well, it's about time!" Jonas's voice booms with excitement. He smiles at us, and then leaves the room again, his boots pounding over the hardwoods. "Who made the fire?" he calls as he enters the living room.

"No comments," Zack says over my head.

"Needs work," his brother shouts back. "Needs work!"

"Needs work," I repeat.

"Okay, okay. I heard him."

I step back a bit and look into Zack's eyes. To be truthful, to be trustworthy, to know that over time, with God's help, I have come from wanting to die in Georgia to embracing the sweetness of life in the mountains of North Carolina—those are the valuable things to know. I risk exposing my thoughts, something that I've found near impossible to do these past months in Bryson City. "I think *we* need work, too."

He looks as though my words have slapped him.

Immediately I want to retract what I said, but it's Jonas's fault, he gave me the idea.

"Work?" Zack clears his throat. "We need work?"

Goodness, surely he, of all the intelligent people I know, understands this. "Needing work isn't a bad thing," I explain. There are times even the best-looking cake could use a little more icing or a few more buttercream roses.

His eyes are hopeful. "But you do think there's potential?"

That's when I tell him what the three Ts really stand for. "Trust, time, and truth."

"You're right. I believe in all of those." His smile makes me think of a picnic by a cool mountain stream. Add a pinch of autumn breeze, a cup of sunshine, and a heap of potential.

When he kisses me gently, it is even better than a slice of velvet cake.

forty

Regena Lorraine, dressed in a bulky peach-colored dress, removes her leopard-spotted glasses from her eyes. Her frame fills the doorway to the kitchen as she watches me pipe rosettes along the top of an almond cake. I've received three cake orders already this first week of November.

People have told me they picked up brochures at the Chinese restaurant and bookstore. This has to mean that the employees I handed them to are displaying them, as they said they would. Even though I'm an outsider from Georgia, I feel I've been given a chance in this little town. I know that Jonas has been instrumental in telling everyone he does business for that my cakes are the best, which means that people are ordering because of his genuine marketing skills. And who can resist Jonas when his eyes flash like headlights as he speaks of dessert?

Marble Gray did pay for her cakes, although she claimed she didn't have the exact amount on her and gave me a dollar less than the price on the brochure. I let it go. I had a feeling if I argued with her, she'd make a scene so voluminous that it would bring the Swain County police to my front door. I don't need that kind of publicity. Regena Lorraine said she was surprised Marble Gray paid anything. "That woman will steal the shirt off your back." And your underwear, I once heard.

As I notice the frosting running low, I open the refrigerator for more butter. I'll need to make more frosting. I'm grateful that not only do I have the mixer I brought from Atlanta, but that Ernest has one in this cabin, as well. On the refrigerator door is a drawing of an owl. The feathers are brown, with shades of gray at the tips. The eyes are as round as demitasse cups. If the picture could sing, I'm sure it would do so loudly and beautifully. This is a tawny owl, and although they hide, they like to be heard. Darren's name is signed in the left-hand corner. I told him he better put his name on the sheet or otherwise, since the drawing is so good, I might think Bob Timberlake drew it.

"Bob who?" he asked.

"We'll have to go to Blowing Rock one day," I said. "He has an art gallery there."

My aunt inserts a finger into the bowl of buttercream frosting, smacks her lipstick-covered mouth, and says, "Cabin is yours now, Shug."

I'm not sure I heard correctly, so I just look at her.

"You don't have to teach cooking at The Center anymore." With a jeweled hand, she reaches inside her tote bag and displays official-looking papers.

My eyes glance at the papers and then at her face. Is she serious? Or, knowing my aunt, is there a long story she needs to tell me first?

"All legal. I was at the lawyer's this morning. This is your place now. Oh, we do have to get you to sign some forms next week."

"So I fulfilled my obligation?" Over six months of grueling lessons to noisy, wild, rude, lovable children.

"Sure did." She smiles, but then shows clear shock at my next question.

"But can I still teach?" I've learned how to love those kids. I would hate to give it all up now. I know that soon they'll have outgrown middle school and graduate on to high school, but there will be others to replace them. I want to be ready for the new kids with my shiny pans and recipes for something other than white sauce.

She regains her composure, places her glasses back onto her face, uses her fingers to delicately adjust them against her nose. "Of course."

Nervously, I ask, "There's nothing that says I have to give up my classes?"

"Oh no, Shug. Besides, I don't think Miriam would want you to quit." She attempts a wink. "The kids would be sad if you left them."

Giovanni, resting at his usual spot, stretches and yawns.

I put the frosting bag on the counter and look at my aunt to ask the very thing that has been on my mind. "Do you think Grandpa knew I needed to teach so that I could change?"

"Change?"

"You know, grow up."

"You are all growed up, Shug." She smiles and turns to go, leaving the papers on the countertop. I follow her down the hallway, guessing she doesn't understand what I mean at all. But I'm wrong. As she opens the door, a blast of cool November air flows into the cabin, and Giovanni races outside to jump into a pile of brown leaves. My aunt pauses, looks at me, and says, "Life is what happens to you while you're busy making other plans."

I nod. I think of the words my grandfather penned in his letter to me. *"Life is never as we expect it."*

"I suppose Ernest's plans, mixed with God's, all came about to teach you wonderful things." She lifts a strand of gray hair from her eyes, considers saying something else, hesitates, and then says, "Ernest was fond of you."

"Really?"

"You and he are more alike than you realize. He saw something in you, something that clicked with him."

My face must have its bewildered look because she clarifies with, "Shug, he knew. He asked for my advice, and I gave it. I told him that I was sure you would appreciate a cabin in these parts. But he wanted you to not just get the cabin and stay holed up in it. He wanted you to receive something and to have to give something of yourself. Receiving and giving, isn't that what it's all about?" She smiles.

"Receive . . . and give . . . ?"

Fingering her sentimental silver ring from her mother, she explains. "Did I ever tell you about the time I wanted a bunny rabbit?"

Without waiting for my reply, Regena Lorraine excitedly dives into her story. "Ernest made me work for it. I begged for a bunny, in spite of the fact that he told me caring for a pet takes a lot of work. He went on and on about how I would have to clean up after it and feed it and be responsible enough to keep it out of Mrs. McGullery's flower garden. I said that I could do all that. That's when he looked me in the eye and said that I had to help the Kinston twins with their math. They weren't very smart, oh no. They weren't the brightest bulbs in the county. But I could teach fractions pretty well." She smiles as though reflecting on a chalkboard filled with one-thirds and three-fourths.

"Did you ever get the rabbit?"

Mischievously, she smiles. "I did. I named her Huckleberry Finn, even though she was female. To everyone's surprise, those Kinston twins passed fifth-grade math." After a moment she says, "I learned patience and how good things take time. Ernest says the twins benefited from my teaching. I gave to them, and they gave to me."

At that, Giovanni pauses from his romping and barks. It is a sweet reaction, and mixes well with the faint scent of my aunt's perfume.

From her truck, Regena Lorraine takes a spiral-shaped brown piece of pottery with two large dots on one side. "Here you are, Shug." She places this object in my hands. "Sorry it took me so long." Then she opens the passenger door and Giovanni leaps inside. She lowers the window, and his nose twitches with pleasure as his mouth produces a bubble of drool.

"Going to play Clue," she says to me with a wave. "I hope I win something good tonight. I could use another measuring cup. My glass one broke this morning."

After the truck edges out of the driveway and starts down

the narrow sloping road, I look at what I've been given. The dots are eyes, part of a face—the face of a raccoon. The pink lips are faded, as though the bowl has been used and washed many times. So this is the famous raccoon bowl. I wonder what peanut soup tastes like from this silly container. I recall the story Regena Lorraine told me about the raccoons attacking my grandpa as he tried to get into the cabin. My aunt still laughs at the memory. Is that what this bowl is about? Being able to laugh at certain memories? Then eat hot soup from it? I think being able to fully taste all the flavors comes with experiencing all of life. Grabbing it by the reins and feeling it pulsate in your heart, in your mind, and in your hands.

Sometimes truly living comes in the least expected or wanted circumstances. Like having to teach middle-school children. Then, before you know it, you have been transformed and you *want* to be with them, you *want* to reach them.

The rust-colored cabin forms a bold and happy presence on the edge of this mountain. To the right of the driveway, the pile of leaves I raked yesterday is no longer a mound, thanks to my aunt's mutt. It doesn't matter. In fact, piles of leaves must be for jumping in—why else would they make such a nice crunching sound? With the raccoon bowl in one hand, I leap into the scattered pile. There is nothing wrong, I tell myself as I lose my balance and land on my bottom, with acting like you're five again. Smiling into the pale blue sky, I note how the clouds look like creamy vanilla pudding.

There will be plenty of opportunities in the days to come to rake leaves in *my* yard by *my* cabin.

Right now I have cake orders to fill.

And after that, a date to get ready for. Zack and I have been invited to Burger King for dinner and then to McDonald's for dessert. The kids are all going to meet us there. They claim I need to expand my horizons.

Sometimes that's just what the recipe calls for.

Chef B's Crispy Potatoes

6 baking potatoes (Yukon Gold potatoes are tasty)
¼ cup extra-virgin olive oil
1 tsp cayenne pepper
3 tsp garlic salt
Salt
Pepper

Peel the potatoes. Cut them into wedges 2 inches wide and about 3 inches long. Place the potatoes in a bowl of cold salted water for an hour. Heat oven to 400 degrees F. Drain the potatoes and pat with paper towels. Coat them with olive oil. Add the cayenne pepper, garlic salt, and pepper and salt to taste. Spread the mixture on greased baking sheets. Bake for 15 minutes and turn the potatoes with a spatula. Bake for 15 more minutes or until light brown and crispy. Serve to any hungry middle-school group or gathering.

Jonas's Favorite White Velvet Cake

4 large egg whites
1 cup milk
3 tsp vanilla
3 cups sifted white flour
1 ½ cups sugar
1 T plus 1 tsp baking powder
¾ tsp salt
12 T softened butter

Mix the egg whites, ¼ cup of milk, and vanilla in a small bowl. In a mixing bowl, combine the dry ingredients and blend on low. Add the softened butter and the rest of the milk. Mix on medium speed for 2 minutes. Scrape down the sides and continue to beat. Add the egg mixture a little at a time. Mix for 30 seconds after each addition. Pour batter into two greased 9-inch pans. Bake at 350 degrees F for 30 to 35 minutes or until an inserted toothpick comes out clean. Let cakes cool in pans for 10 minutes and then loosen the sides with a metal spatula. Invert onto wire racks to cool completely before frosting with buttercream icing.

questions
for
conversation

1. Have you ever wanted to leave a location and start over? If so, why? Where did you imagine you would go? If you have ever made a big move, did it solve any problems? Did it give you a new perspective?

2. Deena falls into the trap of focusing on outward appearances. Do you have any imperfections you try to hide? Have you ever wished you looked like someone else? Why do you think society places so much emphasis on people's outward appearance?

3. In an uncomfortable situation, Deena resorts to the familiar. Can you understand her need to make a velvet cake after her first day of teaching? Do you ever feel like you have to prove to yourself you still have what it takes when things don't go your way? What helps you feel better after a difficult day?

4. How does Deena handle the story of what has happened to Darren? Do you think her reaction is appropriate? Has child abuse impacted your life in any way?

5. Have you ever inherited something, big or small? What was it? Were you surprised to receive it? Did it affect the way you thought about the person who left it to you?

6. What did you think of Jonas? Do you know anyone like him? What was your favorite piece of "Jonas wisdom"?

7. A major theme of this novel is recognizing the need to forgive—and then following through. Have you ever found it difficult to forgive someone? Why are some people easier to forgive than others? Do you ever have trouble forgiving yourself?

8. Grandpa Ernest thought a lot of his granddaughter. Why do you think he left the cabin to Deena? Why did he ask that she teach at The Center? What did Deena learn from Charlotte, Darren, and the rest of the kids? If you were assigned to teach a group of middle-school students, would you welcome or dread the experience?

9. How has Deena's mother influenced the way Deena has turned out? What do you think Deena's personality was like before she met Lucas? Is Lucas really to blame for Deena's problems?

10. What did you think of Regena Lorraine, Marble Gray, and Chef B? What parts did they play in Deena's recovery?

11. Are Deena and Zack a good match? Do you see a future for them? Do you think Deena will stay in Bryson City?

12. What's your favorite kind of cake? What are your favorite foods? Do you have any kitchen utensils or other objects you treasure because of how you received them?